Hey Ma, Your Husband's Dead

A Novel By

Rick Peoples

# # # # # #

This is a work of fiction.
Names, characters, places, and incidents are either products
of the author's imaginations, or are used fictitiously.
Any resemblance to actual events, locals, organizations, or
persons, (living
or dead) is entirely coincidental.

# # # # # #

ISBN-13: 978-1-7321799-0-5
ISBN-10: 1-7321799-0-5

Have a great Summer!

For my wife and my sister,
Two of the strongest women that I know.

Rick!

The Call

It was the type of phone call that she had always expected, but never quite prepared herself to receive. Like most days, she was sitting on her perch. And while my mother, Beatrice may possess several bird-like qualities, for all practical purposes, her perch is a small kitchen pantry, which was converted into a breakfast nook when my sister, younger brothers and I were small. Over the years as we grew (outgrew?) and moved on, she marked it as her own personal space. It still retains its country charm...aged knotty pine paneling that has turned a rich umber color with age. It has a sloped ceiling that is painted every spring with a fresh coat of white to cover the nicotine stains. After all, it's the only room in the whole house that she allows herself to smoke in. The school papers that were once hung with pride over the countertop have since given way to a collection of wicker baskets arranged in magazine style fashion. The three small bar stools with seats that were once painted to match the Formica countertop have long been replaced by a single rattan style stool with a back. And if you swiveled it just right, you could put your feet on the windowsill directly opposite the counter. This was Beatrice's favorite position. She could easily reach her corded telephone hanging on the same wall as the window. She has absolutely no use for those cordless things.

She was sitting here in her command central when the call came in that mid-March afternoon. As she did with most of her calls, she swiftly leaned in to check the number on the caller-id. The last thing that she needed today was to feel guilty about not buying three hundred feet of plastic wrap being peddled by some pesky telemarketer with a speech impediment claiming that all of the proceeds would go to helping some unfamiliar homeless veterans association. She would probably tell you that there were many reasons why she couldn't make out the number. It was an overcast winter day and her normally bright refuge was filled with shadows and, of course, there was the lousy overhead lighting fixture. The house has been remodeled and redecorated several times over in the thirty-five plus years that she had lived there, but for some reason the light that gives off an eerie yellow glow, regardless of the bulb wattage, never got the axe. And when you combine the jaundice lighting effect with the brightly waxed paneling and yellowed ceiling, it would surely tax anyone with twenty-twenty vision. But more than likely, the true reason she couldn't make out the incoming call number was the fact that her eyeglasses were resting on an end table in the den.

Rolling the dice, she reluctantly answered the ringing phone.

"Hello."

"Beatrice? Hi. It's Katie", said the meek voice on the other end.

Since she hadn't heard from her stepdaughter in over twenty years, Beatrice instinctively knew that this was the call. To help calm her nerves, she swooped a Kool into her mouth and lit the cigarette quickly.

"Oh, Katie. How are you dear?" she said as she exhaled.

"I've got some bad news about Dad."

"Oh?"

"Please do not let him be in a coma or a wheelchair! It would be just my luck that he would be in a wheelchair or a coma." Beatrice thought to herself.

"He's dead. They're really not sure from what. I guess he had been gone for some time before LJ found him."

"How long?"

"A week. Maybe two."

"Ewww."

The rest of the conversation was filled with pained pleasantries, sketchy details surrounding his demise and potential funeral plans. And while she listened attentively and asked genuinely sincere questions about how the rest of the family was fairing, Beatrice conducted a mental checklist of her wardrobe.

Black dress? Check. Shoes? Check. Purse? Out of date. Need new. Where the hell did I leave that coat?

There was an awkward kind of silence for a moment, which seemed like an eternity of dead air before Katie asked the question Beatrice had been waiting for.

"Beatrice. There is some paperwork that we need to fill out. According to LJ, you and Dad were divorced."

Katie had a soothing vocal quality that could always defuse even the most difficult of situations. Beatrice often felt that Katie's vocal talents were wasted as a bank teller. She was much better suited for a career as a high school guidance counselor or at the very least a voice model to be used by those state offices, government utilities, or corporations which no longer believed in using live bodies to answer the telephone and thus subjecting callers to a lifetime of voicemail hell.

"No dear, I'm afraid that your sister is wrong."

"Excuse me?

"Your father and I never divorced."

"Oh." replied Katie who was obviously taken back by Beatrice. "Were you legally separated?"

"No."

"Are you sure?"

"I think I would remember dear."

"Was that too sarcastic? I don't want her to think I am sarcastic."

"Oh. Well then, you should be getting a package shortly from Hindes and Dolan...insurance information and such. We're hoping that you can help us out with some of the funeral expenses." Katie said. Her voice wasn't as bright as it had been earlier.

"Of course. You can count on me. Let me know what you need."

Katie promised to call back just as soon as she and her siblings had a chance to iron out all the details regarding the arrangements. They made their goodbyes and Beatrice hung up the phone.

"Did I really just smoke three cigarettes?"

She hit the speed dial for my office. She hated calling me at work, but circumstances being what they were, she thought nothing of it.

"Hello Michael, This is Mrs. Kufasso." she said into my voice mail. My mother felt that I had several false starts from a career perspective. Now that I had such a *big* job in corporate America, she was determined not to give anyone who maybe listening to my voicemail any opportunity to think that I spent most of my days on the phone with my mother. So she borrowed her secret identity from one of her favorite customers at the deli.

"You can reach me at the home office," she continued. "You are never going to believe who just called me."

Reality Check

After The Call

The family network instantly sprang to life. It took very little time for Beatrice to contact her four grown children, and even less time for us to call each other to compare notes, share stories, and laugh. To anyone who may have been eavesdropping, every one of the conversations were similar in content, however each took on a different tone and flavor specific to the unique relationship that my mother had shared with each of us.

"When?"

"A couple of weeks ago."

"Ewww."

"That's what I said."

"Who found him?"

"LJ."

"Is she medicated yet?"

"Is there a time when she isn't medicated?"

"This will probably push her right over the edge. The poor thing."

"Bless her heart."

"Mom, she has been over the edge as long as we've known her."

"Where did they find him?"

"The bathroom."

"In the tub?"

"No."

"On the floor?"

"No."

"No Sah."

"Shut up."

"He was on the t…"

"Somehow that seems very appropriate."

After hanging up with my mother, I sat quietly in my office staring at the framed pictures of my wife and children on the credenza. Memories that I thought that were once safely locked and tucked neatly away came crashing back and dragging me down not unlike a child caught in the undertow at the beach. Suppressed reminiscences of roach coaches, belching and farting in church, being forced to ride in the only car in the free world without a muffler, the get rich quick schemes, the pills, the booze, and the three AM family cage matches came bubbling once more to the surface.

I got out of my chair and crossed over to the window. I stood there for the next several minutes looking at everything and nothing shaking my head in disbelief and lost in my private dark thoughts. Truly amazed that after all that my siblings and I went through, it was nothing short of miraculous that each of us could roll out of bed each morning and function.

And then eventually I smiled, taking great satisfaction in now knowing that...Fred had finally dropped dead.

The Arrival

It was late into the spring of nineteen seventy four or was it nineteen seventy five my parents were in the middle of a nasty separation. Their relationship had all the makings of a made for television movie that would be played continuously for years on one of those cable stations made exclusively for women. It would probably star one of those women from Knots Landing or perhaps that lovely Mrs. Tom Hanks, Rita Wilson. The age-old plot is about a girl from the right side of the tracks falls in love with boy from the wrong side of the tracks. My Father, Butch represented everything that my grandmother hated in a man. He stood about five foot nine inches, which was of course too short in Nana Flossie's eyes.

"You do not want short sons, Beatrice," Nana Flossie would often preach.

Butch was the youngest of six and had been out of high school for two years, making him almost three years older than Beatrice. Like many a man who could be considered vertically challenged, Butch overcompensated by being a little too arrogant and a little too cocky. He was quick to blame others for his mistakes, which infuriated Nana Flossie to no end.

"Beatrice, a man should stand up and he should own his mistakes. It will also make a short man seem taller dear." Nana Flossie would often say.

Butch shared an apartment with a couple of his buddies and was able to pay for his share of the rent by driving a truck for a local brewery.

"Beatrice. No good can come out of a relationship with a man who peddles alcohol for a living. Remember how your poor father turned out." Nana Flossie would remind Beatrice.

Butch was a smooth talker. Little did Beatrice know then, that he was also a smooth operator who had a plan and a scheme for every situation. He always seemed to know someone, who knew someone, who could get them a deal. But they were young, stupid, and in love. Six months almost to the day from her high school graduation, with her two best friends who were coincidently both named Betty, standing at her side, Beatrice and Butch eloped.

It wasn't until the birth of Beatrice's first child ten months later that her mother spoke to her again.

The years following Beatrice lived in a state of euphoria. She had achieved her dream. Four children, a small house in the country, (a gift from her grandmother) two cats, a poodle named Regis Ryan, three hamsters and assorted number of parakeets later, Beatrice thought that her life could stand toe to toe with any of those television families. Like most single income families of the time, there were periods when money was tight and sacrifices had to be made. She would often pride herself on how creative she could be at dinnertime with a few essential staples in her kitchen. As long as she had a pound of hamburger, an onion and a tomato, nothing could stop her from working her culinary magic. We were healthy and our happiness made her happy. She naturally assumed that her husband was also sharing the happiness that she felt.

Looking back, she probably could have kicked herself for not recognizing any of the tell tale signs of a marriage in trouble. Butch often had to work late, even though the shoe store where he had been employed as the assistant manager closed nightly at five o'clock. He often took extended lunch hours claiming that he was getting a quick trim at the barbershop. In those days, he wore a modified crew cut so it was hard to tell if he really did get his hair cut. For years he made "Old Spice" his cologne of choice. But suddenly he was amassing a new collection of colognes and after shaves like "Hi-Karate" and "Brute".

"If it's good enough for Broadway Joe, it's good enough for me." Butch would say when he was questioned about his change of scent.

While it would have been nice to order herself some new outfits from out of the Sears catalogue, Beatrice knew it wasn't practical. My father needed the newer clothes more than she did because as he was often quick to point out, he was the breadwinner and he needed to look good for the general public.

He was quick to criticize and was extremely short tempered. Almost every discussion ended with a screaming match, usually long after we were in bed, which resulted in him leaving the house for a few hours to blow off steam. As time went on, the fights intensified and seemed to happen earlier and earlier. Eventually, he would just stop coming home.

Beatrice had heard the rumors and the stories surrounding her husband. Butch was fooling around. Butch was seen playing cards at the Italian American club. Butch was seen with some skinny blonde at the racetrack. Butch was seen at such and such club really enjoying himself. Considering the source, most of the tall tales were being filtered back to her through some divorced "friends" who were no doubt jealous of her life. Beatrice chose to ignore all of them. Her marriage had hit a rough spot. Nothing more. Nothing less. They would work it out, even if that meant she had to continue to chase him down every Friday and Saturday night. It wasn't until she actually caught him in the arms of another woman that it finally dawned on Beatrice that her marriage was over.

The months and months of screaming fights till all hours of the morning miraculously stopped when Butch moved out. Sure there were still an occasional cross or curse word screeched into a phone receiver from time to time, almost always over the negative cash flow, but for the most part a much-needed blanket of tranquility had wrapped itself around this tiny household by the golden pond. For weeks, the only noises at night that could be heard were the occasional snores from one of my siblings or from the choir of crickets and bullfrogs that lived beside our house. Naturally it was only fitting that this brief respite was mercilessly interrupted with the arrival of Fred.

Fred arrived into our lives the way that he went out...with a thud.

Thud. Thud. Thud.

Huhhh?

Thud. Thud. Thud.

I suppose you could chalk the entire experience up to the overactive imagination of a teenager. Granted, I had just seen that really bad movie about the California earthquake. You remember the one, "filmed in surround sound"...which when translated from the Hollywood hype machine of the time meant that the movie theatre was jammed packed with a bunch of speakers roughly the size of Volkswagen Beetles. These monstrosities were then rigged to roar during specific parts of the movie. The goal was to give the average moviegoer the feeling that they were actually experiencing the earthquake first hand. The only purpose the blaring served was to cover up a host of bad dialogue, compounded by bad acting. All the speakers were able to accomplish was to shake loose the fillings in my mouth.

Thud. Thud. Thud.

Help! I'm trapped in a bad movie!

Thud. Thud. Thud.

No. I wasn't dreaming. The white glow from my alarm clock assured me that it was three o'clock in the morning. The clock was one of my most prized possessions. By today's standards, my box shaped AM / FM alarm clock with faux walnut wood finish would be considered clunky. It was the kind where after a faint click, the numbers flipped over to measure the passage of time or depending upon the severity of the hangover double as a Chinese water torture. The intensity of the noise above my head had me convinced that the drop ceiling in my basement bedroom was about to drop on my head.

Thud. Thud. Thud.

The noises grew louder and louder as I bolted up the cellar stairs and into the kitchen. I tried to rub the disbelief out of my eyes, but no matter how hard I rubbed…he was still there.

At first glance, you would have sworn that some misshapen character from a Saturday morning cartoon show had invaded the house. If you were able to straighten out his bowed legs, Fred probably would have stood six feet tall. The top of his spaghetti squash shaped head was covered with tight brown curls that were slowly snapping back into place. I could only assume that the heavily dowsed Bryl-crèem treatment they received from early this morning was slowly wearing off. He was blessed with a hawk-like nose that sat square on his face. I stood transfixed, staring at his mouth. He had a set of exceedingly full lips that could be considered to be a very attractive feature on most women. But on him, it looked more like a set of those wax lips that I used to buy at Penelope's Penny Candy Store at Halloween. And then he opened his mouth.

Was he actually singing?

It was easy to confuse what little teeth he had with yellow stalagmites. Looking back, I think this probably explains my fixation with dental floss. Trying to put a positive spin on the situation, I suppose you could say his teeth matched perfectly with the two-toned yellow checked sports coat he was wearing. He probably could have used a different size jacket because when he extended his hands above his head, you could see his massive forearms. In true seventies fashion style, he was also wearing brown polyester pants, a black golf shirt and a white Patent Leather belt. A pair of brown and white loafers completed the outfit.

In one hand he held a can of Budweiser beer and cupped in the other was a Winston cigarette with the longest ash I had ever seen. Fred continued to wave his hands above his head in what I was hoping to be in rhythm with some imaginary music that only he could hear. My second guess was that he was having some sort of epileptic seizure, which signaled the onset of some deeper mental health or emotional issues. This three hundred pound man continued his tap dance in front of our refrigerator. It was anyone's guess to which would fall first, the floor or his cigarette ash. If the way he gyrated and hopped was any indication, I was sure that in a short amount of time, I would be able to see the kitchen ceiling from my basement bedroom.

"What the heck is that?" I asked loud enough hoping to be heard over the happy hoofing reject from the June Taylor Dancers. Actually there were several other more colorful words that I have long started using with my friends, but without knowing who else was in the room, there was no way

I was going to flaunt my new found vocabulary. Beatrice was not above giving our mouths a good soap lathering when she felt that they needed it.

It had been a long time since I had heard my mother laugh. But there she was sitting on a stool that would eventually become her perch, tears in her eyes and a hand over her mouth vainly attempting to hold back a cackle.

Did my mother just spit beer out of her nose?

Doubled over in laughter was our neighbor George, who was doing his best to steady himself against the kitchen counter. He wasn't too successful. George quickly found himself kissing the vinyl floor, which sent Beatrice into further uncontrollable fits of laughter. Fred mercifully stopped his dance routine and let out a loud bass guffaw that would surely make both Fred Flintstone and Ralph Kramden envious. Even George couldn't help but giggle as he struggled unsuccessfully to get back to his feet. Eventually he just gave up and did his best to make it look that his new position on the floor was a conscious choice. This of course, sent Beatrice and Fred off on another laughing tangent.

Later that week, poor George would come over and make some feeble excuse that he hurt his foot at work. But the truth of the matter was that due to a slow economy compounded by his love of the grape, George could rarely hold down a full time job. He was what some may call a happy drunk who was doing his best to hold on to whatever shred of dignity he had left. Beatrice would just smile at him and say something like, "I thought that was the case George. If it's not better in a couple of days you better get a doctor to look at it."

And then they would both just smile like a couple of old friends who shared a secret.

"Who is that?" I asked pointing towards Fred, hoping that I could be heard over the kitchen of hyenas.

As if on cue, he shoved his outstretched paw at me. "The name's Fred. Pudda there buddy."

Trying not to wince in pain as he vigorously shook my hand, I knew that our lives would never be the same again.

Reality Check

Tag Team Telephone

It did not take long for the news of our step monster's about-timely death to sink in. But before we could put Christopher's Gantt charts into action, Beatrice insisted that we wait what she called "an appropriate amount of time – for the sake of appearances."

"I will not appear too needy-greedy." she repeated as she blocked our numerous requests for a family meeting.

She left us no alternative. Christopher and I had to tag team her on the telephone.

"Hello?"

"Hey Mom. It's me."

"Hi Christopher. How are you darling?" she genuinely asked.

"I'm here too Ma." I added.

"Michael is that you?"

"Yes Mama. Listen, Chris and I have been talking and…"

"No."

"Mom, we haven't even asked anything yet." Christopher pleaded.

"I know what you are going to ask….and the answer is no. Not now. It's too soon."

"How long do we have to wait?" Christopher snapped back which almost sounded like whining.

"I don't know. I told you I don't want to talk about it. As soon as I am ready, I will let you know." Beatrice stated matter-of-factly. I could tell that she was close to pulling an ostrich. Whenever, my mother was confronted with an issue that she didn't want to deal with, she would put her head in the ground and pray that it would eventually go away.

"We can't wait too long." I added trying my best to sound professional.

"How long do you think we need to wait?" Christopher chimed in.

"I told you, I will let you know just as soon as I do." she repeated herself. "There has got to be a rule for this somewhere."

"I am not sure that Emily Post or Miss Manners have ever covered this in any of their newspaper columns." I told her.

"Don't get flip with me, Michael." she snapped back.

"I cannot understand. Why you are so concerned about appearances?" Christopher questioned.

"Because, I am." Beatrice said defensively.

"Why?" I found myself whining not even the slightest bit worried about how easily I became ten years old again. "Ma. You haven't heard hide nor hair from that fat SOB in over eighteen years. What do you really care about appearances? "

"I told you. I just do. That's all. I love talking with you both, but I am tired of this conversation."

"Come on!" I whined again with the voice of a ten year old that wasn't getting his way. "In all that time, have you ever heard from him? Did he ever call to check up on you? See how you were doing? Send you any money? Did he?" I asked.

"No." Beatrice answered quietly.

"Hell, did he once remember to send you a birthday card?" Christopher added.

"He did send me a lovely cheese basket at Christmas one year." she said in his defense.

"Ma, he filled a wicker trash bucket, judging from the amount of dirty tissues and q-tips still in it, I would venture to guess that he purloined it from someone's bathroom, with three cans of cheese whiz, a couple of sleeves of stale saltines, and a half empty bottle of malt liquor." I jumped.

"I have always told you it's the thought that matters." Beatrice said sarcastically after a beat.

"Would it be possible for us to focus for a minute on the problem at hand you two?" Christopher interrupted. "Mom, we get that you do not want to cause any waves. However, the fact of the matter is we don't have any idea exactly what your greedy step-children are up to."

"Excuse me?"

She took the hook.

"You know how crazy they are. I have to assume that they have already secured a lawyer and are currently figuring out how to cut you out of the will." he prodded.

"Do you think so?"

"I don't know for certain, but we have to assume that they are working on it." Christopher replied.

"Michael, what do you think?" Beatrice asked.

"Christopher is right."

"He was always bad with money. He can't possible have much. No. This is ridiculous. I cannot believe we are talking about this. I don't want to have this conversation."

"Mom, neither do we." Christopher agreed. "But, don't you think it makes sense for us to figure all of that out? What happens if you get stuck with all of his debts?"

"Wouldn't that be just my luck?"

"We don't know what he has; we do not know what he owes. But we do know that his kids are already probably trying to figure that out." Christopher said calmly.

"Do you think so, Michael?"

"No doubt." I lied. In truth I sincerely doubted that they were that well organized. Fred's birth children had little use for him and from what I could gather from past gatherings, little use for each other. But, who knows? There is always the off chance that things had changed over the years and they now share a healthy and strong sibling relationship, not unlike the Brady's or the Olsen Twins.

"We have to strike while the iron was hot." Christopher added.

"You really think so?"

"Yes. It's exactly what I would be doing if I were them."

"Christopher's right, Mom."

"Well, if that is the case then, you guys better get to work." she said reluctantly and then hung up.

"Strike while the iron is hot?" I ragged on him.

"Fuck off, Mister Hide nor Hair." he laughed. "We got the green light."

"Green light? Who writes your dialogue?"

"Shut up!" Christopher said laughing even harder. "I'll find a lawyer and you see if you get some information on his pension and life insurance."

Full speed ahead.

Who Moved My (Welfare) Cheese?

Beatrice had an affinity for the ocean and she tried to instill in each of us a reverence for the medicinal properties of the beach. Whatever the ailment, Beatrice was convinced that a couple hours at the shore and a dip in the ocean would cure it. Suffer from aches, arthritis, mosquito bites, blackheads and other assorted acne? Take a dip in the ocean. You have head colds, nausea, pink eye, assorted rashes, pains and poison ivy? Not to worry. All will be cleared up in no time. Just take a dip.

In addition to being a universal panacea for your physical ills, Beatrice believed that the beach is also a great place to clear your head from any mental stresses that have inflicted you. The warmth of the sun combined with the sound of the waves crashing on the shore filled her with a sense of tranquility and inner peace. It was here that she felt most safe. The beach was a place where she could forget about the stresses in her life and re-charge her emotional batteries.

Without fail, once or twice a week, Beatrice would load up the sky blue Buick wood paneled station wagon with the kids, her favorite beach chair, sand pails and shovels in assorted colors and sizes. The standard beach lunch always made that morning consisted of tuna fish with celery in a hot dog roll. The one exception was Kevin who would only eat peanut butter and jelly on Wonder Bread. We always had plenty of hard-boiled eggs and plums. Occasionally, Beatrice would throw in a sleeve of crackers or cookies or whatever she had handy in the pantry. And of course, she would always fill a jug with grape or orange ZaRex to drink.

Beatrice would do her best to make sure we were at the beach early in the morning and certainly no later than ten in the morning. Between ten and two were prime sun hours. Depending upon the traffic, it would usually take about forty-five minutes or so to get to our usual spot by the second set of stairs at King's Beach. This was our favorite place for a couple of reasons. Somehow, the waves just seemed better at this end of the beach...perfect for body surfing. The snack shack was at the other end of the beach, so our end seemed to be less crowded. At low tide, there were always one or two tide pools where Christopher could hang out if the ocean water was too cold or too rough. And strategically speaking, it was also close enough that Beatrice could watch us from her beach chair as we climbed around and on the rocks looking for crabs, starfish and periwinkles.

In those days, Carrie and I were typically each allowed to bring a friend from the neighborhood to keep us entertained, usually it was Greg LeBlanc and Dale Hoag. And without fail we would always seem to meet up with one or both of the Bettys and their kids. After making sure all of the children were the proper shade of Coppertone white, the mothers would set the twelve of us free.

"Keep an eye on your brother."

"Do not go in past your belly button."

"I do not care if Michael is taller. I said your belly button."

"Don't you awww Ma me!"

"Michael, you and Greg come in a little bit so that Stevie has someone to play with."

"Ladies. Move back this way so I can see you."

"If I have to tell you again, you are getting out."

"I know I didn't just see you throw sand at your sister's face!"

Covered from head to toe with a lotion made of baby oil and iodine, the mothers thoroughly enjoyed each other's company. In between the shouts and the menacing stares, they sat in their beach chairs, smoked their cigarettes and laughed and joked about everything and nothing. They'd talk about family, mostly in-law stories, neighbors, recipes, husbands and their kids, mostly their kids. If they were truly lucky, someone might talk about a book that she was able to steal a couple hours away to read or a television program or just gossip about friends from high school.

And the kids played hard, which was nothing like the structured play dates of today, which always seem to require some form of parental interaction, a clearly defined set of rules, and signed contract of behavior. It was a prerequisite that we made our own fun.

"You have a whole beach to play on. Do not hang on me. Go find something to do."

"Why don't you and Julie build a sand castle down by the water?"

"No. It's too soon for lunch. Go find something to do."

Countless hours were spent jumping waves, playing four square, Frisbee or football, building sand castles or burying someone in the sand. Although most games that required catching a flying object always ended in disaster for the poor family that decided to spread their blanket a little too close to our turf. For the most part we got along well, but due to the sheer volume of kids, there was bound to be a casualty from time to time.

"And then...and then...he held me under the water so I couldn't breathe! I'm not kidding Ma, I almost died!"

We'd stop for lunch around noon or when the mothers couldn't take our collective whining anymore and broke down to feed us and then start over again. Occasionally, one of us wanted to go for a swim immediately following lunch.

"You have to wait at least an hour after you eat before you go back in the water."

"I didn't make up the rule."

"Greg LeBlanc. If you want to get a stomach cramp and drown, you are more than welcome to do that when your mother is with you. But as long as I am watching you, you will keep out of the water!"

As soon as it was two o'clock, we would all break base camp and head our separate ways. If we were good and finances permitted, Beatrice would stop at the Dairy Queen on the way home and allow each of us to get a small vanilla cone with a cherry dip. Being true to form, Carrie always insisted on chocolate.

That summer as the post separation private war between my parents escalated, more and more often, Beatrice found herself loading up the sky blue wood paneled Buick station wagon, now in desperate need of a tune up and a new right front tire and heading off to the beach to clear her head. She still brought along her favorite beach chair, sand pails and shovels in assorted colors and sizes and the standard beach lunch. To our surprise, Greg and Dale became optional. This didn't sit too well with Carrie.

"Mom, I don't see why Dale can't come." Carrie whined. "I won't have anyone to play with."

"Carrie, you'll have your brothers. What more do you need?" Beatrice replied.

"A lot more. I need a friend there! You cannot possibly expect me to play with them at the beach." Carrie pleaded.

"Carrie, throughout your life I hope that you are blessed with a lot of friends...I do. But, please listen to me when I say this...friends will come and go. No matter what happens in your life, you will always have three brothers." Beatrice tried to reason.

"I don't care. They're stupid!" Carrie screamed.

"But they're all you have!" Beatrice shouted back.

"Then I will just hang around you all day and drive you crazy." Carrie said calmly and defiantly.

"No you won't. Now please go get in the car." Beatrice said matching her daughter's tone and continuing to pack the standard lunch into the well used cooler.

"No. I'm not going!" Carrie said rebelliously.

"Carrie." Beatrice began in an all too familiar tone that signaled she was close to blowing, "I am not having this discussion with you. I am still your mother and you will do as I say. Now, please grab the things that you want to bring to the beach and get into the car."

"Why can't she come?" Carrie demanded.

"Because, I have a lot on my plate! Because, I don't feel like watching anyone else's kids right now! Because, I just need you to give me a break!" Beatrice snapped back. She then took a deep calming breath and then tried reasoning with Carrie. "Please. Please, just cut me some slack."

"It's not fair!!" Carrie screamed louder.

"Fair? Whoever said life had to be fair?" Beatrice screamed back losing all self control.

"Do you want to talk about things being unfair?" Beatrice asked barely able to hold back her tears. "If it were fair, then your father would never have fallen out of love with me and he would still be here with all of us. If it were fair, he would realize that he still has four kids that he needs to support and he would be sending us money. But the fact of the matter is...he's not. He's out there somewhere, living with some other woman and supporting her and her kids instead of us. He doesn't care that I am rolling pennies to buy milk and bread or that I just received the second notice on the electric bill or that the car is on its last leg. He doesn't care that I lie awake night after night trying to figure out how the hell I am going to keep the roof over our heads and food on the table. So I hope you can appreciate that I have bigger things on my mind right now other than whether or not you have someone to play with at the goddamn beach. Now, I suggest that you shut your mouth and get your ass in the back seat of that car while you still have the ability to sit down!"

Off we went.

The first fifteen minutes in the car was spent in a very tense silence. In those days Beatrice's brother Cooper who was staying with us at the time tagged along. Uncle Cooper was in between "performances" and needed a place to recuperate and the little house by the golden pond was just what the doctor ordered. It was Cooper's job to keep the mood light and distract us all from our troubles. Taking his cue, he immediately went to work. He blasted the AM radio and started clapping and singing off-key to the latest top forty hit. When he failed to get the response he was looking for, he started to sing even louder and began to dance in his seat. Without fail, Christopher and Kevin usually caved and joined in. Carrie sat arms crossed and a snarl on her face as she looked out the window bound and determined not to crack a smile.

Uncle Coop turned up the heat. He started waving at the people we drove passed who were slowly shuffling down the street in the humid July sun.

"Howdy neighbor." he would shout out the window to the people on the sidewalk. "I've kidnapped my niece and I'm dragging her to the beach."

The car ride seemed to fly by. Uncle Cooper had us all entertained. Even Beatrice managed a smile as we held our breath when we drove by Saint Mary's Cemetery, which had to be almost a mile long. Uncle Cooper convinced us that if we didn't hold our breath, we'd wake the dead and that they would follow us home. Beatrice joined in on the fun and purposely slowed the car down to get a reaction from us. We had taken the same route to the beach often enough that we knew it by heart. We would look for our various landmarks, the Dairy Queen, the old boarded up church that looked haunted, and the four story apartment building that was slowly being demolished so that we could determine how much longer before we could body surf the waves. Needless to say we were all disappointed and aggravated when Beatrice took an unfamiliar turn.

"Mom!!!!" whined Carrie loudly. "Where are we going?"

"Aren't we going to the beach?" asked Kevin.

"Yes. I promise." sighed Beatrice. "But unfortunately, I have a short appointment that I have to go to first."

"What?"

"Why?"

"Figures. I didn't want to go in the first place."

"Where are we going?"

"The welfare office." said Beatrice trying her best to sound positive.

"Arrrg."

"I agree with you Christopher. Arrg is right."

"Why are we going there?"

"What's a welfare office?"

"Well Christopher, it's a place where I have to go to check in with my social worker. That's a very special person who is reviewing our case. And if everything works out, then she will make sure we get some money, some food stamps and health insurance."

"I can't believe we have to come here." Carrie whined.

"That makes two of us, fresh girl." snapped Beatrice as she parked the car. "You guys stay here with Uncle Cooper, with any luck; I will be out in a few minutes."

"Oh man."

"Can I come in?"

"Why can't I come in?"

"I should only be a few minutes and then we can get to the beach. Listen to your Uncle." she commanded as she got out of the car and tucked her purse under her arm. She was both anxious and frustrated. Her palms were covered in a layer of nervous perspiration and she wiped them repeatedly on her skirt as she crossed the street which was busy with traffic. Her heart was beating so hard she could feel it in her throat.

"Damn Butch for putting us through this!"

The doors to the local Aid to Families with Dependent Children office open at eight forty five. At any given time, depending upon the weather there was usually a small line of people waiting to get in. Beatrice had hoped that she if she arrived a few minutes early for her third meeting with her social worker, she could circumvent a long line. Uncharacteristically, today she was in luck. Once she signed in with the lobby receptionist, she opened a side door and used the musty smelling stairwell with the two toned green peeling paint to get to the second floor desk of her case worker, Loretta Hazelwood.

"Good Morning Loretta." said Beatrice with an outstretched hand secretly begging God to keep her palms dry for just another moment longer.

"Good Morning. Please take a seat." Loretta took Beatrice's hand and signaled her to take a seat in the green vinyl office chair next to her desk which was covered in several stacks of file folders. Loretta pulled a box of tissues from the top right hand drawer and began to wipe her right hand.

"Oh, I am terribly sorry." apologized Beatrice. "I am very nervous."

"No need." said Loretta as she tossed the damp tissue into the wastepaper basket she kept underneath her desk.

"I am sure. But..." before Beatrice could finish her thought, Loretta held up an index finger signaling Beatrice to be quiet.

"I need just another moment please." Loretta said almost mechanically as she flipped another page in the file.

"Ok." said Beatrice still shocked at the woman's rudeness. Aside from the inordinate amount of the file folders, Loretta Hazelwood kept a neat and tidy desk. From what Beatrice could see, her social worker was all business and with the exception of a mini poster of a white kitten hanging on a tree branch with the words 'Hang In There Baby' written in yellow mod lettering, there wasn't much in the way of personal effects.

Loretta was a long term employee whose naive passion for helping people had slowly and methodically morphed into a righteous cynicism. Her stern demeanor had long since spilled over onto her taunt and thin face, giving the impression to anyone who did not know her, that Loretta was much older than her forty-six years. Beatrice couldn't help but admire Loretta's coffee colored complexion, which was flawless, even under the harsh overhead florescent tube lighting. Loretta wore her hair natural, but made sure that it was pulled back tight in an attempt to keep it out of her face. She wore an oversized African dashiki beige and brown tunic top with two large front pockets, huge bell sleeves, and matching brown stretch knit bell bottom pants. Something about the loose fitting outfit did not resonate with Beatrice until she saw the framed certificate of achievement from Weight Watchers hidden behind a very tall stack of folders. This was a woman who has recently lost a significant amount of weight and still acted and dressed as though she were fat.

"Mrs. Rogers."

"Please call me Beatrice."

"Mrs. Rogers, have you any contact with your husband?"

"No ma'am."

"I see." said Loretta not looking up and making a notation in her paperwork. "Did you bring in the other paperwork we discussed?"

"Yes." said Beatrice as she nervously opened her purse and began to dig through the contents to pull out a stack of papers. She handed a couple of pages to Loretta who snatched them away in an almost mechanically automated motion. "Here is the checking account statement."

"Any savings?"

"No."

"Stocks?"

"No."

"Bonds?"

"No."

"Other checking accounts?"

"No, ma'am."

"How are you feeding your family?"

"We have been squeaking by. As you can see, we don't have much money left."

"Mmmmhmmm. Are you getting any help from your relatives?"

"Help?"

"Money? Groceries? Gifts?"

"No. They don't know."

"You haven't told them?"

"It's really none of their business."

"Mmmmhmmmm."

"And here are the copies of the birth certificates that you asked for last time. You can see that Butch is listed as the father, although for the life of me, I am still not sure why you needed to check that."

"Thank you. It's a fairly routine question Mrs. Rogers. We need to make sure that we are chasing the right man."

Offended that Loretta had questioned her fidelity, Beatrice attempted to change the subject. "It took a bit, but I was able to find the canceled checks for the gas, the electric and the oil bills. Here you are." Beatrice's hand trembled as she relinquished them over.

"Nervous?"

"Very."

"Don't be. As long as you are truthful and honest, you have nothing to worry about. It can be a very overwhelming process Mrs. Rogers."

Beatrice nodded, holding back her tears.

"It says here that you own your home?"

"Yes."

"Why wouldn't you sell it?"

"Where would we go?"

"Not sure. But you could put off going on public assistance."

"For how long? The house isn't worth much. My children have been through enough turmoil. I don't need to add a new home and new schools to the list. Besides, my hope is that this is just a temporary setback."

"You would be surprised how many times a day I hear that very same thing."

"Well, I mean it."

"I am sure that you do."

Leaning on her elbows on the desk and entwining her fingers with the long manicured nails with burnt orange polish, Loretta looked Beatrice in the eye for the very first time. "Mrs. Rogers, I have to tell you that I have some concerns about the validity of your claim."

"Oh?" said Beatrice as her heart stopped beating.

"You are not the typical family that comes in here looking for aid."

"What does a typical family look like?" Beatrice asked using a tone that reeked of bitterness.

"For starters, you own your own home. You live in what many would consider to be an affluent community. You don't appear to have any of the same challenges that…"

"I am going to stop you right there, Mrs. Hazelwood. I am not going to apologize or made to feel guilty for where I am from. I have worked too damn hard and too damn long for what little I have."

"Mrs. Rog…" before Loretta could finish her thought, Beatrice held up an index finger signaling Loretta to be quiet.

"No. It's my turn. Challenges? How can you possibly know what challenges I am facing on a daily basis? My husband left. Do you know what the impact of that has been on my children? Do you know how many nights they have cried themselves to sleep because their father was too busy to show up? Or he simply forgot to call? Do you know how many times I have tried to calm them or comfort them in the middle of the night because they have had a bad dream about their father? Do you have any idea what it is like for me to try and say something positive about the man after all he has done to humiliate and embarrass me, just so my kids can maintain the smallest shred of self-esteem? Did you know that even though it was mandated by the court, he refuses to pay any of alimony or child support? He claims he doesn't have any money. Why? Because on paper it appears as though he hasn't been able to hold down a job since he left us. Except, I know full well that, he has been working under the table for one of his brothers. The only problem is that, I just can't prove it. Yet, no one else seems to care or question where he got the money to buy a new car or how he can afford to take his girlfriend and her kids out to eat all the time."

Beatrice rummaged through her purse and pulled out her wallet. She violently emptied the contents of her change purse on Loretta's desk. She continued as the tears streamed down her face. "You have the bank statements in front of you. You can see that I have gone through all of my savings, there is nothing left. I have exactly six dollars and eighty seven cents to my name. That's it. That's everything! I have filled out every one of your damn forms. I have given you every scrap of paper, every bank statement and every bill or invoice that you have asked for. I have been on time for every one of these meetings. I realize that I may not be the person that you normally see in here. But I can assure you that my needs are just as valid as any mother who comes in here hoping to get enough money so she can keep a roof over her children's heads and food in their bellies. Believe me. If I had any other choice, I wouldn't be here. But I don't have a choice. So, I am here. What I want to know is, are you going to help me or not?"

Outside in the car, after a robust and potentially combative game of *I Spy with My Little Eye*, we ended up playing a new game that Uncle Cooper invented, where you would add a word or two to a celebrity's name to give it a new funny meaning. The goal was to make the name as silly as possible. Each person playing was not supposed to laugh out loud. If you did, then you had to pay a forfeit, which typically meant being on the receiving end of an Indian Sunburn or a Wet Willie.

"Sonny didn't Cher, so she divorced him"

"Dean Martini"

"Helen Reddy or not"

"Lucille Ball-Breaker"

"Burt Reynolds-Wrap"

"Agnes Moorehead-On Collision"

"Richard Thomas-hole"

"Glen Campbell-soup"

"Clifton Webb-Feet"

"Frank Sinatra-La-La"

"Gary Pooper"

We all laughed so hard, we didn't see a smiling Beatrice quickly cross the street and get into the car.

"How did it go?" asked Cooper.

"Better than it should have." smiled Beatrice as she slipped the key into the ignition and started the car. "We are going grocery shopping on the way home."

"You got the money?"

"I got the money. Who's ready for the beach?????"

"I am!"

"Me!"

"It's about time!"

"Shut up Carrie."

Beatrice shifted the car into drive; she turned up the volume on the radio to drown out the squealing, grinding, and chirping noise coming from the front of the car, which more than likely signaled a failing power steering belt...yet another repair that she would eventually have to deal with and drove off in the direction of the beach.

The skies were overcast and grey. While the sun tried several times to break through the haze, it never happened. A cool heavy breeze coming off of the ocean, the choppy surf, and her nerves still shot from her meeting with Loretta Hazelwood all led to Beatrice's inability to relax and unwind. Add in four whiney children and it was no wonder that barely an hour after they arrived, Beatrice instructed Cooper and the kids to break base camp and load up the car.

"Let's see how these food stamps are supposed to work!"

We followed our normal route home. However when we turned onto Boston Street, Beatrice made an unexpected right hand turn into the parking lot of a large and unfamiliar grocery store.

"What are we doing here?" asked Carrie.

"We have nothing in the house to eat, so I thought that we could save some time and shop here." said Beatrice trying her best to sound upbeat.

"This isn't where we normally go."

"No it isn't Michael. But let's give it a shot."

"Mom. It looks really dirty." said Christopher timidly.

"Let's not judge a book by its cover." said Beatrice again using her forced optimistic voice as we all climbed out of the car. "The parking lot is busy. Let's hold hands and be careful."

"God! He is right! This place is filthy!"

"What am I five?" snapped Carrie.

"God! I am going to kill her!"

Before Beatrice could correct her daughter, Uncle Cooper scooped Carrie up and deposited her on her back into an empty grocery carriage.

Shocked and embarrassed, Carrie began to yell, scream and kick her feet wildly. "Knock it off. Knock it off. Quit it. Let me outta here!"

Uncle Cooper paid her no attention and began to push the cart in the direction of the entrance. The more she screamed, the faster he pushed until eventually he began skipping cross the parking lot, taking large strides with each jump.

The rest of us laughed uncontrollably and also decided to join in on the fun and skipped to the front entrance. Once inside the six of us stood in a small group in sensory overload with what we were experiencing. High above, the faint elevator muzak that was being pumped in sounded tinny and almost as though the radio station that they were using was not tuned in properly. When the manager got on the microphone with his thick Boston accent to announce the daily specials, each of the overhead speakers simultaneously crackled, popped and hummed giving further evidence that they had seen a better day. The overhead lighting gave off an eerie florescent glow that bathed everything and everyone in a harsh yellowy orange light. The place was a madhouse with wall to wall people navigating their carriages around each other and the stock boys and girls who were taking up valuable isle space more interested in talking about school or sports than in restocking the shelves. The brown and beige checkerboard tiled flooring was so well worn; Beatrice had a difficult time distinguishing just how dirty it actually was.

"Wow."

"Do we have to shop here?"

"Yeah Ma, couldn't we just go to the normal place?" asked Kevin.

"No. We are here. Let's make the most of it. Carrie, why don't you take everyone to the cereal aisle? Make sure that everyone picks out two boxes. I don't care what you pick out; just so long as you make sure that you are going to eat it. Kevin, I am specifically talking to you. I am tired of wasting good money on cereal that you won't eat just because it has a toy or a prize inside that you want. Do I make myself clear?"

"Yes."

"Yes, Ma."

"Ok."

"Yes Mommy."

"Stick together. Uncle Cooper and I will meet you in the produce section." said Beatrice as she watched us zip through the maze of people looking for where they keep the cereal. "Ok. Let's do this. How bad can it be?"

For most of her married life and even before, Beatrice always shopped at two local and family run grocery stores: Rickley's Farm Stand where she bought all of her fruit, vegetables, cold cuts, and other luncheon meats and Drinkwater's Market, where she did the bulk of her shopping. She knew the layout of Drinkwater's Market inside and out and over the years had made friends or at least casual acquaintances with many members of the staff. Beatrice would miss her conversations with the meat manager Doug Barbuto, the man she shamelessly flirted with even more so now then when they were both in high school and sat next to each other in accounting or Miss Harrington's Health Education class. She'd even miss getting the latest town gossip from head cashier and her former high school rival Cookie Cusimo. While both women had failed marriages, the last thing that Beatrice's frail ego could take would be Cookie telling anyone and everyone who would listen, that the once proud, high and mighty Beatrice was now using food stamps. And most importantly, she couldn't take the chance that someone was bound to tell her mother. That was a story that she certainly did not want to share or be forced to explain to Nana Flossie.

No. From now on, she would try shopping here. She may not be as comfortable. However, the chances of her running into anyone that she knew were slim to none. It took her a little longer than she would have liked to navigate the unfamiliar store. While some of the prices were comparable to her regular haunts, there were many items that were much cheaper. She did question the quality in the meat department a couple of times. Half way through her shopping, Beatrice remembered that Loretta told her that the food stamp coupons would not cover any of the paper or cleaning products that she had already put into her cart. Since she and Cooper hadn't been to the bank yet, all those items needed to be put back. She met the kiddos in the produce section as promised. She reviewed each of their cereal choices and scrutinized Kevin's selection before grabbing the freshest fruit that she could find. They traveled in mass through the maze of shoppers that seemed to be moving in every different direction towards the front registers. As she suspected, the lines at the checkout counters were long and extremely slow moving. Beatrice was vigilant in her lookout for other people using food stamps, praying to God that she may see how others used them before she was forced to potentially embarrass herself. No such luck. And just like before, her palms were covered in a layer of nervous perspiration and she could feel her heartbeat in her throat as she emptied the contents of her carriages on the conveyer belt. The cashier didn't give Beatrice a second look as she began punching numbers into her register and passing the food along to the awaiting bag boy.

The cashier was a handsome woman in her mid to late forties with long faded red hair that she wore in a loose bun at the back of her neck. She wore small gold hoops in her ears and a plain gold band on her left hand. Her uniform consisted of a brown apron worn over a heavily starched white blouse with lantern sleeves. When she was almost finished ringing the order she looked Beatrice in the eye and smiled. Beatrice had rested her purse on the checkout counter and had both hands inside her purse holding on tightly to her food stamps, which were now damp with perspiration. When she finished ringing, she turned to Beatrice and informed her of the total.

Beatrice felt sick to her stomach. She panicked because she truly did not know what to do next.

"Hon. Are you ok?" the cashier asked with genuine concern.

Beatrice was silent. She bit her lower lip and shook her head no. She slowly lifted the food stamp coupon books from her purse. The cashier took Beatrice's hand and gave it a strong compassionate squeeze.

"First time?"

Beatrice nodded affirmatively.

"No worries hon. Think of them just like Monopoly money, except, you are going to have to pull the coupons out of the booklets. They can be a little tricky, so be careful not to rip them."

The Cashier's kindness and demeanor calmed Beatrice, who began ripping the larger value stamps out first.

"Thanks for not having any paper, cleaning or tobacco products. It certainly makes my life a heck of a lot easier. Next time you come in though, in case I don't' remember, remind me that you are using the stamps so I can separate the order."

Beatrice handed her enough stamps to cover her order.

"See darlin'. It wasn't all that bad."

Beatrice uncharacteristically leaned over the counter and gave the cashier a long heartfelt hug.

"Thank you." Beatrice whispered.

And with that, we left the store and loaded up the station wagon and drove home.

After the car was unpacked, the groceries put away, the sand swept out of the car, and the beach toys hosed off, we scattered to the four winds to play with our friends. Beatrice decided to take advantage of the quiet and opted to take a quick shower. She loved afternoon showers simply because there was plenty of hot water and rarely was there someone banging on the door of the only bathroom screaming to get in. Since she didn't get much sun time in today, she would use this alone time to try and clear her head. Once the water was hot enough, Beatrice climbed into the shower. She exhaled as the warm beads of water massaged her tense shoulders. After a few minutes, she sat on the floor of the tub, resting her chin on her knees and cried.

Twenty minutes later, Beatrice stepped out onto the back deck that overlooked the golden pond combing her wet hair. She took a seat at the round black wrought iron patio set and soaked in the warm sun as she mentally made a list of all the bills that she still needed to pay. She barely had time to light a cigarette before she is interrupted by Cooper carrying two large plastic Tupperware cups filled with iced coffee.

"Here you go." said Cooper as he handed his sister a cup and sat down.

"Thanks."

'That bad?"

"Oh yeah."

"What was it like?"

"I'll spare you the details for now. The good news is that I get a check and the food stamps. The medical cards should be arriving in the mail. Every six months or so, I might be getting a clothing allowance for the kids. It's not much, but it's certainly better than a sharp stick to the eye. The only real drawback is that I have to meet my caseworker every month or so to review my file."

"Is that normal?"

"Not sure. This is the first time that I have been on public assistance."

"Ha. Ha. Gimme one of those things." Cooper asked as he reached for the menthol cigarettes and lit one. "Yuck. How do you smoke these?"

"You out? I'll pick you up some of your own after I go to the bank. Do you mind keeping an eye out for the kids? Won't be long."

"No worries. Before you go, you should know that while you were in the shower some guy named Fred called for you."

"Really?"

"Who's Fred?"

"No one really. He is a friend of George's. He came over a few nights ago."

"Well you must have made a good impression."

"Oh? No. I don't care. He is...I'm not interested in...."

"Well you better be, because you are going out with him on Friday night."

"What???? No I am not."

"Yes you are. Too late. I already accepted for you."

"I'm not going. I don't want to do this. I am not ready for this. He's nowhere near my type."

"Your type? Who cares? You are not going to marry him for God's sake. It's just dinner. Bea, you've had a shitty couple of weeks. Go. Get out. Get distracted; take your mind off of it. What's the worst that can happen? You have a good time? You get a decent meal? You get away from your kids for a couple of hours?"

"I hate you."

"So what else is new? He'll be here at seven thirty."

"I...I...I'll see." said Beatrice as she stood and headed towards the door.

"Well you better see about a box of hair color while you are out. You're getting grey."

"Still hate you." Beatrice laughed as she entered the house.

"Love you too."

Table Manners

Back when my parents were setting up house, Beatrice's had a simple philosophy when it came to buying furniture for her home. "I would rather go without until I can afford something decent," she would often say. "Why buy a cheap piece of junk, when you are only going have to replace it later?" It was this philosophy that she has continued throughout the years. Hindsight being twenty-twenty, it's too bad that she didn't apply this same philosophy to the men in her life.

With my brother, sister and me in tow, Beatrice went on a shopping expedition to replace the den couch.

"We are going in here to look for a new couch. You will be on your best behavior while I am talking to Mr. Gibbons. There will be no loud noises. There will be no running around. There will be no jumping on the furniture." she warned us in the parking lot of Lakeside Furniture.

Pointing to Kevin and me, she said "And you two. There will not be another Kagel's incident."

Beatrice would always use the infamous Kagel Department Store incident as a friendly warning to us that our brief respite from the straight and narrow of good behavior in public places would not be tolerated.

Long before the birth of the shopping mall and the transformation of the storefronts belonging to the local merchants on Main Street into Uechi Ryu dojos, coffee houses or pharmacy chains, people in the area shopped for that special occasion outfit at the local department store. Kagel's fit the bill nicely. Like most of the buildings in the town square it was only two stories tall, three if you included the bargain basement section and took up half of the block on the corner of Main and Nelin Streets. It was here that Beatrice had taken us on a shopping expedition to find Carrie the perfect Christmas dress.

Kevin and I were naturally bored with the whole shopping for Carrie thing and set off to check out the new toys upstairs. Just to get some ideas for the letters we were planning on writing Santa Claus that night.

"You two stick together and no monkey business." Beatrice said as if on automatic pilot as she zipped through yet another rack of dresses.

Off we went weaving through the racks and displays of clothes making our way to the alcove and the stairs to the second floor and the toys. Like a couple of scientists we meticulously studied every car, truck, board game and GI Joe in the room and mentally prepared our "gotta have this or I'm gonna die" lists. Eventually with full brains, we made our way back down; I took two stairs at a time. Kevin slid the banister.

Back in the alcove and directly across from the foot of the stairs was a small door that looked totally out of place. I think we were more surprised that we never noticed it before, and naturally not being able to suppress our curiosity, we did what any little kid in our position would have done. We opened it!

The small room was filled with every one of the toys that we had just seen upstairs. And the best part of it, they were all out of their packages and just hanging around waiting for a couple of kids to play with. Carefully, Kevin and I crawled into the small room and shut the small door behind us.

The small room was actually the department store's Christmas display window. But to us, it was a place where we could "test drive" the toys to see if we really liked them. That way if they turned out to be duds, we wouldn't put them on our lists and waste Santa's time. Seemed logical.

It wasn't long before a crowd of people gathered around to watch us play. According to Nana Flossie the crowd got even bigger when Kevin and I started fist fighting over a GI Joe Action Marine.

Nana Flossie waited tables at the Cottage, a small family owned restaurant, which was about a block away from Kagel's. She was taking a quick break between her double-shift to help Beatrice pick out just the right dress for Carrie. It was Nana Flossie's opinion that the sun, the moon, and the stars revolved around my sister.

When she stopped in front of the store it was to talk with a couple of people she knew from church not to watch the wrestling match.

"Rose. What a pleasant surprise to find you here." Nana Flossie would always say something like that whenever she bumped into someone she knew on Main Street. "What brings you up this way?"

"Oh. Flossie. You're looking well." Rose replied.

"Oh I'm a mess. I just got off work for a couple minutes to buy my granddaughter her Christmas dress."

"She's getting so big. Carl and I could not believe our eyes when we saw her in church last Sunday. She's so well behaved." Rose said sweetly.

"She's her Nana's little angel." Nana Flossie beamed. She always seemed to beam when she talked about Carrie.

"Wish more children today were like her." Rose replied as she pointed towards the window of the store where at the time I had Kevin in a chokehold. "Can you imagine what type of family those two hooligans' belong to? Imagine fighting in the front window of Kagel's Department store—right here in the middle of the square."

Open jawed she stood there with the other on-lookers feeling the blood quickly rushing to her cheeks as she clenched her fists in unison. It was difficult for her to suppress her outrage. After all, Nana Flossie knew everyone in town and everyone knew her or knew of her. Everything that we did somehow was a direct reflection on her. The last thing that she wanted or needed was to be mortified by her own flesh and blood. At this point Kevin and I had graduated to chucking Matchbox cars at one another.

"It's a sin." Nana Flossie said struggling to keep her composure and also slightly relieved to think no one really seemed to know to whom my brother and I belonged.

"Rose, it was good to see you dear but I need to get in and get back to work. If you don't stop into the restaurant this week, I'll see you in church." And with that, Nana Flossie briskly walked into Kagel's. She always walked briskly.

Within seconds, she had found the store manager and informed him that there were two juvenile delinquents destroying his window display. She then stopped at a dress rack before tracking Beatrice down. Quickly she pointed out that the red velvet pants outfit that Carrie was currently modeling just wouldn't do. She then handed Beatrice the perfect Christmas dress and smiled lovingly when Beatrice and Carrie emerged from the dressing room.

"That's Nana's little girl. Oh Beatrice this one is perfect. Look how it matches her eyes."

Mission accomplished, Nana Flossie kissed her daughter on the cheek and pressed some money into her hand to pay for the dress.

"Thanks Mom." Beatrice said appreciatively.

"Anything for my girls. In the meantime Bea, you might want to go check on the boys. I think that by now, they're probably in the store manager's office." Nana Flossie said in a voice just above a whisper.

And with that she turned and slipped out the back door of Kagel's like some super celebrity hoping not to be noticed leaving Beatrice to deal with the mess.

Sufficiently forewarned with the infamous Kagel's incident, we were now free to explore the mazes of couches and ottomans that made up Lakeside Furniture.

"Look with your eyes not your hands" she reminded us.

Beatrice was looking through fabric swatches and talking with Mr. Gibbons about the benefits of this new miracle product that literally repels stains from fabric called Scotch Guard when out of the corner of her eye she saw it.

"Oh my God!" Beatrice squealed in delight not believing her good luck. "This is it!" she said excitedly. "I cannot believe that you actually have this!"

Was my mother actually jumping up and down in a store?

Not twenty minutes before this woman who rattled off a veritable checklist of proper behavior was running and making loud noises in the store.

"It is! It's the exact same set!"

This was the same rock wood maple colonial dining room set that she had fallen in love with when she saw it a month earlier in a home style magazine. Beatrice always dreamed of a special dining room, a place where she and her family would sit down to have a proper Sunday dinner or celebrate Easter and Thanksgiving with the entire extended family including Butch's two maiden aunts, whom she could only take in small doses. Currently her dining room was made up of a mish-mash of hand-me-downs and loaners. Nothing matched, including the chipped pieces of china she was able to amass. But this set. This set would change everything.

The new couch quickly became a fading memory...another item to be added to the list of things to buy when the money was there. Without hesitation, she set up a payment schedule with Mr. Gibbons and five months and a lot of pasta dinners later, the dining room set arrived at our house by the golden pond.

Before the furniture arrived, Beatrice spent a lot of time getting the dining room in proper order, akin to an expectant mother preparing her nursery. The stucco walls and ceiling received a fresh coat of cream-colored paint. Later on when she had the money she would talk her brother into helping her wallpaper. Red. With the same zeal and determination she had with each of her projects, Beatrice combed every store within a four-town radius for the perfect wagon wheel "chandelier" and braided rug that would complement her newly stripped, stained, polyurethaned, waxed and buffed hardwood floor. The room, like most dining rooms was right off of her small kitchen. What made this room unique was the number of windows...eight in all. The left wall consisted of a bank of five windows that not only filled the room with sunshine, but also provided a breathtaking view of the golden pond. There was a pair of windows hanging side by side on the back wall that for two seasons the view of the neighbor's house was mercifully blocked by an oak tree which at the height of fall foliage seemed to be ablaze with colors like watermelon, peach and ochre. The single window on the right offered a view of the tiny front yard. It was a great place Mom would use to check up on us as we played. Since the mahogany trim around the windows was in great condition, it only needed a quick rub down with the Scott's Liquid Gold Polish before she put up her window treatments. It took a bit, but Beatrice eventually decided upon white Cape Cod Country Café Curtains.

At least four or five times a year, Beatrice would take down her curtains. She would wash the windows until they sparkled in the sunlight finishing in just enough time to add a little bit of starch to the rinse cycle. Then she would complete whatever household tasks she had put off that morning just as soon as she hung them on her clothesline. They never took a spin in her gas dryer. And when they were dried, she would gather them up and begin the painstaking process of ironing out every wrinkle and pressing every crease, fold and ruffle using the spray starch generously. Beatrice would often listen to the radio and sing along as she worked. The entire process usually took two days and as the years went on, it took on almost religious implications as she perfected her process.

It was obvious that of all her furniture, the dining room was her pride and joy. As part of her every Saturday morning cleaning ritual, Beatrice lovingly applied Ole English polish to every chair slat and every drawer on the hutch until the sunlight reflected on every surface.

To this day, we are still not allowed to wear shoes into the dining room in the fear that we may accidentally dent a table leg or scratch a chair.

Beatrice was true to her word. The room was used for Sunday afternoon dinners. Never were we allowed in there for our morning visits with the Captain or Tony the Tiger! That's what the breakfast nook was for. No, this is the room where we had the special dinners like the time Kevin only got three D's on his report card.

"Sometimes, you just need to celebrate the small achievements wherever you can take them." she would often say.

It was here that we learned the ins and outs of proper table etiquette. 'Forks on the left, knives on the right' became something of a mantra in our home as each of us took turns learning to set the perfect table. Since the cloth napkins were reserved for the high holidays or the really special occasions, paper would have to make do. Naturally, they had to be folded neatly in a diamond shape, unless of course Kevin needed to soften the blow of some terrible news. As Kevin got older, he chose the dinner table to confess his increasingly terrible transgressions from the straight and narrow knowing full well that Beatrice rarely lost her temper there. Kevin's diamonds gave way to paper roses, swans, or some other origami creature. The bigger the transgression, the more exotic and intricate his napkins became.

Where Beatrice refused to compromise her table setting was the use of water glasses at the dinner table. Plastic cups were fine for lunches or the occasional sip of orange juice at breakfast, but they had no place at her dinner table. 'No use crying over spilt milk' had a different meaning in our home as it usually included a shattered tumbler.

It was in this magic room that Beatrice spent many an hour instilling in us the proper way to sit at a table.

"Sit up straight." she would often say. This proved exceedingly difficult for my younger brother Christopher who could only reach the table with the aid of the family dictionary. To further compound the issue, his sock covered feet provided little traction against the polished seat of the chair he was assigned. To complicate his situation further, Christopher's paper napkin spent more time on the floor than it did in his lap.

Beatrice made up small phrases to help us remember our manners. With your first elbow infraction, she would say in a singsongy tone "Mable, Mable. Elbows off the table." If warned again, she grew sterner and would often say something like; "You can always measure a person's character by their table manners. Please remove your elbow or I shall have to do it for you." The third infraction resulted in being summarily dismissed from the table and sent to our rooms.

We learned how to properly cut our meat and how to chew with our mouths closed. Every now and then, Carrie who sat directly across the table from me and I would engage in a game of train wreck. It was one of those kid games you would play to help relieve the stiffness and boredom of being at the formal dinner table. Playing the game was relatively simple. We would each take a couple of forks-full of whatever was on our plates. And when Beatrice and Butch were preoccupied, we would open our mouths to expose the freshly chewed food on our tongues. First person to wince…loses. As you can imagine, color, texture, and imagination…not to mention a pair of completely distracted parents…were paramount to the success of the game.

With the exception of a few close calls, we never got caught.

With each of Butch's unexcused absences, Beatrice got a little more creative with the types of dinners she would serve…nothing too exotic, maybe a new type of spice or a new recipe for something called Spanish rice. On one occasion, when she actually wanted Butch out of the house, Beatrice served a Sunday dinner consisting of fresh vegetables like boiled potatoes, summer squash, string beans, and steamed broccoli. Each item was heavily seasoned with salt and pepper and covered with melting butter. It was the complete antithesis to a man who ate nothing other than red meat.

And through it all, regardless of whatever food was being served, including franks, beans, and brown bread Saturday nights, Beatrice insisted on proper table etiquette. With that all being said, you cannot possibly imagine the gut wrenching horror we felt as Fred joined us for that first fateful dinner.

It took place on a warm Sunday afternoon in June. Beatrice had been seeing Fred for a couple of weeks and felt that it was high time that we all became acquainted. She was understandably very nervous. Everything had to be perfect. Earlier in the week, she franticly completed her curtain routine...which was a month ahead of her normal schedule. The china was washed; the silver polished; and the linens starched and ironed. There would be no paper at this table!

At the market, she must have sent the butcher out back three times before she abandoned her quest for the perfect eye of the round roast. In Beatrice's opinion, an eye of the round was the tastiest of meats and the one meal that she received the most compliments. Naturally she considered it one of her specialties and it would be the ideal dinner for her family and new beau. Using a controlled breathing exercise, she calmed her frustration.

Or was it panic?

And began pacing the meat display in the hopes something would catch her eye. Eventually she spotted a couple of Dell Monaco steaks and Beatrice quickly pounced on them and swooped them into the carriage just before an overweight woman dressed in a rainbow colored caftan and matching kerchief was able to get her bloated yet beautifully manicured hands on them.

"Curlers? In public? Momma would have a field day with her." Beatrice whispered under breath allowing herself a brief smile of triumph as she made her way to the produce aisle.

Beatrice insisted on setting the dinner table herself and did so in the high holiday fashion complete with the serving platters and water goblets that matched her china pattern. The candlesticks came out and went back more than once, before Beatrice eventually decided to go without.

"It's just right." she said to herself as she went back into the kitchen to check on her appetizers.

Each of us was dressed in the freshly pressed outfits that Beatrice laid out on our beds that morning. Not quite our Easter best, but certainly much better than the jeans and shirts that we usually wore each day to school. Kevin complained as usual about how difficult it was to move in his new pair of Tough Skins.

"Be thankful. There are poor children out there who would give their right arm for a new pair of pants. Now be a good boy and try to keep clean." Beatrice replied. How do I look?" she asked.

Beatrice wore one of her standby outfits...a pair of navy colored pedal pushers with a matching navy and white striped jersey, a pair of white canvas sneakers which always looked as though they just came out of the box and of course the footies style socks complete with matching pom-pom.

"You look beautiful Mommy." Kevin and Christopher said in unison. Carrie and I were convinced that Kevin was trying to score points.

"Thank you Christopher." Beatrice said lovingly as she kissed Christopher on the forehead. "Kevin, I appreciate the compliment my darling. I really do. But today would not be the day to drop one of your bombshells at the dinner table. Do I make myself clear?"

"Yes ma'am."

When the doorbell rang, Beatrice gave us a quick final inspection and then rattled off a series of warnings that seemed as though they had been tape recorded and played back over and over as we followed her to the front door.

"Be on your best behavior. Company manners. I am not kidding. I want to hear 'please', I want to hear 'thank you'. Fred's table manners may be different from ours, so I do not want to hear any wise cracks or snide comments. I do not want to see any eyeballs rolling to the back of your heads. Boys, if he sticks out his hand, you be sure to shake it!"

And before opening the door, she turned to us and said "And above all, no train wreck!"

She knows about train wreck?

One last look in the hall mirror and Beatrice opened the door to reveal Fred. He must have just applied the Brylcreem, because his curls looked as though they were shellacked to his head. He was wearing the same outfit that I first met him in during earthquake season.

We would eventually learn that he only had the one "Sunday Best" outfit. The rest of his wardrobe consisted of cast offs of the uniform he wore to the plant in various degrees of shabbiness. When a t-shirt became too yellowed or if his blue Dickies and matching shirt complete with name patch were too tattered or too stained to wear to work, they made it into the pile of unfolded laundry that eventually became his every-day-attire.

The tableau had the makings of a great horror movie scene. The Quasimodo-Beast stands awkwardly in the front entryway looking lovingly at Beatrice. Eventually, he shifted his gaze to the four of us who were crouched on the stairway glaring down at him. Contempt and disdain flashed from our eyes like daggers. And in that instant, an air of mutual hatred was confirmed and an implicit declaration of war was established between us and her new beau. A beat later, he returned his attention to Beatrice.

"Hi Sweetie." Fred said to Beatrice as he awkwardly kissed her on the cheek. "These are for you."

Grasped tightly in his massive right hand was a bouquet of white and yellow Chrysanthemums that looked as though they were hurriedly picked and then tied together with a pink bow.

"Oh Fred. They're lovely." Beatrice said affectionately. "I have just the vase for them."

"After lunch, let's be sure to check the garden for missing flowers" Carrie whispered to me.

I bit my lip until it bled in the hopes that it would suppress my laughter.

Beatrice threw me the look...the facial expression that every mother shares with some variation with her children as a warning sign that they are about step over the line and that the current behavior had better cease and desist. Failure to comply usually results in yelling, screaming and the use of said child's dreaded middle name. She then grabbed Fred by the arm and said proudly, "Freddie, I would like you to meet my children. This is Carrie. She's the oldest. You've already met Michael Spencer.

Ouch!

"Next to him is Kevin and the little guy is Christopher."

As promised we shook his out stretched paw, which seemed to please Beatrice to no end. And with each introduction, Fred would say something like, "Pudda there partner", "Gosh you are pretty"; "Your Mom has told me a lot about you" or some other such obviously rehearsed phrase.

And then the six of us just stood there staring at each other.

"You looked famished Fred. Why don't we skip the hors d'oeuvres that I had planned in the living room and go straight to the dining room for lunch?" Beatrice suggested.

The uncomfortable hiatus in conversation caused her motherly instincts to kick into high gear, warning her that the pre-meal chat she intended as a way to break the ice would more than likely end in disaster.

We were actually going to use the living room?

We all took our assigned seats around the dining room table. Beatrice was at the head of the table closest to the door just in case she needed to quickly retrieve something out of the kitchen. Kevin and I sat next to one another facing the bank of five windows. We spent many a meal watching the boats and daydreaming how much fun it would be to sail along with them on the little golden pond. Across the oval shaped table sat Christopher and Carrie. I don't know what upset Carrie more the fact that Fred was going to take Butch's place at the head of the table or the fact that he was the only one allowed in the dining room with his shoes on.

With a couple of quick trips, Beatrice had served the Sunday dinner. In addition to the barbecued steaks, there were platters of potatoes, beet greens, corn on the cob, fresh garden tomatoes in Italian salad dressing and cucumber slices that have been marinating in apple cider vinegar.

When Beatrice finished filling the last goblet with cool well water she took her place at the table.

"Everything sure looks good Sweetie," said Fred. "By any chance do you have any rolls?"

"Oh, I'm sorry Fred." Beatrice replied sounding almost embarrassed that she forgot the rolls. "We usually don't eat bread with our dinner."

"Oh. No bread?"

"Well, I have bread in the house. I just don't have any rolls."

"That would be just fine. A couple slices of bread would be just fine then." Fred requested as he rubbed his two hands together. "Everything sure looks good. Who wants some potatoes?"

By the time Beatrice returned to the dining room with a small side plate containing half a dozen or so slices of Wonder bread, Fred had already piled his plate with the steak and potatoes.

"Thanks sweetie," he said taking the plate. "Kevin was just telling me how he won the Pinewood Derby with the cub scouts this year."

"Yeah. And I got my picture in the paper and everything." Kevin added smugly.

"Wow. That's some accomplishment there little buddy," Fred said as he tucked his napkin into his shirt collar so that it formed a bib. Christopher's eyes bulged in disbelief.

"Kevin just loves the scouts. Freddie were you ever a Boy Scout?" asked Beatrice anxious to keep the conversation going.

With a mouth full of potatoes he replied. "Nah. Never was much of a joiner. But I used to love to go camping. There was this one time when my friend Harry and I went skinny-dipping."

Throughout the telling of the story, Fred had both his elbows on the table.

Mable! Mable!

Between taking bites of food, he would use his fork to accentuate certain points of the anecdote not unlike a conductor stricken with Bells Palsy using his baton to guide an orchestra. Once or twice small pieces of food would fall out of his mouth and back onto his plate only to be scooped up and shoveled back in. The captured audience paid less and less attention to Fred's tale and more and more to his table rule infractions. For each violation, I drew a line in my mashed potatoes. Eleven and counting.

He ended his story and to our surprise, Beatrice let out a loud laugh whereupon Fred let loose with a thunderous guffaw. His large belly bumped the table a couple of times as it jiggled and knocked a water goblet into Christopher's lap, which seemed to make Fred and Beatrice laugh even harder.

"Mommy!" Christopher shouted with a tone that proclaimed his innocence.

"Oh no baby. It was just an accident." Beatrice said still chuckling. "Carrie, please help your brother get cleaned up."

"Mom." Carrie protested.

"Please. Just do it."

"Come on squirt." Carrie said as she pushed away from the table. "Let's find some dry clothes."

"I'm sorry little buddy." Fred said trying his best not to laugh. As soon as Carrie and Christopher left the room, Fred started to laugh even harder causing Kevin to let out a small snicker. I responded by kicking Kevin under the table.

"Oww. Knock it off monkey butt!" Kevin protested.

Beatrice who at this time was cleaning the water up out of Christopher's chair shot me the look again.

"Boys. Remember what I said about table manners."

"Aw Bea. Let 'em alone. They're just being boys." Fred said in our defense. "My brothers and I used to have some real knock down drag out fights."

"Well I am sure that you are right Freddie, but somehow I doubt that your mother let you and your brothers misbehave at the dinner table." Beatrice said. "Ok. It's all cleaned up. No harm done. Freddie you haven't tried any of the beet greens."

"Think I'll pass for now Sweetie; still need to work on my corn. Kev, pass the butter will ya?"

Fred then started to tell another of his stories. This one involved a fight he and his two brothers had over the same girl named Brenda Harmon. He described her as a real dish...a regular "hotsy-totsy". Only this time, his trusty fork-baton was replaced with a knife that was now balancing an extraordinarily large slab of butter he just hacked out of the butter dish. Once again I found myself tuning out the story of his youth and fixating instead on the knife. Back and forth his knife waived. It was going to happen. I was sure of it. Any second now the lump of Land O' Lakes would surely be sent flying. I couldn't help but wonder if Beatrice would have the same cavalier attitude when her curtains or walls became splattered with butter.

And just when I thought it was about to take flight, Fred stopped the waving, picked up a piece of Wonder Bread with his free hand and messily smeared the slice of processed wheat that promised to help build strong bodies twelve ways with the contents of his knife.

Whew!

Without missing a beat, the buttered bread quickly joined with his knife-baton in an obnoxious syncopation as he continued his story. Eventually he replaced his knife with an ear of corn from his plate, which he pointed and shook at Beatrice repeatedly as he stressed different parts of his mundane tale until he reached the crescendo at which point he plopped the ear of corn onto the Wonder Bread and proceeded to twist and turn. Carrie's mouth was hanging open as she stood in the doorway. I knew what she was thinking. "My God. This fat guy is polishing his corn before he eats it."

This became known as the Fred Method for buttering your corn.

Beatrice shot all of us the look.

"Come on in you two and eat. Your dinner is getting cold." Beatrice said through gritted teeth.

As my brother and sister took their places at the table, Fred began to gorge himself on his polished ear of corn. As he gnawed, he started to breathe and wheeze heavily. Beatrice later explained to us that poor Fred had a deviated septum that made it hard to breathe when he ate. Christopher sat slack jawed in his seat watching the small fractions of corn kernels bounce off Fred's chin and fall into his linen bib. Once he got hit with a couple of stray kernels, Christopher broke his catatonia-like silence.

"Ewww. Mommy. Help. It's raining corn."

Carrie, Kevin and I started to laugh which caused the overly frustrated Christopher to cry. Of all of Beatrice's children, Christopher was considered to be the only "Ten". He was quite, neat, polite and clean. He hated to get dirty. Thankfully there was a brief time in his early twenties when he was as loud and messy as the rest of us.

The more we laughed, the more Christopher cried. He got up from the table and ran over to Beatrice who did her best to console him.

"Will you three knock it off? Can't you see that he's upset?" Beatrice scolded at us.

Finally noticing what was going on Fred let the stripped cob fall onto his plate. "What's the matter little buddy?" he asked Christopher as he licked the butter from each of his fingertips.

"You got corn on me." Christopher blurted out through his tears.

"Did not."
"Did too."
"Did not."
"Did too."
"Did not."
"Did too."
"Did not."
"Did too."

Eventually Fred wore Christopher down and we finished the rest of our meal in silence.

Reality Check

A Tale Of Two Lawyers

Three calls to the state bar association lawyer telephone referral line later, Beatrice, Christopher and I found ourselves sitting in the leather wing back chairs that helped to make up the plush waiting room of Emerson, Meredith, and Murdock, attorneys at law. One look at Beatrice and you could tell that she was impressed with the room's floor to ceiling paladin windows, exposed brick walls, crown moldings and the blue and green Persian rug that covered the impeccably waxed hardwood flooring. The offices were housed in the old McKay Theatre, which remained empty throughout most of the Nineteen Sixties and early Seventies until it was remodeled as part of the ambitious "Fresh Face for Main Street" urban renewal project run by the town selectmen.

"Michael, are you sure that we can afford this guy?" Beatrice asked in a stage whisper doing her best to make sure that the receptionist didn't over hear her question. Judging from the smile on the young lady's face, I am sure that she had.

"Michael already told you Mama; the fifteen minute consultation is free." Christopher whispered back and at the same time winking at the receptionist who smiled even more as she answered the next incoming call.

"You know," she whispered, "Your Uncles and I spent many a Saturday afternoon here, back when it was a movie theatre."

"Gosh, when I think about it," she continued to whisper, "We used to raise hell."

"Really?" Christopher half-heartedly whispered back to Beatrice. Instead he chose to focus more of his attention on the lovely receptionist with blond hair and an inviting smile.

Grabbing his chin, Beatrice pulled Christopher's face closer to hers. "Hey. Casanova. When I am talking to you I expect you to give me your full undivided attention!" she whispered louder. "You can ogle and drool over that pretty girl on your own time!"

"Ma! Will you cut it out?" Christopher snapped as he pulled away. "Stop treating me like I am twelve years old."

"Do I have to separate you two?" I asked in a half serious tone.

Before either one of them could answer back, another strikingly beautiful woman sauntered over with an out stretched impeccably manicured hand.

"Good morning. You fine people must be my ten o'clock. My name is Randi Gonzales-Ruiz. It's a pleasure to meet each of you." she said in a voice that dripped of honey and quite possibly could have belonged to one of those wives from Stepford. She smiled like a Cheshire cat or perhaps more likely, like someone who was proud of some very recent and very expensive cosmetic dental surgery. She shook each of our hands firmly. Before we had the opportunity to introduce ourselves, she said, "I understand that you have some questions about a will. Why don't you follow me to the conference room and we'll see what answers I can get for you?"

We followed Ms. Gonzales-Ruiz and her blue double-breasted pin striped power suit, through the double frosted glass and brass doors behind the blonde receptionist and down an office lined corridor until we got to the conference room. As before, Beatrice was impressed with the mahogany trim and marble conference table. Ms. Gonzales-Ruiz gestured for us to make ourselves comfortable in the supple leather chairs as she sat at the head of the table and opened her monogrammed brown leather portfolio and uncapped her Monte Blanc pen.

"May I offer you coffee or some water?" she asked. And again before we could respond, she picked up the receiver of the telephone in front of her and pressed two buttons. "Harmony? Would you be a dear and bring us four coffees please? Thanks hon."

She smiled. More teeth. Checked her watch and then made a small notation in her portfolio. Put her pen down. Folded her hands and her rather large diamond engagement ring sparkled under the overhead lighting. Her smile, slowly transformed to a new look of genuinely rehearsed heartfelt concern and said, "First of all, on behalf of everyone here at Emerson, Meredith, and Murdock, please let me express our condolences regarding your loss."

"Thank you." Beatrice replied.

"How can I help you?" she asked in another genuinely rehearsed tone.

"Well, it involves my husband." Beatrice began. "We recently found out that he has passed away."

"Was it unexpected?" Ms. Gonzales-Ruiz asked in a less rehearsed tone.

"Not really. Although we expected him to pass away a heck of a lot sooner." I said.

"Michael, there is no need to be so blunt." Beatrice admonished. "You must forgive my son Miss Ruiz, but my husband led what many would consider to be an unhealthy lifestyle."

"May I ask how he died?" she inquired.

"Honestly, we are not too sure. My husband and I were estranged. We haven't spoken in a number of years. We only got the news recently. I believe it was some form of heart attack. But if you think the cause of death has any relevance, I would be more than happy to get that information for you."

Ms. Gonzales-Ruiz shook her head no.

"Apparently he had been dead almost two weeks before my poor step-daughter found the body. It was quite a shock as you can imagine. They were very close."

I sat back in amazement and watched as Beatrice played the grieving widow. She had the perfect range of emotion, not appearing to be too callous or too distraught. I was equally astonished to hear her leave out certain facts. For example, Fred died on the toilet on a Wednesday. We know this, because we were told that the men from the coroner's office had a very difficult time trying to pry away the open TV Guide that thanks to rigamortis, Fred was permanently clutching in his frozen hands.

"My husband and I never divorced. When he left, I never made any formal arrangements for any financial support. I suppose, most women today would think I was crazy. And, to tell you the truth, I probably was a little crazy. But, I could honestly say, I didn't want anything from him. I had my pride and all I wanted was my independence." Beatrice said in a manner that, if delivered by Sally or Meryl, would have gotten them another Oscar nod.

"I can appreciate how you may feel. However, legally I would have advised you against it." Ms. Gonzales-Ruiz said smiling.

Again with the teeth.

"I guess that it's all water under the bridge at this point." Beatrice shot back.

"Since we have had very little contact with my step-father, we have no clue to the state of his finances. Now that he is dead, would my mother be responsible for his debts?" Christopher asked.

"You see, my concern at this point is my home." Beatrice chimed in. "The house is all that I have. It was mine before the marriage to Freddie. I am sure you can appreciate how difficult it is for a single mother to keep a house afloat on a fixed income. I have worked very hard to keep my credit rating, such as it is. I am not sure that I would be able to swing everything if all of a sudden I had additional bills to pay that weren't mine."

"I can appreciate your concerns. No one likes to deal with unexpected financial burdens. Can you tell me if he had a will?" asked the robo-lawyer.

"Not that I know of...I really don't think so. " Beatrice replied. "He was always talking about writing one, but I would imagine that he would never get around to it. My husband used to plan to do a great many of things. However, Freddie often spent so much time planning that he never would get around to executing them."

"Unfortunately, people like your late husband are not all that uncommon. I could tell you all sorts of horrible situations that my clients have found themselves in that could have all been avoided with just a little estate planning. Are your wills in order?" the Stepford Lawyer questioned hopefully looking for a sale.

"They most certainly are." Beatrice said proudly and I knew that she was lying through her teeth. "Mine is in my safety deposit box with the rest of my important papers."

"Good for you." Another smile. "The key here is to find a copy of the will. Without knowing for certain it exists, we could spend a lot of time speculating. Is there someone you could call?"

"I suppose that I could try one of my step-daughters..."Beatrice said reluctantly.

"Marvelous." she beamed. Lifting up her pen, she then asked, "Now what can you tell me about his assets?"

"Well, I know that he had a pension, and some stocks." Beatrice listed.

"Mmmhmmm." the lawyer half-heartedly answered as she began to concentrate on making her notes. And as her custom, Beatrice immediately stopped. Noticing the awkward silence, Ms. Gonzales-Ruiz looked up and motioned to Beatrice to continue.

"Oh. Are you ready for me dear?" Beatrice asked in a tone that Christopher and I both immediately recognized as trouble. "I didn't want to get too far ahead of you."

Taken back, the robo-lawyer looked a little confused. And then said, "No. I'm fine. Please continue."

"Well, to the best of my knowledge there might be some other items like camper..." Beatrice began but stopped to make sure that Ms. Gonzales-Ruiz maintained eye contact. "And a couple of cars. I am sure that they can't be worth much. He always refused to spend money on a good car. He did have a piece of property that he was living on at the time of his death."

"I see. Do you have an idea how much the house would be worth?"

"Well, I am not sure that I would actually call it a house." Beatrice said almost embarrassed.

"I'm sorry?" Ms. Gonzales-Ruiz questioned in the hopes that Beatrice would finish her thought.

"Before we married, Freddie bought a small parcel of property, near a lake. It wasn't much. A little under an acre I think. It was always his hope that one day we would retire there. Between you and I, that was never going to happen. I think that I knew deep down on some level, we would never last. And truth be told, retirement always seemed so far away. But to keep the marriage going, I went along with his little pipe-dream home. I always figured, in the worst case scenario, we would have an investment that we may be able to sell later. Since, he didn't make much money working at the plant; he would scrimp and save some money. So that once a year we would have enough to tackle some project or another. He thought that not only could we save a lot of money if we did the majority of the work ourselves, it was also a way that we could all work on something together as a family. Not that he had any real experience building a house, but he wouldn't stop until he had all of the information he needed. You see, for all of his faults, there wasn't anything that Freddie couldn't do, once he set his mind to it. So, one year he had us all digging the septic system, another year a well. The last project that we all worked on was the foundation. Remember boys? That project nearly did us all in. We separated shortly after the foundation was finished and Freddie went up there to live full time."

"In the foundation?" Ms. Gonzales-Ruiz asked in disbelief.

"Yes." Beatrice said with her version of the robo-lawyer toothy smile.

"He did manage to put a roof over it" I added.

"Oh" Ms. Gonzales-Ruiz replied obviously still in disbelief. She paused for a nanosecond to gather her thoughts. "Well, if the dwelling is as bad as you describe, I am sure that we would be able to convince a realtor to sell it as a fixer-upper. In most cases people who purchase lakefront property usually knock down existing structures and build a home more to their liking."

"I never said it was lakefront property dear. I said it was near a lake." Beatrice politely corrected her.

"My mistake." she replied without her toothy grin. "Either way, we will need to contact a realtor and have them do an appraisal to see what the market will bear. You are more than welcome to use a realtor of your choice. If you would like, I can recommend several that we have used in the past. Now, a simple title search will tell us if there are any liens on the property. What is the address?"

"Route 11. Middletown, New Hampshire." Christopher dictated.

Upon hearing the address, Ms. Gonzales-Ruiz returned the cap to her Monte Blanc pen, folded her hands on her now closed monogrammed brown leather portfolio. She took a rather large cleansing breath and flashed her toothy smile as she said, "On behalf of my firm, I find that I must apologize to you and your sons for wasting your time here today. Obviously one of our clerks failed to explain to you that we are only licensed to practice law in the state of Massachusetts. Since your husband was living in New Hampshire, I am afraid that you are going to need to work with a New Hampshire based attorney."

Before we could say a thing, Ms. Gonzales-Ruiz stood up reached out her hand to shake ours and said, "I wish you the best of luck solving this situation. I will ask Harmony to come show you out. I will also see to it that she has some referrals for you as well."

And then she was gone. I guess our fifteen minutes were up.

Less than two and a half days later, we found ourselves driving north into New Hampshire to make our ten o'clock appointment with Louisa A. Nickels Attorney and Counselor at Law. Beatrice was impressed that she had both titles. Christopher and I were hard pressed to figure out what the difference was between the two and more importantly why would someone want to advertise that they were both? Beatrice was equally impressed with the receptionist when she called to double check the driving directions.

"He said that their offices were located on the second floor in one of the oldest historical landmarks in the county...the old General Store built in the 1800's. It's now the Public Library. It sounds lovely. Have you ever noticed that nearly all attorneys have the most incredible office space?" Beatrice said.

"Have you ever noticed that funeral parlors have the best houses?" Christopher asked.

"It is really a shame that you boys didn't go into business with Uncle Chicky."

"Ma! How many times do we have to go over this? I didn't want to be an undertaker." I snapped back knowing full well where the conversation was going.

"But it could have been you and your kids living in that gorgeous home instead of cousin Beverly and her idiot savant husband." she said.

Touché!

"Ma. He's not an idiot. He is just socially retarded." Christopher said.

"Christopher...don't use that word!"

"Sorry, Mom."

"I do admit Christopher that there are...socially underachieving people in this world, and I have known plenty in my day. Hell I have even been married to a couple of them. Socially defective people usually lack the ability to match their clothing from time to time. Now do not confuse this with colorblind people who wear yellow and brown or different shades of pink and red. Colorblind people cannot help the way that God made them. Socially defective people wear checks and plaids together as a fashion choice. Their pants are usually way too short. On occasion, they have been known to have toilet paper attached to the bottom of their shoe when they come out of the restroom. They usually show up too early and stay way too late at a function. They want to fit in, they just do not know how. However, it has always been my experience that socially defective people were always clean and pressed. They take baths and showers. Sure, sometimes they were too liberal with the cologne to hide a biological problem that they could not control through any fault of their own. But it's different with Cousin Beverly's husband. While he may only possess a room temperature IQ, he cannot be held accountable for that. However, he always smells like low tide. If I didn't know better, I would swear that he doesn't know how or worse yet, simply chooses not to bathe. He always looks dirty. Can you imagine? You've just lost your loved one. You're shelling out God knows how much for a funeral and the guy arranging the whole thing has greasy hair and no matter what he wears always look like he just rolled out of bed." Beatrice stopped for air before she shuttered.

"Of course, Cousin Beverly is no real catch either!" I added. "Why didn't Uncle Chicky and Aunt Celeste pay to have those things capped?"

"It's not really their fault. They were a product of the times." Beatrice went on to explain. "Back when I was raising you kids, people didn't believe in orthodontia like they do today. Crooked teeth added a sense of character to a person's face. It was a simpler time. Not like today. Today parents slap a set of braces on their kids the minute they turn eleven. It's awful."

"Hey Michael," Christopher asked. "When is Kennedy getting her braces again?"

"Now Christopher, you leave your brother alone. My granddaughter's braces are a necessity." Beatrice chided.

"Michael can't help it if his children didn't inherit his straight teeth."

Changing the subject as fast as I could, I said "At least Cousin Beverly had the good sense to have those ugly yellow horse teeth bleached."

"But now the poor thing has big really, really, really white horse teeth." Beatrice laughed with a whinny.

We continued laughing as I drove the car onto Main Street. But the laughter slowly died as we approached the dilapidated building with the blistering white paint and forest green crooked shutters on the corner of Main and Hamilton Streets.

"Well, we certainly shouldn't judge this book by its cover." Beatrice began while struggling to find something positive to say. "After all, it's probably one of the more recognizable buildings in this town."

"No doubt." I muttered under my breath.

"Well, let's try to stay positive. That nice receptionist said that there was plenty of parking in the rear. Turn here, dear." Beatrice commanded.

We parked and climbed the dark steep stairs to the second floor landing, which we assumed served as the waiting room for Louisa A. Nickels Attorney and Counselor at Law. This space was a sharp contrast to our previous lawyer's waiting room. Several mix-matched chairs of various sizes, textures, and cleanliness replaced the high backed leather chairs. The brown and yellow oval frayed braided rug showed signs of wear and tear and scarcely covered the battered and stained hard wood flooring. A couple of end tables collected small piles of back issues of People and New Hampshire Living magazines as well as a set of mismatched chipped ginger jar lamps. The walls were painted industrial mint green and looked as though they could have used an additional coat of paint.

We stood there for a couple of minutes, taking in the sites and aroma (Was that mold?), when an overweight sweaty man in a sweater vest and black rimmed glasses walked by with his arms full of files.

"You here for Lou?" he asked, barely stopping for our reply. "I'll let her know that you're here. Take a load off. She'll be with you in a minute. There's a bubbler around the corner if you want a drink."

"I need a cigarette." Beatrice announced. "Do you see an ashtray around here?"

"Me too." a gravelly voice said from around the corner. "Thank God a client that smokes. Hi. My name is Louisa Nickels. My friends call me Lou."

Before us stood a tall thin woman with wiry grey hair which she loosely piled on top of her head and held into place by a half chewed number-two pencil. She used her left hand to try and push the fly away sprigs of hair from her sparkling dark eyes and extended her right hand for Beatrice to shake, which of course Beatrice did immediately. Lou had sharp facial features and high cheekbones, which offset her triangle shaped face. She wore no makeup, except for some peach colored lipstick. Her lawyerly wardrobe consisted of a faded navy blue pocket t-shirt, a tan broom skirt, and a pair of leather flip-flops on her feet. She wore no jewelry, except for two silver chains around her neck. Attached to one chain were a set of dirty half glasses; at the end of the other was the top of a silver fork. Each of the tines had been delicately hammered so that they now curled outward.

"What an interesting necklace." Beatrice sincerely commented.

Holding it in her hand and admiring it as well, Lou replied, "Thanks you. It's a heavy bugger. My brother was a silversmith artist in the early seventies. Remind me to show you the matching spoon rings. Of course, our mother was not too happy when she found out that Derek was using the family silver to make jewelry. Oh she cursed him for days. Now he sells tennis bracelets for a chain jewelry store at the Mall Of New Hampshire. He had such a promising talent. "

"My mother used to have the exact same necklace. Do you remember boys? She still has it in her jewelry box." Beatrice said.

"You are fast becoming one of my favorite clients." Lou said with a sincere laugh. "Come on let's see what I can do for you."

She took Beatrice by the arm and together they walked down the mint colored hallway to her office.

Beatrice and Lou stood by the window of this cluttered space. Beatrice smoked one Kool after another as we explained our situation. We told her about the separation, the unknown bank accounts, the small piece of property in Middletown, Fred's fondness for drinking and driving and the crazy stepsister. All the while, Lou stood there puffing away on her dark Moore cigarette listening attentively and occasionally nodding and murmuring the affirmative "a-huh".

Where was her legal pad? Why wasn't she writing any of this down?

When Lou was certain that we were finished, she threw her cigarette out the window, breathed the last of her smoke through her nose and crossed to where Christopher and I were sitting.

"So how long has it been since you found out that he was deceased?" Lou asked.

"A little over a week." I answered.

"Well If I were you I would get up there and secure the property." Lou commanded.

"Can we do that?" Christopher asked.

"You bet your ass, you can." Lou said with a little excitement in her voice. "Since you never filed for divorce or were never served with divorce papers, technically you are still married to him…so that makes you his widow. Sorry."

"No worries." Beatrice answered.

"But they hadn't lived together for years." Christopher questioned.

"Doesn't matter. Still married in the eyes of the law." Lou said matter of factually.

"What do we do next?" I asked.

"The first thing you should do is secure the property and see if your husband left a will. This could all be for nothing if he has a will."

"What do you mean by that?" Beatrice asked.

"If your husband has left a will, that means he could have left his estate to any number of people…his children, his first wife, his cat. Anyone actually." Lou rattled off. "Now I am willing to bet, from your brief description of his life style, this was not the type of man who took care of stuff like a will. But we have to be positive."

"How do we do that?" Christopher asked.

"You have to get a look at his personal papers, which I am sure are probably on his property in Middletown." Lou instructed. "Chances are if there was a will, you would have heard by now."

"I suppose that you are right." Beatrice admitted.

"Look, I want you people to understand something. This type of stuff is not like television or the movies. If there isn't a will, then it will take a long time to settle his estate. Are you prepared for that?" Lou sincerely asked.

"As I told you on the phone, we don't think the man was sitting on hidden millions. As a matter of fact, we are pretty sure that he owes more than he is worth. All we want is to make sure that our mother isn't responsible for his debts." I explained.

"Understood. What we will do is petition the court to make your mother the executor of his estate. Once that's established, then any debts will be subtracted from his remaining assets after they are sold for a fair market rate. Whatever is left over, minus any expenses will belong to your mother."

"How do we start?" Beatrice asked.

"Get up there with a camera and a really decent lock to secure the joint. If your step-daughter is as crazy as you say, there is no telling what she has taken or has given away. So there may be nothing left to fight over. Start taking an inventory of everything that is there. And I mean everything, electronics, jewelry, pots, and pans, even down to the number of aspirins. Excuse me for a second." she stepped away and walked towards the door. "Hey Francis. Come in here a minute will you?" she screamed. "Better than intercom." she smiled as she walked back and sat behind her desk. "It sounds like we are not talking about a lot of money. And the last thing that I would want to see is that whatever money you do have coming to you be eaten up by my fee."

Here it comes.

"How much is your fee?" Beatrice asked.

"I typically bill out at a hundred dollars an hour. But considering your circumstances and the fact that I like you, I am going to recommend that you and your sons do a lot of the legwork. Hunting down bank accounts, stocks, pension and insurance policies, dealing with realtors and such. Of course, I'll be there to offer direction and advice every step of the way. But if you take care of all the messy stuff, I'll reduce my fee to a couple of thousand dollars."

Before we could react to her proposal, the sweaty balding man in the sweater vest appeared in the doorway. He still had files in his arms, which lead me to believe that they were either surgically attached or he constantly lugged them around in a vain effort to show Lou and the rest of the world his dedication to the job.

He took the apple out of his mouth long enough to say, "Whaddya need?"

"Francis. Have you meet everyone? Everyone this is Francis. Francis this is everyone." Lou said from behind her messy desk. "Francis is my right arm around here. Francis, we are going to help Beatrice and her family settle an estate. That is of course if it is something that you want us to do for you?"

Beatrice shot a look at each of us and then stood up to shake Lou's hand.

"We have a deal."

"That's fantastic. I couldn't think of a better way to start my day. Francis, please draw up a contract for Beatrice, while I explain about the need for a bond."

I couldn't help but wonder if Lou had been a used car salesmen in a previous life.

The Great Lasagna War

It had been a very long winter for the people who had made their homes around the golden pond. In those early days of spring, the eager residents emerged from their freshly paneled dens and rumpus rooms with rust colored shag carpets and dark wood accented plaid couches. Like a well choreographed Broadway musical or some other profoundly synchronously religious ritual, each resident almost simultaneously tucked their iron rakes or hoes tightly under their arms; stared into morning sun soaking in its warmth and glory; and covered their hands with well worn leather gloves which were saved specifically for yard work. After a quick and ceremonious wave or a nod hello to their neighbor, each resident went about the business of clearing the harsh winter from their property.

Beatrice loved this time of year and all it symbolized. With her trademark Kool hanging from the side of her mouth she got on her hands and knees, pushed her long black bangs away from her face and began to clear the debris from her flowerbeds. She smiled with anticipation as she removed each branch and handful of withered and wet oak leaves and placed them in the same large olive green bucket she used year after year. It would be a matter of just a few short weeks and she would find herself visiting each of the smaller florists and garden shops that did business within a thirty-mile radius of her little house by the golden pond. Carefully and meticulously, Beatrice would snap up her favorite colored pansies, red New Guinea impatiens, alyssum, Sweet William, petunias, red Martha Washington geraniums and coleus. While some people made yearly pilgrimages to Mecca or the Holy Land, Beatrice often had a near religious experience on her annual trip to Chapman's Greenhouses.

Money had been scarce that winter and she briefly considered the idea that she may have to find a way to do without as many flowers. But the thought went as quickly out of her head as it entered. She would find a way. Perhaps she could water down the ZaRex or better yet cut it out all together and make the kids drink more water. Perhaps she could find a way to cut down on the electric bill and she knew that she certainly could save money by not ordering those short sets she admired in the Sears catalogue. She would find a way.

Each spring, the scent of the moist pungent soil became her perfume. She cherished the earthy bouquet and inhaled it in an almost passionate manner. The time that Beatrice spent in the dirt each spring was necessary for her emotional and physical survival as the oxygen she breathed. Certainly it was a close second to her cigarettes and beer. As she tenderly turned over the dirt in each of her flowerbeds, she often took off her gloves so that she could feel the soil between her fingers not caring when it became trapped underneath her nails. The state of Beatrice's nails in the spring and early summer often sent Nana Flossie over the edge and was just one of the sources of their habitually heated arguments.

Beatrice could tell by touch just how much fertilizer or lime she needed to add to the dirt in order to make it a perfect resting place for her future plants. All the while, she mentally and meticulously arranged each of her future gardens, by color, size, and bloom time. As she worked, she sang along to the latest top forty songs blaring from an old transistor radio, that her father had given her as a wedding present.

"That dang radio lasted longer than my marriage. It is certainly more dependable than Butch."

Shortly after daylight savings time began, Beatrice adjusted her daily routine to include several hours of gardening. Just as soon as the beds made, the breakfast dishes were cleaned and put away, a load of laundry in the machine and the bathroom scrubbed down with lemon-scented ammonia, she would steal away an hour or two to plant and weed. And at just before sundown, when supper was finished and the dishes were washed and put away and after the kitchen was wiped down and the kids were tubbed and in their pajamas and plopped in front of the television, Beatrice would steal another hour or two to water and feed her treasured flora.

As long as I can remember, thus was Beatrice's daily routine each spring until the first frost. Whenever I asked her why she spent so much time in her gardens, Beatrice always had the same response.

"Pardon, the pun, but it keeps me grounded." she said. "It may sound silly and as I say it out loud, it may sound even a little selfish, but my gardens were all about me. Your sister had her sports teams; you had your art and your brother had…well he had his 'friends'. My gardens are the only thing that I did for myself. It had nothing to do with any of you. I wasn't defined as a mother or as a housewife."

The courtship of Beatrice and Fred began to bloom during the late spring of nineteen seventy-six. The country was in the beginning stages of bicentennial celebration, which eventually became something of a fever pitch. You couldn't turn on a television or read a box of cereal without coming across some tidbit or another about the revolutionary war. Our town chose to show its patriotism by painting every fire hydrant in the municipality to resemble a drummer from the revolutionary war. It was at the Kelly's annual Saint Patrick's Day party that most of the men in our neighborhood decided to show their newfound patriotism by growing mustaches and taking up Tiparillos. Beatrice found both activities utterly ridiculous. When Fred made the unfortunate mistake of removing a tiny cigar from his pocket, she sent him home, although not without a fight. I went to sleep that night thinking that was the last we would see of Fred, only to be disappointed when he returned the next day with a small bouquet of wilted carnations as a peace offering.

Since her separation from Butch had been so difficult on all of us, Beatrice felt it important to keep us close and entertained. In those early days of their courtship, Beatrice insisted that all activities she and Fred planned had to also include the four of us. There were trips planned to Salem Willows for skeet-ball tournaments and chop suey sandwiches; waterskiing on Squam Lake and barbeque; mini-golf and soft serve ice cream cones. It was also (not so fondly) remembered as the year each of us had gained twelve pounds.

On a trip back from fishing and Chinese food, Fred was illuminating us with tales of his culinary masterpieces and how once, while he was trying to impress the skirt off "some gal I used to know—in the biblical sense", he had miraculously transformed the kitchen dining room of his small apartment on Clinton Street in Lynn into an authentic Italian piazza.

At the time, I didn't understand what he was talking about, but years later, after I had gotten to know him better, I am sure the apartment's transformation more than likely consisted of: dim lighting, which he was able to achieve by unscrewing a couple of bulbs from the overhead lamp, a dripping candle atop an empty bottle of Chianti, a Perry Como album and a picture of the Pope, which I had no doubt was hanging on the wall askew.

"The room set the tone, but once I served the meal, that's all she wrote." he bragged. "She was all over me, like white on rice."

"Freddie, what type of narcotic did you slip into that poor unsuspecting woman's food?"

"Har-har!" he chuckled with the deepest belly laugh. "Sweetie, when I turn on the charm, there isn't a woman in the world who can resist me."

"Well, Freddie, in that case, I hope that you will give me plenty of advanced warning. "

Ewww!

The rest of the painfully long car ride Beatrice and Fred would talk about nothing in particular...the weather, their childhood, or their favorite movie. Fred would think nothing of driving three hours to find the perfect fishing hole...let alone the perfect egg roll. And every now and then, Fred would revisit the "success" of his perfectly prepared Italian meal.

Later that evening, when it was time to say our goodnights, we found them both sitting in the living room, which was usually reserved for special company at the high holidays like Thanksgiving or Christmas. Beatrice was nursing her glass of rose on the rocks. In those early days, Beatrice was careful not to let us see her drink more than one glass of wine or a can of beer even though there was usually an empty wine bottle or a half dozen drained beer cans in the morning trash. Fred drained another can of his Schlitz beer and placed it next to his other empties which he lined up on the dark pine end table.

The fat man is not using a coaster!!!!

We each took our turns hugging and kissing Beatrice goodnight.

Why is she not commenting on the coaster? What's wrong with my mother?

I waited for her to pounce on Fred for his clear disregard of proper coaster etiquette. He was still talking about his Italian masterpiece, only now he was referring to it as the culinary equivalent of the Mona Lisa, the Statue of David or as he called it "the Sixteenth Chapel." Beatrice had finally had enough of his boasting and starting talking about her world renowned lasagna recipe.

Of course, I don't ever remember my mother serving lasagna – let alone having a world-renowned recipe. The simple truth of the matter was that considering their Irish heritages, neither had any business boasting about their previous successes with Italian cuisine.

We said our goodnights and made our way to bed. It would still be a few months before the bullfrogs that inhabited the golden pond would sing us to sleep with their croaking chorus. Instead, in those days our nightly lullaby consisted of a kaleidoscope of clattering which was composed of the "hssst" from the pull tab of a can of beer, the crack of the ice cube tray, the glugg, glugg of wine being poured from its box, the splintering of broken glass, "sshhh's" being said in a loud stage whisper followed more often than not by giggling.

Beatrice finished her morning routine early the next day and then managed to sneak away for a pot of coffee at Gina Cappabianca's house. Gina and her family lived up the street and around the corner. Gina was a second generation Italian American who was recently transplanted from her familiar neighborhood, which was situated smack dab in the middle of the Chelsea projects. Thanks to being the sole beneficiary of her grandfather's generous life insurance policy,

Gina and her husband Anthony were able to make a down payment on a house in the country. Back in those days, any town away from the projects was considered the country!

In her heart Gina knew that the open spaces, the fresh air and the school system would help to give her four children a fighting chance at a life they would never be able to have if they stayed in the projects. But secretly, she longed for the hustle and bustle of her busy city street. Aside from not having a decent butcher…has no one out here ever heard of prosciutto?…Gina missed three of her four sisters who also lived on her block. They were always together, through thick or thin, constantly intertwined in each other's lives, meddling, laughing, crying, and fighting. Gina traded all of that in for a three-bedroom ranch, which was located on an acre corner lot and a series of short long distance calls made on Sunday afternoons.

Over another pot of coffee and a package of Kools, Gina confided in Beatrice that she found her new suburban life very frustrating. She didn't have too much in common with her neighbors and so no reason to go out of her way to talk to them, let alone be nice to them. Gina felt trapped. The town didn't have public transportation and the nearest cab company was three towns away. Gina never learned to drive! She was cut off from her sisters and only got back to see them on the occasional Sunday, when her husband Joe wasn't working, which was hardly ever.

"I've already told Anthony, I am slapping the for sale sign up on our way to the last one's high school graduation ceremony."

For the next hour or so the two women smoked, talked about their kids and gossiped about the neighbors. The morning passed quickly for the two lonely women and before they knew it, the clock on the wall struck noon and Gina's children appeared in the doorway looking for their lunch.

"Go away! I'll call you when it's ready!" Gina shouted at her children. "Bea, you would think that I never fed these kids."

"Well, I better get going."

"Are you sure you can't stay? It will only take me a second to throw the animals some sandwiches. Then I will put on another pot of coffee."

"No thanks Gina, I'm floating as it is." she replied as she headed towards the kitchen door. "Besides, I have to get home to my kids, there is no telling what they have been up to. "

"Thank you for coming by. I don't get much company. Well, company that I can stand."

"I know what you mean. Why don't you come down next Thursday and we can do this again?"

"I'd like that."

Beatrice had one foot out the door and then she turned to Gina and asked, "Gina, I almost forgot. Can you do me the smallest favor?"

A short explanation and a half hour later, Beatrice returned to her little house by the golden pond with a recipe card for Gina's grandfather, Nonno Galuzzo's lasagna. According to Gina, you couldn't get any more "old world Italian" than that. He was fresh off the boat and the recipe belonged to his grandmother. She quickly pulled together a quick lunch consisting of bologna, tomato, lettuce and mayonnaise sandwiches, pickles and cold milk. She wiped down the nook and loaded us into the car.

Two hours later, we pulled down the hill and back into our unpaved driveway.

"Carrie, help Michael with the groceries and then you can go to your friend's house. Be home before five."

My brothers and I unpacked the paper grocery bags that were filled with foreign food stuffs. We lined the kitchen counter with garlic, basil, ricotta cheese, olive oil, cans of crushed plum tomatoes from Italy, tomato paste, grated Pecorino Romano cheese, hamburger, Italian flavored breadcrumbs, sausages, noodles, mushrooms, onions and peppers. Christopher arranged everything by color, size and food group.

Looking back now, we should have seen this quirk as an obvious foreshadowing of his need to control everything and everyone. Of course to some of his former assistants, this may have been the birthplace of his OCD.

While Christopher rearranged the food, Beatrice stuck her head underneath the counter and wrestled with her pots and pans until she retrieved her favorite cast iron skillet and stainless steel stock pot.

"You boys need to go find something to do." said Beatrice as she tried to shoo us from her tiny kitchen.

"Momma, I want to help."

"Sorry Christopher. But I have to make some spaghetti sauce first before I can make the lasagna and I don't have time for all of your usual questions." she said as she lifted up her gas stove top to relight the pilot.

"But, why?"

"Christopher this is just what I was talking about. Now Mommy loves you, but you need to go find something to do."

"I don't want…"

"And I don't want to spank your bottom and throw you into bed, but I will if you do not GET OUT OF HERE NOW!"

And with that we scampered.

For the next several hours, Beatrice chopped, measured and sautéed just as directed by Nonno Galuzzo's recipe card. In the beginning she was confused about the measurements. The recipe called for a handful of chopped onions, mushrooms, and peppers. Her man-sized hands as Nana

Flossie called them were clearly much larger than Gina's. A quick phone call to Gina, which also allowed her a couple quick puffs on her Kool, helped her realize that it just didn't matter. As long as she was consistent with her proportions, the rest it just didn't matter. Besides, Gina assured Beatrice that that Nonno Galuzzo's hands were the size of sledge hammers.

Beatrice knew from her conversations with Gina that the longer you cooked your sauce…

"Gravy! It's called gravy!"

…the better it would taste. However, she was running out of time. She still needed to boil the noodles and mix the eggs, parsley, cheese and ricotta. She turned up the gas flame on her stove top to a high simmer and filled up another pot for the lasagna noodles.

Thirty minutes later she began to assemble her creation. Naturally she had too much for her pan. Another call to Gina and one Kool later, Beatrice created two more pans of lasagna, covered them with aluminum foil and put them in the freezer section of her harvest gold side by side refrigerator. She reserved a small saucepan of her famous spaghetti sauce…

"Gravy! It's called gravy!"

…which will be used later to cover the cheesy deliciousness before serving. The remainder she poured into her Tupperware. This was the special white Tupperware containers that she always used for her spaghetti sauc – gravy. Even bleach could not remove the faded red stains, so she set them aside to be used for this reason only. She washed her pots, scrubbed down her kitchen, sat in her perch, smoked a Kool and waited for Fred to arrive.

Beatrice didn't put it past Fred to go out and purchase some lasagna from a restaurant in the North End and try to pass it off as his own. So they set up some ground rules for the great lasagna bake off.

Rule Number One: They each had to purchase the same ten by thirteen inch baking pan. Fred insisted that they use a ceramic pan, because based on his research the ceramic pan would cook the lasagna move evenly. Beatrice wanted to use a metal pan, because she knew that it would less likely stain, like her special Tupperware and be easier to clean up later with an SOS pad. After a brief spat using loud stage whispers in the cookware aisle of a discount department store in Lynn, Beatrice conceded her point and they purchased matching ceramic pans.

Rule Number Two: Beatrice insisted that they could each prepare their lasagna in their own kitchens. She told Fred that she did not want him interfering or stealing ingredients for her award winning lasagna. The real truth of the matter is that Beatrice had seen him prepare a meal before. She knew what type of mess he would make, and she certainly did not want to deal with cleaning up the fallout! Fred agreed. However, both pans of lasagna would need to be cooked in Beatrice's oven. After all, Beatrice would have an unfair advantage because her lasagna would be hot and his would cool off on the drive over.

Rule Number Three: The judging panel would consist of Carrie, Kevin, and me. Christopher was too young for a vote. In an attempt to keep things balanced, Fred insisted that George, our "happy-drunk" neighbor and his wife Vivian be part of the judging panel. Beatrice liked the odds and agreed immediately. By the time the lasagna was served, George would more than likely be three sheets to the wind. Chances are that he wouldn't make it to the first bite before he passed out. Vivian on the other hand was the wild card. She and

George had been our neighbors for years, moving in next door shortly after the birth of their second son. She could be described as a long skinny drink of water. She had bleached blonde hair cut into a Florence Henderson style shag and wore cat eye shaped eyeglasses. She was very quick witted and sarcastic, two characteristics that kept us in stitches on more than one occasion. She enjoyed her Benson and Hedges one hundreds almost as much as Beatrice did her Kools and would often come over sit on our front stoop, smoke and laugh. Vivian would more than likely vote for Beatrice, provided that George behaved. If George had too much to drink too soon, he would get affectionate, which always ended in Vivian threatening to beat him within an inch of his life.

Beatrice looked at the clock over her refrigerator and saw that Fred was already a half hour behind schedule. She dialed his number quickly on her nicotine stained yellow rotary phone. No answer. He was never on time so she saw no need to worry. Instead, Beatrice went about her business. She snapped on the gas oven to pre-heat and then started peeling and chopping the cucumber for her garden salad.

Forty five minutes later, Fred's car screeched to a halt in our stone dust driveway creating his usual cloud of grey smoke. Giddy as a school girl he leapt from his dented Pontiac, balancing his pan of uncooked lasagna in one hand and a loaf of Italian bread in the other and barreled into the house.

Like many of the houses around the golden pond, our home was once a summer cottage. Beatrice did her best to add a sense of decorative cohesiveness to the little abode that certainly lacked a sense of architectural cohesiveness that are the measure of the modern homes of today. Over the years a couple of small additions were added and a three season's porch was enclosed to make up the "happy" little house. The front entryway was proportionate to the size of the overall house. The broken plastered walls were long ago covered up by knotty pine tongue and groove paneling which Beatrice kept gleaming with a monthly treatment of Scott's Liquid Gold polish. Visitors needed to climb five stairs to enter the handsome kitchen. Off the kitchen was the dining room, Beatrice's nook and the living room. Off the living room were three small bedrooms, a bathroom, and the former three season's porch turned den. With the exception of the bathroom, each of the rooms had a spectacular view of the golden pond. Beatrice hated the flow of her home. "You always had to walk from one room to another." She often fancied about having the bedrooms on another floor. Not that she ever would, but just once she would like the option of not making a bed or just leaving the kid's clothes on the floor. Instead because of the layout, Beatrice was meticulous in the way she kept her home clean. Everything cleaned and put away in its place. The only room in which she relaxed her cleanliness standard was the play room which was located downstairs.

Yes, knotty pine tongue and groove paneling! Butch knew someone, who knew someone, who had a friend. So the "price was right."

There was also a workroom turned bedroom, an enclosed one car garage that served as storage /laundry area, all of which had a great view of the golden pond.

An hour later, Beatrice and Fred proudly served their culinary masterpieces to the judges gathered around the dining room table. She was able to talk Fred out of the blindfolds, but needed to concede on separate plates and silverware for each of their cheesy concoctions. A compromise she only agreed to because he promised to help with the dishes as there were no dishwashers in the homes that dotted the golden pond.

"Sweetie and I want to thank all of you for being here tonight." Fred began with an aristocratic tone to his voice. "Tonight you are in for a treat. We have both make our famous lasagnas. And it will be up to you decide whose lasagna's is better. Hers is good, but I am sure when all is said and done, you will see that mine is better. Bon Appetite and dig in."

While it was supposed to be a blind taste testing, Fred could hardly contain his excitement as the first plate of saucy, cheesy, and hopefully deliciousness was passed around the table.

"I see that your nervous tick has come back Fred." quipped Vivian, who was in an obviously good mood since George was nursing a second glass of ice tea.

"No, no", he giggled like a school girl. "Bea and I are just excited. That's all. Come on. Enjoy your food."

"Well kids, I bet we know whose lasagna got served first." Vivian said in her usually delivered in a sarcastic tone and rubbing her hands together.

Once Vivian instructed the table on the proper etiquette for eating lasagna, doing her best imitation of a grand dame at a society high tea....pinky finger extended high in the air, she scooped a most delicate forkful into her mouth.

"Mmmmmmmmmmmmmmmmm" she moaned in a deep voice as she slowly chewed the cheesy concoction. "It has a most pleasant bouquet." she said using a clenched jaw trying her best to sound like one of those television millionaires who were marooned on a deserted island. "It has a nice medium body to it. The noodles are just the right texture and the nuttiness of the parmesan cheese shines through, the blend of spices is really quite artful." She continued holding back an imaginary tear. "And the finish...well what can I possible say, it is probably the beh.....the beh...." Vivian stopped midsentence. She put one hand across her heart and the other in front of her mouth as though she was trying to suppress a major burp. "Excuse me," she said in tone reeking of sarcasm.

For those of you who know Vivian, you are aware that she could teach master level classes in sarcasm.

"I don't know what came over me. It's…it's…it's as though something is not agreeing with my delicate constitution. I…I…I…" Immediately, Vivian's eyes opened wide and she jerked her head front and back like a pecking chicken while she made some loud choking noises. The noises and the head movements intensify until they reach a natural crescendo. Vivian let out a death cry before she slumped down in her chair. Before anyone can react, she revived and died once more.

A short beat later and the entire table burst out in laughter. Naturally, Fred was the loudest. But at this point it didn't matter. For the first time in months there was no tension in the little house by the golden pond. My mother, my siblings and our neighbors were genuinely enjoying themselves. The jokes and the laughter continued throughout the meal almost as if we were a scripted for a CBS television sitcom family or a Hallmark commercial.

Even Fred was engulfed in the happiness and levity filling the cream colored dining room with the wagon wheel chandelier. Maybe he knew that odds were stacked against him considering the makeup of the judge's panel. Maybe he knew that his lasagna could neither compare nor compete with Gina Cappabianca's gravy recipe. Or maybe he just wanted to savor the lack of tension and enjoy the moment. Whatever his reason, Fred called off the vote and with much fanfare, he conceded the title to Beatrice.

The rest of the evening was uneventful. We all pitched in to help with the dishes; sweeping the floors and restoring everything back to its magazine photo shoot ready cleanliness.

Beatrice checked homework, made sure that we had scrubbed our teeth and behind our ears and popped us off to bed before relaxing with Fred in the living room with a glass of wine. In those days Beatrice might sip a glass of wine at the end of her day to help her unwind.

Having a bedroom in the cellar was certainly not without its perks. I had access to the playroom which was also covered in tongue and groove pine paneling and red carpet. It had plenty of built in storage, bookcases, toy boxes, and a desk. Most importantly, it also came furnished with a black and white console television and an all in one stereo system that included an AM / FM Receiver, an eight-track, and a turntable that could play both forty-five and thirty-three and third rpms. And yes, it was tastefully covered in wood veneer.

On the flip side however, all sound coming from up the stairs always seemed to be magnified by at least ten. So I really couldn't make out the noise that woke me. I just knew it was loud. My flip alarm clock radio slowly faded into focus showing me that it was three thirty AM and the noises also became clearer. Beatrice and Fred were arguing in what can only be described as a drunken Irish Stage Whisper.

"You're wrong! You don't think I know the truth? Do you think I am crazy?" slurred Fred.

"Shhhhhhhhhhhhhhhhhh!" Beatrice slurred. "You're gonna wake up the kiddos."

"I don't care if I wake up the whole damn pond…."

"Will you shut the hell up and talk like a normal human being?"

Instinctively, I covered my head with the pillow and rolled over with my back now facing the door hoping to God that this pointless exchange would eventually peter out or that they would both pass out. Both were distinct possibilities. The make-believe idyllic family dynamic had slowly faded away and we were left once again with what was the dark reality of all those who lived in the little house by the golden pond. For this was not the first time that Beatrice and Fred's "unwind time" in the living room had turned ugly.

Beatrice always made a point to downplay her alcohol consumption in those days. She may sometimes reward herself with a nice cold beer after a lot of yard work on a hot summer's day or share a cocktail or two with friends on those rare occasions that she found herself at a party or a cookout. We didn't really have an affinity for the volume of her consumption or the personality metamorphous she underwent as a result, until the arrival of Fred. And while he may not have been the cause, he most certainly more times than naught was the catalyst.

Try as I might, the noises of their argument still made it through the polyester filling of my pillow. I knew from experience inserting myself into that chaos wasn't a battle worth fighting. I tried to distract myself by trying to mentally design a new costume for Superman and practicing how to conjugate French verbs in the Imperfect Tense for my test which was just a few hours away. Once I heard the splinter of furniture, I bolted from my bed.

As I raced up the stairs, Fred was standing with his back to the opened front door. The cool spring air did little to lower the heated temperatures that were still rising in the hallway of knotty pine paneling.

"And I want my lasagna pan." Fred demanded his voice resonating throughout the hallway.

"Oh, you want your pan? Here, take your fucking pan!" screeched Beatrice as she threw the pan of half eaten lasagna at him, clocking him off the head. Congealed lasagna rained all over the amber colored pine paneled hallway as the blow sent Fred ass over teacups out the door and onto the front lawn.

"Now get the hell out of here and never come back before I call the police on your fat ass!" she yelled.

I stood there in amazement as Beatrice quickly slammed the front door closed and locked it. She shut off the outdoor lights and commanded that I close my mouth and get back into bed. And with that she turned and walked back to her bedroom trailing the Italian gravy and cheeses that now clung to her feet.

The next morning we would wake to a cheery Beatrice and a spotless home smelling of Pine Sol, bleach and Scott's Liquid Gold. The post dinner party early morning events were scrubbed and cleaned away as if they never had happened. She even managed to rake and remove any evidence of Fred's clumsy landing from the front walkway. She handed Carrie and me our lunch money, wished me luck on my French test and sent us off to school.

The next few days sans Fred were quiet and happy ones. But unfortunately, they would not last long. It was barely a week before he returned with an apology, a half dead bouquet of daisies and an engagement ring.

AAAAAARG!

Reality Check

Hunting For Buried Treasure

More than thirty years have passed since that fateful night Fred tapped danced his way into our lives. Carrie, Kevin, and I have all since moved away, married and started families of our own. Christopher stayed at home helping to support Beatrice and the bills associated with living in the little house by the golden pond. He was the only one of us who knew the full extent of Beatrice's lack of financial resources. When you combined that with Christopher's insatiable appetite for new projects and his hatred for Fred, it was no surprise that he decided to take the lead in figuring out what sort of mess Fred had left behind. This was Fred we are talking about. Of course there would be a mess left behind.

Christopher methodically created one list of "to do's" after another. To help keep the project organized and on target, he kept a leather-bound journal to chronicle important dates, facts, and numbers. For people he spoke to, Christopher also made a point of documenting their demeanor. Next to their names he placed some sort of geometric shape that correlated to a sliding scale that he long ago develop to measure people's willingness to help. A triangle meant minimal support and the person was deemed useless and a complete waste of time. A circle meant that they might be of some use, but not a person that you should invest a lot of time and energy on. A star meant that you had struck gold. This person would bend over backwards to give or get you anything that you may need. Over the years he has honed his organizational skills to such a level that Christopher could probably have marketed his "formula" and easily put to shame those self help gurus that seem to be on every cable television channel when you cannot get to sleep in the middle of the night.

"Those people are such con-artists and cheats. They're crooked as they come." Beatrice would often say. "Now, if you need help pulling things together, there is no one better than my Christopher. He has a real knack for adding structure. Don't know what I would do without him."

"It's too bad that he never found a way to make money doing that stuff. He has such a talent. He's wasting his time working in that office job of his." Nana Flossie would almost always immediately add.

Christopher had long giving up trying to explain to both of them that "his office job" was being the senior project manager for a rather large financial planning institution. His job was all about adding structure to chaos. He was doing what he likes to do. He was good at. He's been the employee of the month four times! But, they didn't get it. Christopher, like all of us, learned that once Beatrice and Flossie were on a tear, there was no use trying to explain anything to them. Instead he would just shrug his shoulders, smile sarcastically and move on. Eventually they would take the hint and talk about something or someone else. If not, Christopher would just go into the next room.

And thus, as it is customary in our family to poke fun of the underdog, Christopher's job became something of an inside family joke that we manage to work into conversation at almost every family function.

"Oh Christopher, is that a new coat?"

"You have such flair. Have you thought about being a model?"

"Can you help me organize my closet?"

"Christopher you have such a knack for passing the mashed potatoes, have you thought about doing it professionally?"

"Yo, Chris. The way to stink up a bathroom...Bro, I know you can make some serious money doing that!"

In all the years that they lived apart, Beatrice and Fred never divorced. When Fred was "sick with the drink" as he put it, he would often call Beatrice and try to reconcile. It was always at that magic hour between three thirty and four thirty AM, when you were forced to stay up for the day because returning back to sleep always certainly meant you would be late for work or school. A divorce for him was out of the question if there was some glimmer of hope that he and Beatrice would one day reconcile and everything would be right as rain again in the little house by the golden pond. It was quite sad actually watching this man's emotional dignity evaporate over the years.

Beatrice's lack of interest in a divorce was brought on by a couple of reasons. With two failed marriages under her belt, she was rightfully gun-shy and wanted to take her time.

"I'm no Liz Taylor!" she would often joke. "Besides, after Butch and Freddie, I've sworn men off. Who needs them? I don't have to share my bathroom any more. That means the toilet seat is always down and I don't have to clean up all those little hairs in the sink."

The other reason Beatrice was in no hurry to divorce was purely financial.

"One day I am going to need social security." she told her friends the Bettys. "As awful as that sounds, unless someone else comes along, and I am not thinking that's too likely, I might as well use his."

So naturally, the first thing on Christopher's to do list was to get a copy of Fred's social security number. That task was assigned to Beatrice and she accomplished it rather easily. She found it on an old tax return that she had saved and squirreled away, just in case.

Mrs. Glory Anne Metcalf at the Social Security office was first rated a star in Christopher's chronicle. Once she realized that we didn't have a copy of the death certificate, her attitude changed and thus her rating quickly changed as well to a triangle.

As it turns out getting several copies of his death certificate was a fairly simple and straight forward process thanks to the friendly and helpful people at the town clerk's office.

Stars for everyone!

I spent the extra money to make certain that each certificate had the proper notary seal which would be mandatory for some institutions.

Darlene Gaffney-Jones, the People and Culture Representative at the plant Fred worked eventually returned my call after four messages. She remembered him "fondly".

"I'll tell you what, that man kept me on my toes. He must have been in this office for one thing or another every week for as long as he worked here. Total pain in the ass. A loveable man...but a total pain in my ass."

She offered her condolences once she heard the news. With a couple strokes on her computer keyboard she confirmed that Beatrice was his beneficiary for his life insurance and his pension. She remembered that he requested to make a change on five separate occasions since he retired, but never got around to returning any of the paperwork. So as far as the company concerned, the money belonged to Beatrice.

No sharing with the steps!

Ms. Gaffney-Jones also explained that Beatrice was eligible to continue her medical coverage through Consolidated Omnibus Budget Reconciliation Act (COBRA).

"Excuse me. Did you say she could have COBRA?"

"Why yes. That is the law."

"I apologize. My mother was under the assumption that she didn't have any medical coverage."

"No sir." Ms. Gaffney-Jones said while she tapped on her keyboard. "According to the system your mother has been on the medical and dental plan since she married Freddie."

Son of a bitch!

We confirmed addresses and contact information.

"Once I get a copy of the death certificate, I will begin the process to pay out his life insurance and the remainder of his pension. Do you know if your mother would like the pension in a lump sum or would she prefer to have it payout monthly?"

"Do we have to make that decision now? I am not sure about the tax implications."

"I totally understand. I will send you a worksheet that works up the numbers both ways. At first glance I can tell you that the money that she would receive monthly would more than enough to cover the cost of COBRA and give her almost as much to spend on other bills. And after eighteen months when the COBRA plan finishes, there will still be enough money for her to take in a lump sum payout if she would like."

"That sounds like a great option. Let's go with that."

"Perfect. Your mother will just need to sign, date and notarize the forms before she returns them to me. The sooner the better. I don't want her to miss out."

I thanked her repeatedly for her time and her help. She offered her condolences again and suggested that I call her cell if we should have any other questions. Once we hung up, I gave her two stars.

Christopher on the other hand had a little more trouble unraveling the deluge of mail that arrived daily at the little house by the golden pond. Mixed among the coffee of the month, cheeses from around the world, seed catalogues, and assorted collector's item Wizard of Oz plates from the Franklin Mint, were the bank statements, credit card bills, second and third demands for payment from the utility companies as well as various magazines, some of which arrived in brown paper wrappers. We decided to forward those to Kevin in Japan.

"So far I have found three checking accounts from three different banks. According to the statements he also had two pass book savings accounts. All of which were in his name."

"So she is going to have to share those."

"I'm not finished." Christopher added. "It looks like he also had a Christmas Club Account through a credit union. Some money in a 401K and in a Roth IRA. Looks like Mom is the beneficiary on the 401K. I can't get any information on the Roth until after they get the Death Certificate and the letter from Louisa A. Nickels Attorney and Counselor at Law naming Mom the executor."

"Sounds promising."

"Yeah, except that it appears that he owes almost as much as he has squirreled away. I am still combing through the bills. But we are going to have to get up to the foundation and see if we can find the passbooks and whatever paperwork he may have had."

"Keep an eye out for a package from the plant." I shared my conversation with Ms. Gaffney-Jones.

"She has had healthcare all along?"

"And dental."

"Son of a bitch."

"That's what I said."

"Do you know how pissed she is going to be?"

"Yup. Well on the bright side, she can now afford to get her teeth fixed."

"Don't think I would lead with that. In other good news, according to one of the bank statement that I got this morning, it appears that there were three ATM withdrawals totaling a little under a thousand dollars."

"So?"

"The transactions happened the day after he died."

"LJ?"

"That would be my guess. Either way, the bank manager seemed most interested. They have cancelled the cards and frozen his accounts. There is a local branch here, so I am going to drop off the paperwork at lunchtime. She said that she was going to try and check to see if they have any video footage of the transactions."

"And then what?"

"Not our concern. The bank is insured so they will replace whatever money was missing after the time of death and then they will let the police handle the rest."

"I am sensing LJ will be getting a new orange jumpsuit for Christmas."

"Probably before then. I'm going to check the other accounts to see if she has pulled the same thing."

"Smart move. I'm supposed to see Carrie tonight at the basketball game. So we will coordinate family calendars and get back to you."

"The sooner the better."

"It's going to take a small army to clean up that place. Once we have a date, I'll order a dumpster."

"Is it really that bad?"

"Bring your camera and make sure you have spare batteries and memory cards. No one is going to believe you. Alright. Gotta bolt. I'm already five minutes late for the budget meeting."

"Smell ya later."

LJ

Fred married Liberty Duncan on the last day of their junior year of high school. The pair had driven to New Hampshire to elope.

I am still somewhat convinced that the pre-trip preparations involved chloroform, some parachute cord, and a couple of Rolling Hitch Knots.

When the couple returned from their blissful honeymoon at the Magic Castle Motel which was just off route sixteen smack dab in the middle of the White Mountains a few days later, they were met by both sets of crazed parents who were relieved and ready to kill them at the same time. It was the talk of Salem High School and Immaculate Conception Church, when Libby gave birth to Freddie, Jr. less than five months later.

The couple struggled like most newlyweds. They set up house in a small shotgun style apartment on Roselyn Street. Fred dropped out of high school and began his series of failed town jobs that his father continued to arrange for him. After work, he spent most of his time at his friend's garage and worked on cars. He frequently went out for a couple of pops with the boys and rarely made it home for dinner with his wife and infant son. When he did, he was often three sheets to the wind and with an empty wallet.

Over the next five years, he and Libby managed to have five other babies, John, after her father, Katie, after her mother, Elizabeth and Daniel, the Irish twins and finally Liberty, Jr. whom everyone called LJ.

While I certainly have an appreciation for honoring a family member a generation removed by naming a child after them, I have never quite understood the indulgence of juniors. Most certainly the name is always morphed into some other derivative like: Sonny, Junior, or CJ, TJ, or MK. In those severe situations like my cousin, he was referred to as Little Joe which was considered adorable as long as he remained below four feet tall and spoke with a lisp. The "Little" title was eventually transformed into Young Joe once he finished his post pubescent growth spurt and reached 6 foot 3.

His lisp, like his face eventually cleared by the time he was a high school sophomore thanks in part to a solid speech pathologist named Mrs. Soares. It should also be noted that Beatrice warned us with bodily harm that under no circumstances were we ever to refer to his father as Old Joe.

Nana Flossie had a simple approach to naming children and I share this advice often. <u>One:</u> Everyone at some point in their lives will get a chance to name a child or a pet. It's their turn. It's a huge responsibility and none of your business. So keep your opinions to yourself. <u>Two:</u> Once you have decided on a name, open the back door and scream it...that meant first, middle and last name at the top of your lungs. If after six or ten times, you can still stand it and pronounce it, then it's a potential keeper. <u>Three:</u> Never share any potential baby names with ANYONE! Because without a doubt no matter who you tell, they will know someone or of someone with that name and that person was either a scoundrel or the type of girl that you would not want to take home to meet your mother. This is why she always recommended that perspective parents have a couple of fake names, like Clark or Eucalyptus, to put people off the scent. Once the baby is born and real name revealed, people always forget all about those other no good nicks.

Fred's marriage imploded on a fatal Thanksgiving at his in-laws' house in Marblehead back in the mid nineteen sixties. Beatrice insisted that she didn't care to know all the sorted details. It was quite painful for Fred and he did not like or want to discuss it. It wasn't until much later that Beatrice shared what little she did know.

The argument started with a small grease fire in the kitchen. It intensified as exorbitant amounts of alcohol were consumed. Beatrice wasn't quite clear about how or exactly when the dining room table was broken; other than there were an assorted number of aunts, uncles, and cousins who were on the receiving end of the flying peas, potatoes, and gravy. The whole commotion came to an abrupt end when the police arrived thanks to the call from a concerned neighbor. When they entered what was left of the dining room, it took more than three officers to pull Mr. Duncan off of Fred, who with the help of his new carving set recently picked up thanks to cashing in some S & H Green Stamps was trying to cleave Fred's head off at the shoulders. Both Fred and his father-in-law were arrested. When Fred was finally released from jail, he came home to a completely emptied apartment. Libby had even taken the butter dish but making sure to toss the unused butter into the sink.

LJ was the only one of his children that remained close after his marriage ended. Truth be told, she was the only one of his children that spoke to him. She had a heart as large as the Atlantic Ocean and a brain that was…significantly smaller. Unlike her other more successful siblings, poor LJ inherited all the worst qualities of both of her parents along with Fred's looks. As a matter of fact, slap a long frizzy-haired blond wig, Coke-bottle-bottom glasses that changed color with the intensity of the sun, some Janis Joplin jeans and a blouse on Fred and you had LJ.

She had several bouts with depression and experimented heavily with drugs and alcohol as a way to enhance her more flamboyant and creative nature. She tried her hand at poetry and pottery; with the help of her Deviant Moon tarot card set, she worked at a carnival telling people their fortunes; she was a groupie, an exotic dancer, and a trucker. She had several extended stays in prison on both the state and local level. Over the years, she managed to have a number of children with various men from various ethnic and socioeconomic backgrounds, which the state in their good wisdom removed from her care before she was allowed to leave the hospital.

Thank God.

LJ would keep tabs on her children throughout the years and on occasion might "borrow" one or two of them plucking them from their backyards, a neighborhood park, or school playground. Her babies were almost certainly returned to their adoptive parents a few hours later often without the aid of the police none worse for the wear. Their little bellies often filled with ice cream, cookies, candies and other assorted junk food. Their little heads were filled with stories of LJ's escapades. She always left them with a small toy. It wasn't much; just something that she could afford or perhaps shoplift from the Good Will…a dirty doll or small truck, a thread bared stuffed giraffe or hippopotamus. Just something that could watch over them when she wasn't there.

If you had a cold, a hang nail, or any other type of illness, or you had just broken off a relationship, LJ was the first person on your doorstep. Sober. Not unlike a disheveled version of Mary Poppins. She would arrive with a sympathetic ear or a shoulder to cry on...whatever you needed as long as you needed. She would create the most magnificent stews, broths, and puddings out of the most meager of ingredients that she found while riffling through your cupboards. She would hold your hand and listen intently as you shared a cup of tea. She freely admitted that she made a shambles of the kitchen.

"I can't be bound by the conventions of cleanliness while I am creating." she would often say followed by her trademarked nervous laugh.

However as soon as she knew that you were comfortable and tucked in for the night, she would go back to the mess that she created and spent most of the night restoring it to some semblance of order. And then as suddenly as she arrived, LJ was off again back to her gypsy vagabond lifestyle and her next great adventure.

When asked to describe her stepdaughter LJ, Beatrice would say, "She was so much like her father. She had these tremendous highs when she was fun to be around. She would laugh and smile contagiously. She would hum all the time and tell these silly stories and rhymes. The stories and the rhymes would sometimes become more singsongy...a little more intense. And then that's how you knew it was all going to change. It was like someone flipped a switch. Her mood would suddenly change. She became this dark, scary other person who there was no reasoning with. We tried to get her help, but she just didn't want it. Her parents had her committed a couple of times, but it just never took. Here is what I believe. Deep down she is a good soul constantly fighting her demons. At her core, she is a nurturer. The real tragedy is that her mental illness prevents her from caring for her own children."

When Fred and Beatrice were married and off on their honeymoon, they left us for two days under the watchful eye of LJ. She spent most of her time nursing a bottle of vodka, smoking weed on the dock, and playing the Billy Joel Stranger album over and over again wondering why people couldn't be nicer to one another.

It took several days for Beatrice to return her kitchen to some semblance of normalcy.

The Entrepreneur

Bill and Maggie McMullen had a prearranged marriage, which ended four days shy of their sixty-first wedding anniversary, when one December evening a drunk driver caused them to swerve off the road and sink to the bottom of Silver Lake in Tewksbury, Massachusetts.

Bill was the drunk driver.

Together they had managed to raise seven children five boys and two girls, who served as the bookends in Salem, Massachusetts where Bill has worked hard to become the desk sergeant of the police department. Like most couples of that time, Maggie focused on her children's physical, emotional, and spiritual well-being, while Bill made sure that he pushed his sons hard to live up to their potential.

Looking back you could say for the most part that they were successful. Both daughters managed to marry affluent men of the community.

Twice. And in the case of the youngest daughter, four times.

One son became an anesthesiologist, another a pharmacist, while another son owned a lucrative insurance company. Then, there was the youngest son...Fred.

His son had barely finished grammar school, when Bill determined that Fred was destined for a career that would require lots and lots of physical labor. And while Fred may have shown lots of aptitude, he had showed no interest in any of the trades. He seemed quite content to hang out at his friend's father's gas station and work on cars, smoke cigarettes and drink stolen beer. When Fred dropped out of school, no one was surprised. For the next two years, he managed to get himself fired from every possible job Bill was able to set him up with. Fred worked at laying pipe for the Water Department; paving roads for the DPW and cutting grass for the Parks Department. Systematically, each time Fred was fired from a job...never his fault by the way...Bill called in yet another favor from another town official. When he got the call about the accident Fred had which involved a town trash truck, a fire hydrant, and the front store window of Lenny's Liquorland, Bill knew that no amount of fixed parking tickets would ever secure his son another job with the town.

At the end of his patience, Bill dragged his youngest son kicking and screaming to see his friend and hunting buddy Burt Martell, who happened to be a floor foreman at the Sylvania plant in Danvers. A couple of years earlier, Bill had helped Burt with an embarrassing incident involving a "niece" at a party that was held in a couple of rooms at the Hawthorne Hotel. Bill kept Burt out of jail and spared him an impossible argument with Mrs. Martell and her divorce attorney. Since then, the two had been good friends.

The "niece" promised never to work a party at the hotel ever again. However, she did join them from time to time on hunting trip or two.

Bill knew that Fred needed to work at a big company, where he would be offered stability and good benefits. Since the company was so big, Fred was sure to be overlooked and if he minded his P's and Q's, he might just be guaranteed a job with longevity. Burt was good to his word. Fred started work on the assembly line that afternoon and stayed doing the same job for the next forty years.

In the fall of Nineteen Seventy Six, Fred moved into the little house near the golden pond with Beatrice and the rest of us. We celebrated each morning as he left for work at five thirty and quietly mourned his arrival home shortly after he punched out at three o'clock.

Fred considered himself a man of vision. He had dreams. He knew that he made enough to just cover the bills and tuck a little away for a rainy day.

Of course, the bills he was paying had nothing to do with the little house near the golden pond.

Fred believed deep in his soul that if he was going to make some real money to live in the style he thought he deserved, he needed another source of income. So he daydreamed. He toyed. He investigated. Each new concept brought hours of research and interrogation. He would think nothing of hopping into his wreck of a car with no muffler and drive for hours to talk to the successful business owner who uncovered that untapped niche market that would eventually become Fred's ticket to financial freedom.

When we were forced to accompany him, Carrie and I would duck down behind the seats in the hopes that none of our friends...or strangers for that matter would see us.

Now that I am older, I should probably have had a better appreciation for Fred's investigation skills. Obviously if mentored or groomed properly, Fred could have had a career as an investigative reporter, a police detective, or an enforcer for a mafia crime family. But instead, all that I can remember is the sense of sheer embarrassment I felt witnessing his scrutiny of the poor cornered owner. He would ask questions about funding, the customer base, suppliers, equipment, and secret recipes. Typically, the grilling lasted an average of eight minutes before the owner politely and sometimes not so politely would ask us to leave. A normal person would have been discouraged, but not Fred. He simply smiled, thanked the man for his time and went on to his next victim, who had a business located usually at the opposite end of the state.

Carrie once asked him why he couldn't just go to a library to do his research like any other normal person. He said, "The stuff I am looking for can't be found in a book. I need to talk to the person who's doing the job now. I want to look into his eyes and see if he really likes what they're doing. If I talked to six or seven people who like what they are doing, it may be the business for me."

And all this time I thought it was because he couldn't read.

Next came the in-house laboratory experiments. He would go shopping and spare no expense to buy whatever gadgets and supplies he thought he needed for his new business opportunity. When he was seriously considering opening up an envelope stuffing business, he filled the house with boxes of number ten regular and number ten window envelopes. He bought envelopes that were square flapped, pointed flap, and foil lined. He bought envelopes that were gray, white, natural and pastel colored. He had brown craft envelopes and gray craft envelopes and shipping envelopes that were made with bubble wrap and corrugated cardboard and plastic mailers. He bought envelopes that had clasps, that were self-sealing, and three different kinds of flavor sealed envelopes. He quickly ruled out the self-sealing envelopes after seeing how much they would eat into his profits. But after spending several nights licking his different envelopes, he decided it was time to research different ways to seal the envelopes.

So he spent time and more money researching different products for moistening envelopes and stamps. He bought boxes of angle tip moisteners and a gross of tube moisteners. He spent long hours at night practicing using an aqua ball moistener and a sponge cup moistener to see which one was better. He tried five different brands of envelope sticks in his quest for the better product.

After narrowing it down, he then went on to which rubber fingertip was most efficient and speedy for handling paper. He bought box after box of deluxe grade rubber tip in assorted colors and sizes. He spent many nights agonizing over the perfect selection, often waking the whole household, which was usually around two AM to show us his choice and demonstrate why it was the best product.

Fred spent a lot of time figuring out which office accessories were best. He purchased five different types of letter openers, before settling on the eight and one half inch chrome plated letter opener with serrated blade.

Of which he bought two.

He had cartons of moist towelettes. No one was sure why he needed so many the towelettes. But he had them just the same. It wasn't until many years later that Christopher noticed that the moist towelettes were on the same page as the deluxe grade rubber tips in an office supply catalogue. This was the closest we would ever get to solving that particular mystery. He preferred the heavy-duty two roll multiple tape dispenser and purchased enough packing tape to wrap around the house twice. Because his fingers were so large, only the round magnetic paperclip dispenser would work for his jumbo paperclips.

Surprisingly enough, Fred never bought a stapler.

And to help keep all of his things organized Fred built an elaborate shelving system in a section of the garage which he converted into his workroom. When he thought he was close to the perfect combination of materials, he would convert the red papered dining room with wagon wheel chandelier into an envelope-stuffing assembly line. With his newly purchased stopwatches, he would time us as we stuffed reams of blank paper into his assorted envelope supply all the time jotting notes on one of his six clipboards. When we finished, usually after ten PM, he would then interview each of us to see how many envelopes we stuffed and which products we liked better and why. The post interview took almost as long as the actual stuffing.

Eventually, he grew bored of the envelope stuffing business, which yielded nothing in profits and about twenty-five hundred dollars of supplies.

On a positive note, Beatrice never had to buy an envelope again in her lifetime.

A trip to the North End of Boston refocused his energies into the booming pizza industry. The next thing we know, we were completing a similar process for perfecting the idyllic combination of tomato, cheese and seasonings. He experimented with thick, thin, stuffed (Yes! He was truly a man ahead of his time!) and Sicilian crust and the pans that would give you the best result. After he determined that he needed a full size pizza oven to conclude his experiments, he spent months tracking down the right oven.

Thankfully the doors to little house near the golden pond were not big enough to accommodate an industrial size pizza oven. Secretly we also gave thanks to our neighbors Bitchy and Shitty who complained to the town zoning board when Fred tried to set up his oven on the front lawn.

He next tackled donuts. From there he went to Chinese food. After the boiling the Thanksgiving turkey in peanut oil debacle of Nineteen Seventy Eight, he shifted his focus to hamburgers. Eventually he decided that he needed to take his recently acquired culinary skills on the road. And thus the idea for the Roach Coach was born.

So once more we were forced to file into the battered Pontiac with the missing muffler not knowing where we were going to end up or more importantly how long we would be gone. It was easy to let your imagination wander and pretend that you were snatched off the street and taken from your home against your will, forced to travel with crazy people who were not your family. But unlike Patty Hearst, there was absolutely no way these hostages would ever feel anything but contempt for our kidnapper... Fred. After we successfully escaped the town limits, Carrie and I came up out of our hiding positions in time to catch Fred's latest scheme.

"Sweetie. You should see this guy. He shows up to the plant in the morning with some coffee, some donuts and a couple of bananas. He parks his truck at the front gate and gets people to buy his stuff as they walk by. Everybody. And I mean everybody stops and drops down a couple of bucks. He's gone by eight o'clock. Then he shows up at lunchtime with nothing more than a couple of sandwiches, a couple of bags of chips and some tonics. Boom. Makes his coins and he splits by two. I mean talk about a cash cow. He gets double the business come pay day. He puts in a couple of hours at most and makes a ton of dough. And do you know what the best part is baby? It's a cash business. Uncle Sam doesn't have to know about a lot of it! It's a sweet deal. But I know that I can do it one better."

This particular road trip was mercifully shorter than most. Fred quickly maneuvered his battered Pontiac with the missing muffler through the backstreets of Lynn. It was yet another short cut, which much to our regret and against our collective wills; we were becoming increasingly more familiar with. As usual, Fred had the radio tuned to his favorite sports talk station.

Carrie and I were convinced that it was the only station that he could tune in.

And also, as usual, if we actually had any interest in what the DJs were talking about, it was almost impossible to understand a word of what they were saying through the crackling and hissing of the blown speaker. If you were lucky you might be able to make out every third word. And as usual, again, the squawking ultimately became a sort of white noise that was eventually replaced by the sound of my Nana Flossie's voice singing over and over in the back of my head. "Lynn. Lynn. The city of sin. You never come out, the way you went in."

You could say that again!

Once we reached the Post Office on Maple Street, Fred ceremoniously rolled down his window, reached out his bloated hand with the sausage like fingers and searched for the door handle. It took the prerequisite three tugs and a shove, before the latch released and the door squeaked open on its rusty hinges. Using a speed that no one thought possible for a man his size, Fred climbed the stairs up to the front door two at a time wheezing all the way. Less than forty-five minutes later, this wait was also mercifully shorter than most. Fred skipped down the stairs and squeezed himself back into the car.

"You wouldn't believe the line in there, Sweetie." he said almost apologetically, as he repeatedly pumped the gas and turned the ignition until it finally took.

"All that and I need to go around back and speak with a guy named Al. You would have figured they could have told me that when I called." he complained as he shoved the transmission into gear. The customary clicking and whirring noise betrayed the fact that his battered Pontiac with the missing muffler was once more drained of power steering fluid as he cut the wheel all the way to the left and pulled out of the parking space and turned the corner looking for the back entrance.

Even we were surprised to see how easy it was to drive through the back gated entrance to the Post Office receiving docks. Sure it was a simpler time, when people didn't have to worry about peanut allergies, CPAP machines and the only choices of diet soft drinks were TaB and Fresca. Sure it was decades before the mass populace enlightenment of "Condition Orange" and other terrorist warnings, but shouldn't someone have tried to stop us? Or at the very least demanded that Fred replace his muffler?

Finding a quick spot to park, he freed himself from his wreck of an automobile and climbed the stairs to the loading dock and entered the Post Office through an open bay door. Carrie and I looked at each other in disbelief that no one even bothered to try and stop the obviously misplaced gargoyle as he walked up and down the aisles looking for his friend. We knew better than to question Beatrice who just sat in the car and stared out the dirty windshield. She often had a far off look in her eyes when we all waited for Fred to complete his business. She was lost in thought – miles away on some secluded beach or another finding her happy place only to be drawn back to the reality of our lives by one of my younger brothers tugging on her shoulder complaining about being hungry or being bored.

"Only boring people are bored Sweet Pea." she would say to us in a soothing voice and trying her best to comfort us into believing that it wouldn't be much longer before Fred returned. Beatrice could always try to find some positive morsel of good when it came to our adventures with Fred. When we were no longer distracted with playing games like "I spy with my naked eye" or "I'm thinking of a number", she would bring up stories about how we met the ringleader of the Shiner's Circus and fed the elephants or when we met Captain Carl, the lobster fisherman with the wooden leg and the pet rat.

Looking back, I had to assume that deep down Beatrice was equally displeased with the emotional roller coaster of complex dynamics that had come to define our family in those Fred years. She had to be. Any sane person would have to be. But we were far from becoming named the first family of positive mental health. To the average observer, on the surface at least, we must have looked like any other television family laughing and joking in the car waiting for 'Dad' to return.

He did eventually return just like a case of genital herpes or at the very least a bad case of acid reflux. Naturally he didn't emerge from the bay door he entered. Fred rarely came out the way he went in. We should have been prepared. But we were not. No. In typical Fred style, he pulled up next to us proudly sitting behind the wheel of a rather large and rather ugly colored blue mail truck.

He did like to make a flashy entrance.

It was an unusual color of blue which was certainly not surprising for anyone who knew Fred. It was a shade of blue that that you did not see every day. If it were a crayon, it would be a close relative of a neon turquoise blue. He flashed Beatrice his ear-to-ear smirk as he bounced up and down excitedly in the driver's seat. He waved his left hand with all the skill and cunning of a seasoned beauty pageant winner.

Although there was certainly no beauty there to speak of.

And all the time his right hand was seemingly permanently affixed to the horn of this rather large and rather unsightly colored mail truck.

"Freddie?" Beatrice said in a phony surprised tone as she shoved open her car door. "What are you up to now? Kids, get out here and take a look at what Fred is up to now." Which of course was code for get out here now and act really surprised or there will be hell to pay later.

He flashed his yellow stalagmite smile and slid open his window. "Isn't it a beaut Sweetie?!" he squealed like a four year old who got his first look at all the presents under the tree on Christmas morning.

"It's all that and a bag of chips, Honey" Beatrice replied in her most sincere voice. "Isn't it great kids?"

"Oh wow!"

"It certainly is something."

"How many miles to the gallon do you get?"

Beatrice shot us each a look that immediately told us how she disapproved of our apparent lack of enthusiasm for Fred's new project. "Sweetie. What's it for?"

"Kids. You and your mother are looking at the beginning of our financial independence."

We all stood there dead panned with confused looks on our faces. Barely a beat passed, he went on to say, "In just a few short weeks, I plan to transform this Post Office Mail LLV Van Truck into Bea's Traveling Kitchen."

Still deadpanned confused looks.

"We're gonna make a killing. Isn't the color something?"

It's something all right.

"Mother, tell me he is not going to park that thing at our house!" pleaded Carrie.

Much to Carrie's disappointment, the blue monstrosity also came to take up residency alongside the battered Pontiac with the missing muffler in the driveway of the little house by the golden pond, where night after night Fred began his own personal marathon towards financial independence.

Like all of his projects, Fred became all consumed with turning the blue behemoth into his own personal mobile cash-making machine. When he returned from the plant, he stood in the kitchen, smoked his Winston's and slurped on his cup of freshly brewed coffee that waited for him each afternoon. He shared with Beatrice all the happenings at the plant; feinted interest in Beatrice's day and then reviewed all of his ideas and drawings. He kept them all in a very small notebook that fit in his top shirt pocket along with his pencil.

Fred also had an endless supply of the little notebooks from the time he thought he could make a lot of money being a stringer for the local paper. He scored a deal where he would be paid by the word. After all, he knew many words and with the help of his stash of newly purchased thesauruses, he was bound to make a killing. Unfortunately, his career in journalism at the town's weekly newspaper was cut painfully short due to a deadly combination of lack of typing skills and his command of the English language.

As he perfected the ergonomically correct interior layout for Beatrice's Traveling Kitchen taking a mere five or six notebooks worth of lists and drawings, Fred removed the shelving unit used by the prior owner to sort and store mail and added a bucket seat intended for his new co-pilot Beatrice.

Night after night he tinkered and he toyed, often demanding that he and Beatrice take their dinner at the makeshift tool table he set up alongside the parked traveling kitchen.

"Sweetie, it's got good bones. Before I drove it out of the parking lot, they replaced the muffler, the tires and put in new shocks and struts. I'm telling you, when it comes time to getting cars for the boys, they are going to buy them from the Post Office."

And when he was finished, he would kiss Beatrice on the lips and thank her for his dinner and back to work he went. As he lost the afternoon light, he lit up the newly purchased lawn torches, which admittedly cast off very little light and did even less to ward off the mosquito population. But he loved the smell.

No one else seemed concerned that Fred was working so close to our house with gasoline, oil and open flames.

From behind the bedroom curtains, Carrie and I watched as he turned on the seven hanging flashlights that he had jury-rigged inside the truck. The concentric circles of additional light lit up the interior. As usual, as soon as they were lit, he covered up each of the windows with a newly purchased flower power sheet set that he got off the clearance table at some heavily discounted department store in the shady part of town two towns away. All we could see was his misshapen silhouette which moved back and forth. Like clockwork, we would next hear the clanging of hammered metal.

"What do you think he is doing in there?" Carrie would ask.

"Not sure."

"It's just a matter of time before he tries to drag us into helping him. I over heard him say that when he wasn't selling food, he was planning on taking us camping."

"Camping?" I asked. "What for? We already live on a pond."

"No shit Sherlock. No one ever said he had any common sense. All I do know is that it will be a cold day in hell before I ride in that thing."

"Me neither." I agreed.

"How many "D" batteries do you think he uses?"

"I don't know."

"I bet he buys Duracells for his stuff. Did you know he changes them out every afternoon? He has to have a hidden stash around here somewhere."

"Yeah. He keeps them behind a loose piece of paneling in the playroom."

"Are you kidding me?"

"Nope. Caught him last night."

"Did he see you?"

"Nope. Why?"

"Show me. I need to make a withdrawal."

"Huh?"

"Last night I asked him if we had any batteries for my tape recorder and he told me that we didn't. And then he dug around the junk drawer and tossed me some half charged generic battery and told me that was the best he could do."

As Carrie and I left the window in order to plunder Fred's secret cache of batteries, he continued working like he always had until eleven or twelve at night. Methodically, he first turned off his flashlights; locked the doors; circled the truck twice, making sure that all possible egresses were tightly secured. He then meticulously extinguished the torches one by one. Once inside the house he washed his paws with his personal bar of Lava soap that he kept under the kitchen sink in a Tupperware bowl and dried them with a nearby dishtowel. Next he poured himself a generous bowl of cornflakes and hobbled into the dining room so that he could spread out the newspaper and scribble notes into one of his notebooks for fifteen minutes. Before retiring for the night he polished off two packages of Drakes apple pies which he kept hidden in the back of a kitchen drawer where Beatrice kept her supply of clean dishtowels and a large glass of milk for dessert. A generous and thunderous release of natural gas from both ends and he was off to bed.

And thus Fred kept up the same pace and the same routine day after day for the next three weeks. Each time he completed a modification to the once mail truck, we were assembled and forced to "ooo" and "ahh". We flashed our fake smiles and quietly groaned at the same time as he demonstrated the new flashing yellow light that he installed on the roof. We ceremoniously golf clapped and gasped in horror when he unveiled the neon orange Bea's Traveling Kitchen sign that he had made and affixed to the side of the truck. With each alteration, we also got the half hour lecture on how he accomplished his project. We learned where he found the eight-track player and how with just a few feet of wire from Radio Shack and some speakers he picked up alongside the road; he could turn it into a powerful stereo system. He educated us on the workings of the CB Radio and how useful and economical they were especially after the craze and how easily they could be installed. We learned that the new roof top mounted speakers on either side of the flashing yellow light could play music or be used to project his voice announcing the arrival of Bea's Traveling Kitchen.

"Step right up. You know you're hungry. You're in for a real homemade treat when you eat at Bea's." Fred's voice roared through the crackling speakers.

"Please tell me that he's not serious." Carrie said in disbelief.

"And think about how useful it would be, when we are trying to round the kids up." Fred said seriously. "Carrie, Michael it's time to come home now. Your mother needs you."

"Ma!" Carrie, Kevin, and I whined in tandem.

"This is cool." said Christopher. "Can I try?"

"Sorry partner. Maybe a little bit later, after I work out all the bugs."

"Oh Sweetie," Beatrice chirped. "This is quite an accomplishment."

"And that's not the half of it. Get a load of this." he slammed his mitt on the truck horn.

Nothing.

He did it again.

Still nothing.

"Honey, what am I supposed to be listening for?"

Fred squished his face up, which he did whenever he was trying to unravel a puzzle or a problem. He also used the same expression each time he happened to be constipated, so it was difficult to know the difference on more than one occasion. He relaxed his expression as he rubbed his chin with his right hand and ceremoniously tapped his nose twice with his index finger. And then with a gleam in his eye he disappeared under the dashboard. Beatrice was able to finish two cigarettes before Fred reappeared.

"I think I have it this time, Sweetie!" he said huffing and puffing. "Let's see what happens now. Contact!"

Once again his oversized mitt thumped on the horn.

Nothing.

As customary, Fred once again squished up his face. He sat that way for about thirty seconds before his facial features eventually returned to normal. He took his usual three deep cleansing breaths and showing more determination than before, whacked his fist even harder on the horn.

At first, there was not a sound. We stood in the driveway disenchanted once again. Not so much with poor Fred and his failures, but knowing that his continued lack of success meant that we were held once more against our wills standing around the driveway being eaten by mosquitoes. What felt like a lifetime later, the speakers came to life with a light hum. It was soft...almost inaudible at first.

"Did you guys hear something?" Kevin asked not believing his ears and our eventual good fortune.

"Shhhhhh." Carrie said with her eyes closed and her hands folded and resting on her chin.

"What are you doing?" I asked.

"Praying for lightning. I think it's working."

Eventually, like the trickle of a leaky faucet a small amount of static crackled and oozed from the speakers. Gradually the clatter grew louder and louder and ultimately recognizable as "Pop Goes The Weasel". However, since it was a Fred project, it did not surprise us that the song did not sound right. It was distorted. Sounding as though the album was being played on an old turntable at seventy-eight instead of thirty-three and third. We stood there watching him sit behind the wheel of this truck that had consumed our lives, smirking and conducting the music (?) with his fingers. To us it was just noise, but to Fred, the noise was as sweet and as beautiful as any symphony ever written.

I leaned over to whisper something to Carrie and noticed that she was still standing there with her eyes still closed and her hands folded and resting on her chin. "What are you doing?"

"I am still praying for that lightning bolt."

Several weeks and several hundred dollars later, Fred's dream of financial independence came to a crashing halt. During the maiden voyage of Bea's Traveling Kitchen, Fred happened to serve a western omelet to "an undercover city health inspector" named Brian Abbott. While Brian did admit that he was happy with the way the food tasted, he was disappointed that Fred could not produce any of the necessary documentation that would allow him to continue to serve food. Words were exchanged. One shove lead to another, which eventually led to the two men rolling around in the street. Thanks to the timely interference of a passing patrol car, Brian only suffered a broken nose and a missing front tooth. Fred considered himself the victor had the beginnings of a black eye. Of course he was arrested and Bea's Traveling Kitchen impounded. It took quite a few hours for Beatrice to cool off enough and bail Fred out of jail. On the other hand, Bea's Traveling Kitchen stayed in the impound lot until Fred worked enough overtime to pay for its release.

Three weeks later, after the release of his precious truck, Fred received two letters in the mail. The first one was a letter from the City of Peabody stating that due to all of the code violations, he was being fined a thousand dollars and would never be allowed to operate Bea's Traveling Kitchen within one hundred miles of the city limits. The second letter was from Mr. Brian Abbott's Attorney also asking for a thousand dollars. This was to replace Brian's missing tooth. The letter also requested that Fred keep at least five hundred yards distance between him and Mr. Abbott at all times.

Reality Check

Wakey Wakey

Beatrice received another phone call from Katie to let her know that due to the condition of his body, she and her brothers and sisters felt it would be more advantageous to have Fred cremated.

"That does sound very practical dear." said Beatrice trying to sound calm and collected. She was in her perch and instantaneously lit herself another Kool.

"As you can imagine this has been very upsetting for LJ"

"The poor thing must be devastated."

"You are right. Mom has her hands full trying to console her."

Beatrice knew that LJ's sobriety was too fragile and that being the one to discover her father's corpse would prove to be too much for her. She would be as unpredictable as always. The rest of the very pleasant and yet very awkward phone call was filled with congenial updates about her family and details regarding the services for Fred. Two quick cigarettes later, the call ended.

"Well regardless of the circumstances, I look forward to seeing you and your brothers and sisters, Katie." lied Beatrice. "And again dear, I am sorry for your loss."

After she hung up the phone, Beatrice sat in her perch staring out of her window contemplating her next move. She sat quietly for about a minute or so with her head in her hands trying to relax herself with some cleansing breaths.

"Fuck this shit. And fuck him for putting me through this shit." she muttered to herself before she crossed to the refrigerator and opened a cold beer. Standing in the middle of her kitchen she took three or four large and very satisfying chugs of the light beer. She returned to her perch, the rattan swivel stool with the back facing the counter so that she could rest her feet comfortably on the window sill. She lit another Kool and reached for her corded landline phone and dialed each of us in reverse birth order.

Later on that same evening, I meet up with Carrie and Christopher at Stormin' Norma's, a small pub which happens to be equal distance from each of our perspective homes. And thanks to the modern age of technology, Kevin also joined via FaceTime. Kevin troubled youth made good is now a Marine Lieutenant Colonel Weapons and Tactics Intelligence Officer stationed with his wife and three sons in Okinawa, Japan.

I still get great satisfaction out of the fact Kevin was out ranked by his wife.

"How are the boys?" Carrie asked.

"They're doing great. They all made the local wrestling team….For some reason, wrestling is huge over here. Wish that I could be there to witness this shit show live." Kevin said sarcastically.

"Liar." I quickly replied just as the waitress brought over the loaded vegan nachos and another round of cocktails.

"Oh man. Are you at Norma's? Oh man, I miss those nachos. Gimme a close up. Gimme a close up. Damn!"

"Enough." snapped Christopher. "I am gonna have to get going soon. Let me tell you what I found out. I spoke with Francis at Louisa Nickels'' office after talking with Mom. He did do a search at the probate courts in Massachusetts and New Hampshire. There are no records of Fred ever filing a will."

"Shit." cursed Carrie as she took another sip of her martini. "So what does that mean?"

"According to Louisa A. Nickels Attorney and Counselor at Law, that means that the surviving spouse, i.e., Mom, becomes the executor of the estate. She gets to keep anything where she is designated sole beneficiary. All other assets, she gets to keep fifty percent and the remaining fifty percent is split equally among his surviving heirs. Lou is supposed to send a letter to each of his kids later this week. Beatrice is looking up the addresses."

"Great!" Kevin chimed in. "How much do you think we will get?"

"Nothing you idiot." Carrie said in disbelief. "We aren't his blood. Thank God. The rest goes to his spawn."

"Ok I get it Carrie. So how do we know how much he is worth?

"It can't be much. He was living in a foundation with a roof." I added.

"The land has to be worth something." Carrie insisted. "Didn't he always say it was all paid for?"

"Yes. But who knows. He may have taken a mortgage out." Christopher added. "We are going to have to get a hold of his bank records."

"Already a step ahead of you." I said with a mouth full of nachos. "I took a trip up there today."

"Wha?"

"Are you kidding?

"When?"

"I took the day off and drove up this morning. I was curious. I wanted to see what we were going to be getting ourselves into. Plus there was the LJ factor. Who knows what she had done up there."

"Did you actually go into the foundation?" "Kevin asked as his image fluttered in and out.

"I went to the police station first and introduced myself to Chief Wentworth. Great guy. I explained a little about our situation and asked if he could have his guys keep an extra eye on the place for us. He liked Fred a lot, not a big fan of LJ's. He is the one who suggested that I make arrangements to secure the place. So he took me over to the hardware store and the next thing I knew he was driving me over to change the locks."

"Are you kidding me?"

"What was it like? Was it disgusting? Could you still smell him?

"Did you ride in the back seat? Did he cuff you?"

"No asshole. Reliving your past life Kev? The Chief was great. He even took me over to the Post Office and we helped get all of his mail forwarded to Mom."

"Get you."

"We did check with Mrs. Duncan at the Town Hall and all his taxes and registrations are current and up to date. I am sure that there must be more records at his place, but I didn't have a lot of time to go through everything."

"Was it gross?" asked Carrie.

"I've seen cleaner death camps. The place is going to need a lot of work to get it into shape."

"You don't think she would want to keep it?"

"I doubt it."

"Whatever. It's up to Mom to decide. But we are going to have to get up there sooner rather than later."

Christopher shifted immediately into Christopher mode, "We are going to have to start making a list of all the things we are going to have to tackle. So email me anything that you can think of and I will start tracking it. The bigger issue of the day is that his wake is in two days and Beatrice plans on attending and she wants one of us to be her escort."

Simultaneously we all put our fingers on our noses and say, "Not it!"

"You were late Kevin!" I was quick to point out.

"Gimme a break bro. I am on the other side of the planet. Cut me some slake for poor internet connection."

"There is no way in hell that I am going." barked Carrie. She pointed at each of us with the last of her gin soaked blue cheese stuffed olives. "One of the three of you is going to have to step up. And yes I am including you..."Mr. IamsoimportantbigMarinemilitarycareerandlivinginJapan!"

"Carrie, even if I could pull the leave on short notice, it isn't physically possible for me to get there in time. Japan. I get a pass."

"Then it's up to either one of you two. I hated the bastard. There is no way in hell that I am going."

"I'm not going"

"No. No. No. No."

"You have to do this? She likes you better than me."

"Then what a perfect opportunity for you to share some prime bonding time with your mother."

"The kids have a band concert."

"You're kids aren't in the band."

"Whose side are you on?"

"Mine."

This little family skirmish would go on for some time. Eventually we came to realization that the only way that we were going to come to any sort of resolution was to break out the old family standby for breaking disputes...Rock, Paper,

Scissors. Using the rules published by the World RPS Society, which serves the needs of decision makers since Nineteen Eighteen, Carrie accepted her defeat with a best three out of four challenge.

While Christopher, who still lived at home with Beatrice would start sorting through the mail and tackle any banking related matters, I was assigned to get multiple copies of his death certificate and to work my magic on the Human Resources Department of the plant where Fred worked to check on pensions and other social security benefits. Poor Carrie was forced to go shopping for clothing.

How do you dress to attend the wake of a mad man that you hate with every fiber of your being?

Beatrice and Carrie did not have what anyone would consider to be a typical Hallmark mother daughter relationship. Just like Beatrice's relationship with Nana Flossie, both were strong willed and opinionated woman who loved each other fiercely. It's that sometimes they just don't like one another. It was in those dark days after Fred moved into the little house by the golden pond and the darker ones that followed after he left that the rift between mother and daughter slowly began.

After her marriage to Butch ended, Beatrice felt like the preverbal fifth wheel. All of her friends including the Bettys were happily married and she felt out of place and awkward in any social settings. Add in the fact that he refused to pay her any money, Beatrice was forced to borrow from her older brother Joe and eventually apply for Welfare which was a devastating blow to her ego. When Fred came along, he was the polar opposite of her husband. He was loud. But he made her laugh and that is just what she needed. He alienated the neighbors and the friendships that she once shared slowly drifted away one by one. She drank more to help her through the changes. Perhaps if she drank less, then she might have spotted the issues with Fred sooner.

The days and weeks following that final fight with Fred that involved the entire family, Beatrice felt humbled and humiliated without anyone to confide in. And as she became more of a recluse rarely leaving her perch, Carrie was coming into her own. The lust for life and Beatrice's fearlessness seemed to transfer into Carrie. And for a period of time, Carrie truly felt that positions were now reversed. She had become the parent and Beatrice the child.

Once Carrie was married and had a family of her own, she and Beatrice began to work on repairing their relationship. And while they often clashed over the littlest of things, there was always an undercurrent of love and respect for each other. The night of the wake was no different.

The McCarthy and Hollatz Funeral home is a brick Federal Style house that is located on the corner where Washington Square and East Washington Square transect in Salem. It was built in 1830 by John Samuels, whose innate sense of proportion and attention to decorative detail made him one of the most celebrated architects of his time. Like most of the charming houses in the area, it had intricate woodcarvings and neoclassical ornaments on the mantels, and doorframes. It also has a magnificent double parlor, which can accommodate multiple services. It has been freshened up over the years. It was unfortunate that the previous owners didn't share an appreciation for Mr. Samuels' creation. That was until Nineteen Ninety, when it underwent a major restoration shortly after it was purchased by Misters McCarthy and Hollatz. No expense was spared to restore this beauty to its former glory and naturally they added some modern touches like HVAC, a state of the art kitchen, and media room in their upstairs living quarters. When the project was finished, it was featured on the cover of North Shore Magazine. The interior was breathtaking and the grounds the envy of the neighborhood. Unfortunately, the footprint of the property did not allow for the creation of any additional parking. And thus, Carrie and Beatrice were forced to circle the block three times before finding a parking spot a couple of streets over.

"What type of shit show are we walking into her?" Carrie asked.

"I do not know baby girl. To be honest, I am more than a little nervous."

"Who do you think is going to be there?"

"Who the hell knows?" Beatrice was about to light a cigarette and then realized that she just rescued her good black coat from its month long visit at the dry cleaners. She didn't want it to reek of smoke and couldn't afford to have it cleaned again right away. So she put her cigarette back into its package and popped a breath lozenge instead. "Probably Joey."

"He the orthodontist?

"No. There isn't an orthodontist. Joey has an insurance business. He was closest to Freddie. You're thinking about John the anesthesiologist."

"To be honest with you, I am not thinking about any of them. I have spent a lot of money and many years in therapy trying to suppress those memories."

Beatrice gave her the look.

"Relax. I was joking. Well mostly."

"I am sure Felicity will be there. She was his older sister. Married a stock broker and after she put him in the ground, she married his partner. She was such a condescending witch. You'll spot her right way...doesn't move her jaw when she talks."

"What about his kids?"

"I don't know. Most of them wouldn't speak to him. I tried to bring them together. Thought we were making some progress when we were invited to Katie's wedding. But that just seemed to cause more issues with the others."

"Well I bet they show up just to make sure that he's dead. I know that is one of the reasons I am here."

"Well that and the fact you lost Rock. Paper. Scissors."

"Ouch."

"Listen baby girl, I know that you do not want to be here. I know that you hate Freddie for what he did to you and that you will never forgive him. Hell, you have barely forgiven me."

"Mom…"

"No darling. We are not going to rehash anything right now. I know how you feel so let's just put it aside for now and know that I do appreciate that you are here with me now. Deal?"

"Deal."

"Good." Beatrice put her arm around Carrie and gave her a tight squeeze as they continued walking. "I absolutely hate these things. But if I don't show up, there will be hell to pay later on."

"LJ?"

"Oh yeah. So let's just concentrate on getting through this for now. You know, your Uncle Cooper and I have these things down to a science. We go in, unusually forty five minutes after the service starts. You don't want to be the first to arrive because you will be forced to talk a little bit longer to the family. It can be terribly awkward for everyone involved. Sign the guest book. Make your way through the line. Eyes down but try to make eye contact with a couple of people. You want them to remember that you were there. Always have a couple of tissues in your hand." Beatrice hands Carrie a wad of tissue.

"What is this for? You can't possible think that I am going to shed a tear."

"Not at all. You keep them in your hand to absorb any sweat coming off your palms. There is nothing worse than having to shake a clammy hand. Also they make for a good prop. If someone is coming over that you don't want to talk with, cover your eyes with the tissue like you are having a good cry and then wave them off with the free hand."

"Does that work?"

"Every time. Now, Freddie is being cremated. So we won't have to deal with the casket protocol."

"There is a casket protocol?"

"You betcha. But there is no time for that now. I am sure that they will have his urn on display."

"Tell me that they used a garbage pail."

"Quite possibly. You know how fond he was of picking through the neighbor's rubbish. When we go through the receiving lines flash a fake smile. No Teeth. Say things like, 'I am sorry for your loss. Or he was so full of life."

"Hope he rots in hell comes to mind."

"If there is any justice in the world, I am sure that is where he is headed. And don't think that you are the only one in the room thinking that. But keep your opinions to yourself. This is their time to grieve. You are here as my backup!" snapped Beatrice. It may have been her voice, but the words and mannerisms attached to them were pure Nana Flossie.

"Yes ma'am."

"Oh God. We are here. I promise we will not be here long. If all else fails, mentally redecorate the room and we can compare notes when we get out. Ready?"

Carrie nodded her head and in they went.

They crossed the tastefully papered vestibule and made their way to the guest book where Beatrice signed in for both. Each of Carrie's senses was overwhelmed from the minute she entered. The air was thick and heavy with the smell of the gladioli, carnations, chrysanthemums, roses and lilies that were liberally used in the floral tributes. Visually the space was very appealing. The walls were a freshly painted hue of Grey Owl. A color Carrie had recently chosen for her guest bathroom. One of the rooms to her right featured an eclectic cluster of café style tables and chairs so that families could casually gather before or after a service. The combination of compact florescent light and light emitting diode bulbs made the space feel more like a coffee house than a funeral parlor. The only thing missing were the warm pastries and hot coffee.

When she first heard the noise, Carrie couldn't believe her ears. "Mom?" she whispered. "Is someone actually playing a drum?"

She and Beatrice exchanged a look of confusion just before they were greeted by a pair of women. One, much older, wore an Armani black suit. Her poker straight blonde hair pulled back into a low ponytail appeared almost white. She had a thick gold bangle on her left wrist and large gold earrings. Her lips were painted the same red color as her nails. She couldn't have been more than five foot four in her high heeled shoes. The other woman was taller by half a foot and much younger. If Carrie had to guess, she would say that she was in her early forties. She was a brunette with freshly highlighted with shades of auburn and caramel. She was much more plainly dressed in a black pencil skirt and matching top.

"Beeeeeeeeeeeeeeeatrice." gushed the older woman ensnaring Beatrice in the tightest of embraces as she exchanged "air kisses".

"Felicity." said Beatrice as she tried but ultimately failed to break free. "Felicity, this is my daughter Carrie."

"Carla?" she repeated as she reached out with her left hand and squeezed Carrie's outstretched hand like she was a young debutante in a period drama all the while never releasing her grip on Beatrice.

"It's Carrie."

"Oh I am sure it is. Beatrice I am just so distraught...our poor Freddie."

Carrie stood there transfixed on the fact that her mother was correct, Felicity's jaw did not move when she talked.

"Beatrice, I know it's been a while, but I am sure you remember Freddie's daughter Katie."

Beatrice managed to break free of Felicity's hold, long enough to share a heartfelt hug with Katie. "Don't be silly Felicity. Of course I do. Katie. I am so sorry about your loss. I hope you know he used to talk about you all the time. Saying how proud he was of you and your brothers and sisters."

"Thank you Bea." Katie said quietly trying to hold back some tears.

"Beatrice, I know that you must be so busy with your own family, let me take you in to meet everyone." Felicity said while she took Beatrice's arm and lead her into the next room. Carrie and Katie followed behind.

The visitation room was the largest that McCarthy and Hollatz had to offer. It was painted in the same Grey Owl color as the rest of the other rooms, which seemed to make the beautiful ornate woodwork and hardwood floors stand out even more. It had several large windows which stretched from floor to ceiling. Instead of the typical heavy damask drapes that traditionally adorned the windows of most funeral homes, the gentlemen opted to frost each of the windows instead. This allowed all sorts of natural light to flood the room and at the same time allow the grieving family privacy from any prying eyes and or neighbors. In the middle of the room on a marble pedestal rested a solid cherry wood cremation urn. It sat under a single overhead light. The urn was handcrafted and had cast pewter side brackets adorning each of the corners and a round picture frame, complete with a picture of Fred from high school.

We would later learn that LJ had designed the urn and had help with its creation by a few of her more talented artisan friends.

Immediately to the left of the entrance to the room sat two gentlemen in ceremonial Native American Indian clothing. They were on opposite sides of a thirty-two inch deer hide shaman drum.

"Bea, this is Grandfather Ashwood. He is the Shaman of the...let me see if I can get this right...the Cowasuck Band of the Penacook Abenaki People....I think that is correct. And his grandson, Zachary. Freddie and Mr. Ashwood became great friends while he was living up there in the heart of the wilderness."

"Felicity, I am not sure that I would call where he was living the heart of the wilderness." Beatrice tried to correct her sister-in-law.

"Beatrice, any place that does not have easy access to a Barney's or a Neiman Marcus is considered the wilderness in my book. Mr. Ashwood and LJ insisted that he play. The Shaman's drum is supposed to help his spirit with the cross over. The only thing that it is managing to accomplish is having my sanity slowly cross over to crazy town. Honestly. I should be grateful that he at least stopped with the infernal chanting and my poor parents – God bless their souls, didn't live long enough to witness this spectacle. Darn. There they go again. Honestly. I never will understand the need for chanting. "

The receiving line stood in front of the flowers that were arranged around the outskirts of the room. Beatrice was reintroduced to her brothers-in-law John and Joseph. Both were taller more professional polished versions of their dead brother.

"Johnny, Joey, you remember your sister-in-law Beatrice."

"Oh yeah. How are you Bea?"

"Been a while Beatrice. How have you been?"

Both men gave Beatrice a brief uncomfortable and affectionless hug.

"I'm fine, thank you. I am truly sorry for your loss. I am not sure you have ever met my daughter Carrie."

Carrie shook each of the men's hands while Felicity introduced the stoic identical women standing next to John and his brother Joseph.

"Beatrice, these are...."

"Mary Jane and Alice." Beatrice said interrupting. "I recognized you the moment I entered the room. My, you ladies haven't changed a bit. You are both as beautiful as always. How are the girls Alice? They must be in college by now. Mary Jane, this is my daughter Carrie. Carrie, these beautiful women are twin sisters. They lived across the street from Freddie and his family when they were all much younger. They married Fred's brothers Uncle Johnny and Uncle Joey."

Carrie suppressed the urge to scream they are not my uncles.

"Don't you have a sharp mind for details Beatrice." added Felicity. "We probably should be..."

"Mom, I don't mean to be rude. But didn't Fred have another brother and sister?" Carrie asked while trying desperately not to throw up in her mouth.

"That's my girl!" Beatrice beamed proudly to herself.

"Oh my gosh. That's right. I know that we were a little late Felicity. I hope that we didn't miss them."

"No dear. Steven and Joan's families all vacation together every year for a couple of weeks in Cozumel. They stay in an all inclusive. They have been doing it for years. Well with everything happening so quickly and with so much that was up in the air until the last minute, we didn't think that they needed to ruin their annual retreat. And you know, Freddie would want them to enjoy themselves."

"Sure."

"Now before you ask, my husband George isn't here either. There was so much going on at his firm…you do know he owns an investment firm Beatrice?"

"You make damn sure that everyone knows he owns an investment firm."

"He must be under a tremendous amount of stress Felicity."

Beatrice felt a small tug on her left elbow. She turned around to and came face to face with a handsome heavy set woman wearing a navy blue suit with a white silk blouse accented with pearls. Her wiry strawberry blonde hair was arranged in a loose twist. She had a very pale completion and her faded blue eyes were red from crying.

"Beatrice?"

"Libby?"

At first the two women stood there silently looking at each other. They had spoken on the phone a few times and met for a couple of minutes at Katie's wedding. It had been many years since the two of them were in a room together. They shared a look that only two women who were married to Fred would know as if simultaneously sharing each other's pain, sadness, and relief. And then the women hugged each other very tightly for several minutes.

"You know, it really should be you standing up here, Beatrice." Libby said in a husky cigarette voice.

"Oh no. Regardless of what her nibs may think, this is really about your kiddos. How are they?"

"It's been a hell of a week. Daniel refused to come. And Elizabeth is looking after LJ."

"How is she?"

"She's not doing well."

"My heart breaks for you."

"I am at the man's wake and I am so full of rage. I thought that I had put all of these feelings behind me. It's been years since we were married. He left so much unresolved – and for no reason. I can't tell you how many times I begged him to patch things up with them. I'll tell you what. If I could, I'd kill him again for what he has put me through this week."

Beatrice rolled her eyes and then smirked. "I know exactly how you feel."

Both women shared another hug.

"Tell LJ that I will be in touch as soon as I untangle some of that mess he left."

"Mess? Are you talking about the same Fred? He was always so neat and organized."

Both women laughed.

Beatrice finished the receiving line by spending a few sincere minutes with Katie and her husband Jerry and then with Fred's oldest son Freddie, Jr. and his wife Hillary. She held each of their hands tenderly and tried to assure each of them that Fred loved them in his own peculiar way.

Felicity then guided Beatrice and Carrie through the maze of people who were gathered in small groups scattered about the room. Felicity, a natural born hostess introduced Beatrice as 'Our poor Freddie's second wife.' She told a funny story or an anecdote about how they were connected to Fred as Beatrice met neighbors and friends, distant cousins and school chums. Carrie stood behind her mother taking careful stock of each person that Beatrice shook hands or offered a small kiss on the cheek. It didn't take long for Carrie to realize that the people gathered here today didn't really know Fred at all. They were all here because they knew his children or were acquaintances or clients of his brothers. There wasn't one person in the room who was here because they felt the slightest bit of remorse for the loss of Fred. No one really cared.

And then, Carrie smiled

.

Doing Hard Time In Vacationland

It was a Sunday afternoon in late May when we were seated in our usual spots around the oval dining room table, waiting for Beatrice to serve dinner. Much to our disappointment, Sunday dinners also now included Fred who had become something of a regular fixture, especially at mealtimes. He was seated at the head of the table furthest from the small kitchen. Carrie and I set the table earlier that day using Beatrice's favorite and only bone white China. The dinner plates each had a thin silver edge and a platinum inlay of tiny gardenias. The set was a wedding gift from one of Butch's maiden aunts and was typically only used for high holidays. Since Butch left, Beatrice insisted that we use it every Sunday, along with the good water goblets with the silver rims. She vetoed the linen napkins because she didn't have time in the schedule on laundry day to wash, dry and press them.

"Sweetie, it smells damn good from in here." bellowed Fred.

"Almost ready. Kevin? Carrie? Would you come help me please?" Beatrice called from the kitchen.

Two minutes later, Carrie and Kevin returned to the cream colored dining room with steaming bowls of boiled carrots, potatoes, onions, turnips, and cabbage, all had been heavily buttered. Beatrice followed right behind with a platter of meat and a basket of refrigerator rolls fresh from the oven.

"Ok. I think that is everything folks. Let's eat." said Beatrice as she slid into her chair.

"Looks even better than it smells. Sweetie." said Fred as he rubbed his hands together. "Kids be sure to thank your mother for this delicious looking meal."

"Thanks Mom."

"It looks good."

"Can't wait to dig in."

"I hate cabbage. Don't give me any cabbage."

Beatrice made sure that each of us had an appropriate amount of each of the vegetables, including Carrie, the cabbage hater. She cut up Christopher's food before serving herself.

"I just love a boiled dinner. It was my favorite growing up. Do you like the smoked shoulder Freddie? I like it some much better than corned beef. I think it adds much more flavor to the vegetables."

"This is fantastic. Best I have ever had." replied Fred with his mouth full of food.

Christopher, still gun shy from the corn on the cob incident as well as several other food deluges winced a little hoping that he wouldn't get hit with any food that may eventually escape from Fred's mouth.

Normally our meal times were loud and festive and the conversations typically were light and upbeat...most of the time. With the addition of our ever so frequent guest, meal conversations were almost non-existent. We continued to eat our meal in relative silence with the exception of Fred's heavy breathing and slurping as he ate. Eventually, Beatrice broke the conversation silence.

"Hey kids. I have some good news. Freddie and I were talking and we think that it is time that we took a family vacation."

"Oh?"

"Where?"

"When?"

"Do I have to go?"

"Are we going to get to go to the beach?" asked Christopher.

"No, we are not going to the beach." replied Beatrice.

"Why not? We always go to the beach. It's tradition." whined Carrie.

"The beach?" repeated Fred as if he couldn't believe his ears.

"Freddie. For the last few years, we would take the kids to stay at a cottage on the beach either on Cape Cod or on the New Hampshire shore."

"I think I remember you saying something like that."

"Well you are right Carrie, the ocean has been somewhat of a family tradition. However, now that Freddie is part of the family, we thought that it was time for us to build some new traditions."

"What if we don't want any new vacation traditions?" asked Carrie as she rolled her eyes into the back of her head.

"Before you pass judgment young lady, why don't you listen to where we are going? Tell them Freddie."

"A buddy of mine at the plant told me about this place. It's a cabin up in the woods of Maine."

"Maine?"

"The woods?"

"We better keep a close eye on Christopher so he doesn't get eaten by a bear." sneered Kevin.

"A bear? A bear is going to eat me?" panicked Christopher.

"Either that or a coyote!"

"A coyote?"

"Or a wolf."

"A wolf? Mom, I don't want to be eaten by a wolf."

"Don't worry Christopher. Kevin was only teasing." said Beatrice in a smoothing reassuring voice while simultaneously dope slapping Kevin off the back of his head.

"It's called Sunflower Cottage. It's a little off the beaten path. But there are plenty of things there to keep you kids busy. Tell them Freddie."

"You guys are gonna love it. The cabin sits right on a river. There are canoes, a dock that you can fish and go swimming off of. It has a Tarzan swing that will take you half way across the river. There are plenty of hiking trails and a place to have campfires and make s'mores. I tell ya, it is right outta Huckleberry Finn."

"Doesn't that sound like a lot of fun?" said Beatrice hoping to get a positive reaction from at least one of her children. Carrie and I exchanged a look of "man, this is so going to suck" across the table and stuffed potatoes into our mouths so that we couldn't speak without breaking a cardinal table manner rule.

Beatrice, fully aware of what we were up to, gave us each the evil eye and then set her sights on the next kid in line. "Kevin? Doesn't that Tarzan swing sound like a lot of fun, honey?" prodded Beatrice.

"Sure does ma." agreed Kevin who followed our lead and shoveled the boiled carrots so quickly into his mouth that the butter started to drip from a corner of his lips.

"Christopher? What do you think? Doesn't it sound like we will have a great time?"

"Except the part about the bears and the wolves." replied Christopher earnestly.

"Well then I guess it's all settled, Freddie. We have booked the cabin for the first week in July. And before any of you ask, the answer is no friends will be coming along. It's strictly a family only vacation."

Before any of us can raise a voice of decent, Beatrice added, "You know how I feel about you speaking with your mouths full. So save it for later. Freddie, would you please pass the vinegar?"

Over the next few weeks, our collective and repeated requests for an exception to the family vacation rule or to make arrangements to stay with another family and forego Maine all together fell on deaf ears. Carrie was being uncharacteristically quiet when it came to the subject of the family vacation, not really putting up much of a fight as Kevin and I pushed, begged, and pleaded with Beatrice. As a matter of fact the more that we pushed and begged the more Beatrice dug in her heals. And the quieter Carrie got!

We soon learned that while we were busy working on Beatrice, Carrie was working on convincing Nana Flossie to take her on a girl's retreat, a little grandmother granddaughter bonding time to a Booth Bay Harbor bed and breakfast the exact same week. Knowing that Beatrice could not say no to Nana Flossie, Carrie was triumphant in her bid to circumvent the process. She would have a quiet and civilized vacation by the ocean being spoiled and we would be stuck in the middle of nowhere with Fred.

Aarrrg!

"Asshole."

"All's fair in love and war, Michael." Carrie sneered.

Beatrice thought that the last minute addition of Uncle Cooper to the family vacation would somehow take the sting out of Carrie's coup.

It didn't.

"Life is too short for you to be pissed off all the time Mike. Cheer up and try to make the best of it." said Uncle Cooper as he rubbed the top of my head messing up my hair.

I knew deep down in my heart that he was right, which just pissed me off even more. Somehow, I was going to have to find a way to swallow my resentment and take a more positive posture. Who knows, we may actually have a decent time. After all, how bad could it be?

It took a little over two and a half hours of driving on a Saturday morning for the grey battered Pontiac with the missing muffler to get from the tiny house by the golden pond to Magoo's General Store in somewhere off the beaten path Maine. Christopher was in the front seat between Fred and Beatrice who were both hung over and perhaps still a little drunk from their pre-vacation cocktails last night at the Blue Star Bar. They later let it slip that they had closed the place. From the way that they snapped at each other, you can assume that the night did not go as smoothly as planned. There were long periods where they did not utter a word and both chain smoked all the way up. Christopher was given the responsibility to find some decent music each time we drove out of range of a radio station. Which was quite frequently. Uncle Cooper, Kevin and I shared the backseat and fortunately I had the one working window, which I naturally kept open desperately looking for fresh air. Kevin and Cooper played slaps for most of the trip.

Magoo's General Store was a big red building with a wrap around covered porch that stood at a fork in the road, where Old Sachem Road converged from route sixteen. There had to have been a dozen or so rocking chairs in various shapes and sizes that were just screaming out for company to come sit a spell. The siding was decorated with vintage metal signs advertising everything from gasoline to potato chips, candy bars and worms. Fred pulled in and parked the Pontiac along side of one of the two gasoline pumps that were in front of the store. We were very close to the cottage and he wanted to fill the tank and check the oil before we got there and settled in. He gave Beatrice ten dollars to go inside and get whatever additional supplies that we needed for the week.

"This isn't enough." whispered Beatrice tensely.

"It's what I have." snarled Fred.

"No it isn't." Beatrice snapped back. "You told me not to buy milk, eggs, and butter until we got up here. We are going to need a couple of other things as well."

"Like what?"

"How about cream for your coffee, asshole?"

Fred shot her a very intense look of hatred. He reached into his front pant's pocket and pulled an additional three ten dollar bills from his gold plated money clip and handed them to Beatrice.

"Thank you." she said curtly and walked into the store. Kevin, Christopher, and I followed. At the same time a rather thin teen age boy with an oily completion and dark oily hair wearing dirty blue coveralls and a cheap pair of sneakers came out of the store to help pump the gas.

We were greeted by both a bell and Mrs. Magoo, a heavy set woman with silver white hair that she kept in a long tight mermaid tail braid, who was standing behind a counter in the center of the store, helping a young child with his penny candy selection and ringing up a customer's order, while another customer talked quietly on the payphone which was hung on a wooden column a couple of feet away.

"Good morning folks. Welcome. I am Mrs. Magoo."

"Good Morning. I am Beatrice and these are my sons, Michael, Kevin, and Christopher. Say hello boys."

"Hello."

"Nice to meet you, ma'am."

"Hi."

"What a great store you have here." admired Beatrice who was taking it all in. The right side of the store had a small breakfast counter with six stools, a couple of café tables and a glass deli counter. Two of the parameter walls on the left side of the store were half covered with shelving units filled with various canned sundries and food stuffs. The other one was covered with coolers filled with milk, other dairy products, ice cream, sodas, and beer. There were long wooden tables scattered about that were stacked high with tee shirts, sweatshirts, camping and fishing gear. The magazine rack was stocked full, although a little out of date with the adult men's magazines covered in a brown paper wrap on the top shelf.

Beatrice handed Kevin one of the ten dollar bills and told him to spend it all on penny candy. She also reminded him that he would be expected to share everything that he bought with Christopher, Uncle Cooper, and me. As Kevin and Christopher ran to the candy counter, Beatrice walked the store. She went from shelf to shelf, cooler to cooler and selected the items that she needed and handed them to me to carry for her. Mrs. Magoo had just finished ringing Kevin up when Beatrice and I put the groceries on the counter.

"Looks like they have quite a sweet tooth." smiled Mrs. Magoo.

"I don't normally allow this." Beatrice smiled back. "It's a special occasion. We are on vacation."

"That's wonderful, dear. Are you staying someplace local?" asked Mrs. Magoo as she pushed numbers into the large brown cash register.

"Not too far I guess. It's called Sunflower cottage."

"The Cresta place?"

"I don't know. I guess so."

"Oh, you'll love it. It's a beautiful place. Overlooking the river."

"That's what I have heard. I can't wait to see it for myself. Oh, would you please throw in a couple packages of Kools, Camels, and Winston boxes?"

"Sure thing dear." said Mrs. Magoo. "I do hope the weather cooperates with you."

"Weather?" I ask.

"We are due for a bit of rain this week."

"Ma!" I whined.

"Enough! Not a word." commanded Beatrice.

"Oh, me and my mouth." said Mrs. Magoo apologetically. "I hope that I didn't…"

"No worries Mrs. Magoo. You cannot control the weather." said Beatrice as she handed Mrs. Magoo some money. "We will make our own fun."

"Please call me Sylvia."

"Ok Sylvia, it is."

Mrs. Magoo handed Beatrice back her change.

"Ok boys. Please take the bags and say thank you to Mrs. Magoo for all of her help."

"Thank you Mrs. Magoo."

"Thanks."

"Thank you."

"It was nice to meet you Sylvia. I am sure we will see each other again this week. Have a nice day."

"You too dear. I could be wrong about the weather."

"Let's hope so." Beatrice smiled as we left the store and hopped back into the freshly gassed and oiled Pontiac with an impatiently waiting Fred. We drove northeast for two miles on Old Sachem road before the pavement gave way to a dirt road. Another mile and a half later and we had finally reached our destination.

Sunflower Cottage was aptly named. It was a modest A-Frame style home with a roofline that stretched from each side of the slab foundation and met at the top forming a sharp point. With the exception of a small bump out on each side of the house, it reminded me of a huge triangle. The shaker shingles were painted the same deep yellow orange color of the sunflower petals closest to the seeded center and the trim was painted cream. There was a large weathered deck for the front landing. A pair of chipped green Adirondack chairs flagged either side of the front door which was all glass. Over one of the chairs was a white rectangular Welcome sign with faded sunflowers painted on it.

The front door emptied directly into the utilitarian kitchen with a green linoleum checkered floor that was peeling in the corners. A stained glass sunflower hung in the window over the sink which was immediately to the left of the entrance and gave a full view of the front yard. The lower cabinets were painted white, while the uppers, which didn't have any doors, were left a natural wood color and were heavily shellacked. The butcher block counters were stained with watermarks and desperately needed to be sanded and resealed. Throughout the space you could not help but notice the several ant traps that were not too well concealed. Towards the back of the kitchen, there was a double wide open doorway which led to the pass-through dining space. The walls didn't have any windows and were painted a high gloss white. In the middle of the room on top of a stained blue braided oval rug rested a whitewashed picnic table that was also heavily shellacked. A pair of white captain's chairs flagged each end of the table. A pot of plastic sunflowers sat in the center of the table on top of a matching sunflower table runner. Behind each of the captain's chairs was a door. One led to a small bedroom with a queen's size black cast iron bed that was covered in a sunflower quilt. The other door led to a small bathroom that consisted of a sink, a toilet, and a claw foot tub.

Beyond the dining room was the two story living room with well worn and gouged wide plank pine floors. The walls had large pine beams every few feet that went from floor to ceiling and were stained a maple color. Matching tongue and groove paneling hung horizontally between each of the beams and also went from floor to ceiling. With the exception of the sliding glass doors which opened up to a deck and a set of backstairs that led to the dock, the rest of the exterior wall was made up entirely of a series of oversized windows that gave an expansive view of the small river and the herd of goats that were grazing in the clearing which was surrounded by large trees on the other side.

There was an orange cone shaped free standing fireplace with a curved base in one corner of the room. On the opposite corner sat a bookcase filled with books, puzzles and older board games as well as a dark walnut black and white television console. The furniture which consisted of a couple beige fur (although I would have assumed that they must have been white at one time) butterfly chairs, a couple of end tables that had thick green glass ashtrays, a large plaid couch, a matching chair and ottoman was arranged to make small conversational areas around the large room.

A spiral staircase led to the door of an enclosed loft space which sat over the kitchen and dining room. It was a wide open room with wooden walls and a ceiling similar to the living room. It had red shag carpeting and a set of full size beds against opposite walls that were each separated by small painted dressers with decoupage sunflowers. It smelt heavily of stale cigarette smoke. After claiming my bed, I banged open the front yard facing windows which were stuck in the hopes that it would air out the space.

The windows looked directly into the driveway where the rest of the family I assumed was unpacking the car and lugging the stuff into the cottage. My heart froze with fear when I heard Beatrice's scream and witnessed Fred punch Uncle Cooper straight in the face. Blood squirted from his nostrils like it was a running spigot as Cooper fell on his back. He tried to hold his nose to prevent the blood from rushing out, turning his white T-shirt a deep red. "Stay the fuck down!" shouted Fred while pointing his crooked right index finger at him.

"Cooper!" screamed Beatrice again. "What did you do? What the hell do you think you are doing, Fred?" Beatrice screamed as she grabbed his right arm with both of her hands, thinking that she could prevent him from striking her brother once more.

"I have had enough of this shit!" Fred screeched back, his face turning almost purple with rage. "I ain't staying here another minute! Get offa me! Get the fuck offa me!" With a quick and powerful jerk of his right arm, Beatrice lost both her grip and her footing and fell hard to the ground. Fred started to walk away from Cooper and headed towards the driver's side door of the grey dented car.

"Stop it! Stop it! Stop it! Stop it!" cried Christopher.

"No. No. No. You are not doing this to me!!" screamed Beatrice as she pulled herself up from the dirt driveway not caring about the rocks that were now embedded in her bleeding palms and knees. She wrapped her arms tightly around his waist and dug her heels trying in vain to stop the man who was more than double her size.

"I'm serious. Get the fuck offa me!" he roared almost spitting his words.

"No! No! You are not going to do this! You are not leaving me here!" she yelled back almost matching his ferocity.

"I said get the fuck off!" he screamed even louder and swatting her with his free hand striking her in the face. The blow sent her flying. At that point Kevin jumped on Fred's back and started to hit him repeatedly in the head, while Christopher latched on to Fred's left leg and bit him for all he was worth.

I rushed down the stairs and through the kitchen determined to help. In the time it took me to get to the front door, Fred had managed to remove Kevin and Christopher and get behind the wheel of his car and started the engine. Beatrice whose right cheek was red and swollen was back on her feet. She lunged for the interior car handle of the passenger side door and held on for dear life.

"Stop. Stop Freddie. You can't leave me here!" Beatrice cried.

"Mommy! Stop!" screamed Christopher.

"Get away from the car Bea. Let go of the car Bea. Beatrice!" he shouted as he put the car in gear and began to pull away.

"Don't. Don't. Please don't do this." shouted Beatrice, who didn't relax her grip and was now running along side of the car. "Noooooo!"

Fred gunned the engine. Beatrice ran as fast as she could but eventually tripped and hung on the door with all of her might dragging her feet, hoping that he would eventually come to his senses and stop the car. Instead with his left hand gripped firmly on the steering wheel, he reached over and pounded on her hands with his right fist. Ultimately, Beatrice let go and collapsed in a heap as the battered Pontiac with the missing muffler sped away.

Beatrice eventually rose to her hands and knees and stayed there for a beat or two trying to control her anger, frustration and her tears with her breathing. Once she acknowledged that it wasn't working, Beatrice stood up, adjusted her shirt, brushed her black bangs out of her face and walked back down the long unpaved driveway. A couple of the suitcases had popped open in the melee and their contents were blowing about the front yard. She rummaged through one of the boxes of food that she packed and pulled out a gallon bottle of Vodka.

"Kids. Do your best to pick this all up and bring it into the house please. I am sure he will be back once he cools off. I am going in to get myself cleaned up. Please hurry. I think Mrs. Magoo was right. It looks like it is going to rain." Beatrice said as she entered the house. She rummaged through one of the cupboards by the sink and found a large ice tea glass and filled it half way with ice from a metal tray in the freezer before she filled it to the rim with the vodka. She stared at the glass for a minute or two contemplating her actions. With a heavy sigh, Beatrice lifted the glass to her mouth and drained it dry.

Outside, Kevin, Christopher and I picked up our clothes and stuffed them back into the suitcases.

'What got him going?" I asked.

"He was pissed about the candy." Kevin said.

"Fucker."

After we settled in a bit, Beatrice took to her room for a nap, which was something that she rarely did even when sick. Coop suggested that we get our suits on and check out the river.

"Let's see if this Tarzan swing is as good as they say." said Cooper doing his best to keep us distracted. Thankfully his nose had stopped bleeding. His eyes however were beginning to turn black. He would have a heck of a double shiner.

We quickly changed into our swimming trunks and each grabbed a towel and headed down the back stairs towards the dock. The noon time sun was now engulfed in heavy clouds of silver and charcoal and the air smelt electric as the winds began to blow and gust. We ran down the gangplank which connected the dock to the shore and could not find anything remotely resembling a Tarzan swing. Gone also were the canoes and the fishing rods that Fred promised.

"Ooo the water is cold." said Christopher as he stuck his toe in the water.

"It's fine. You gotta get used to it." said Kevin as he pushed Christopher off the dock and into the water.

A split second later, Christopher broke the surface screaming, "Kevin! I am so going to tell on you."

"Oooo, I am so scared." mocked Kevin as he somersaulted off the dock and into the river.

I did one of my patented cannonballs into the water and then the three of us swam across the river to check out the other side and see if we could find the herd of goats that were there earlier. In the meantime, Uncle Cooper liberated a red canoe from the "neighbor's" house and eventually was able to paddle over and join us on the other side. We followed a path through the woods for a little bit until we heard the first sounds of thunder and decided it was best if we headed back. The intensity of the thunder may have gotten louder as we got closer to the boat, although it was nothing compared to the baritone voice of an irate Mr. Anderson, who was standing on his dock demanding that we return his boat "toot sweet" before he called the sheriff.

"Hello there. My name is Cooper. I am assuming that this canoe belongs to you? I told them not to take it! Just as soon as I realized what they had done, I swam over to make sure that they set it right. Boys you are in so much trouble! Return that poor man's boat and get your asses in the house. NOW! I am going to greet you with my belt as soon as you get in the door." bellowed Cooper sounding almost exactly like Fred. And with that, Uncle Cooper dove into the water and swam to our dock, leaving the three us confused, red faced and red handed.

With Christopher in the middle, Kevin and I hopped into the canoe and made the short paddle to the dock of the awaiting and angry Mr. Anderson. He insisted that we help pull the boat out of the water and put it under his deck to protect it from the rain storms that were coming. Once finished, he threatened us with the sheriff if he should ever see our hoodlum hides on his property again. He chased us off his dock and into the water. We swam the few yards to our dock just as the first few drops of rain started to fall. Once we were safely on our "property" we grabbed our towels and made the ascension up the stairs to the back deck, just as the skies opened up.

It turned out that Mrs. Magoo downplayed the storm, in reality it was a tempest of biblical proportions. The rain came down hard and sounded like a thousand hammers driving tiny nails into the roof. The thunderclouds seemed to stall directly over Sunflower Cottage. Their incessant booming and cracking caused the windows in our loft bedroom to rattle, as the lightning bolts made the night skies shine like it were noon instead of midnight.

The next day, Kevin, Christopher, and I tried to keep ourselves entertained as the storms continued in their intensity. The winds were blowing and it appeared as though the rain was now coming down at a ninety degree angle. We played Parcheesi, Sorry, and whatever other board and card games we could find, while Beatrice and Uncle Cooper nursed their wounds with ice compresses, cigarettes and glasses of "special lemonade." Beatrice was tired and stressed from her ordeal, so we were left to fend for ourselves when it came to meals and snacks throughout the day. After watching the Creature Double Feature on the black and white television console, we each kissed Beatrice and headed up the spiral staircase to bed. The rain had become a sort of white noise to us at this point. However the loud crashing and booming of the lightning did keep us on edge. We didn't hear the crashing and the booming coming from downstairs.

Come morning, we climbed down the stairs and looked out the massive wall of windows in the living room. The rain seemed to have slowly petered out. The skies were still monochromatic and ominous, but the wind seemed to have dissipated as well. The goats were back in the clearing on the other side of the river grazing on their breakfast of grasses and bushes. Uncle Cooper was asleep on the couch snoring to beat the band. Christopher was the first to notice the remnants of the ginger jar lamp that once sat on an end table now taking up residence on the floor.

"What happened here?" Kevin asked.

Before I could get off a wise ass answer, Beatrice emerged from behind the creaking door of her bedroom. She was wearing last night clothes that were wrinkled and dirt stained. Her right eye was the color and shape of a plum and her hair was in desperate need of a brush.

"Hello my babies." she said in a raspy voice. She gave a big closed lip smile which quickly turned into a wince as she leaned down to hug Christopher.

"Ma. You look like...."

"Hell. I know Michael." she said while obviously having a difficult time standing up. "I need you kiddos to do me a favor." She said as she shuffled to the plaid chair in the living room with her cigarettes, lighter and ashtray.

"Over on the counter, I left some money and some change." she winced again as she lowered herself in the chair and lit a cigarette.

"Mommy. What happened to the lamp?" asked Christopher trying to get in close.

"Don't worry about it baby. It was an accident. Uncle Cooper knocked it over last night. I will pick it up before you get back."

"Back? From where?" asked Kevin as he pinched Cooper's nose closed in an effort to stop the snoring.

"I need you guys to go to Mrs. Magoo's. Michael, I wrote down a couple of numbers were Freddie may be. I want you to call him and ask him to come back and get us." she said as she held my wrist with both of her hands.

"Ma. I don't want..."

"Michael. Please. He should have come back by now. I would have thought he would have been back by now." she pleaded. "I put some extra money there too. Why don't you see if Mrs. Magoo has any donuts? Doesn't that sound nice? Or get something else that you would like to eat for breakfast. Please do me a favor and don't try and fill up on a bunch of junk. I want you to buy some American cheese. I'll make grilled cheese sandwiches for lunch when you get back. Doesn't that sound good?"

Beatrice hugged Christopher and Kevin. "Hurry up now. By the time that you get back, I will have myself and this mess all cleaned up. I must look like a fright. Sound like a plan? Ok? Shoo. The sooner you get going, the sooner you will be back."

We made the trip down Old Sachem Road to Magoo's General Store in record time, only having to stop a couple of times for poor Christopher who complained that he couldn't keep up because his legs were not as long as ours. The greasy haired teenager from the other day was there sitting in one of the rockers on the front porch smoking a cigarette.

With all the second hand smoke, I felt as though I'd smoked a carton of cigarettes this week!

"Hello boys." Mrs. Magoo welcomed us from across the store and behind another counter. She was putting away some homemade peach preserves. "What brings you in today?"

"Good morning, ma'am. We are here to get something for breakfast and to use the payphone." I said.

"The phone is right over there. Let me know if you need any change. Menus are on the counter. Take a seat and I will be with you in a moment." she said as she continued arranging the peaches.

Kevin took Christopher by the shoulder and led him to the breakfast counter, while I used the rotary dial payphone to track down Fred. Miraculously, he picked up the call on the first ring of the first call.

"Hullo."

"Fred?"

"Yeah. Who is this?"

"It's me Mike."

"What do you want?"

"For starters, how about coming back and getting us?"

"Why would I want to do that?"

"Cuz you left us here in the middle of nowhere with no way to get home."

"I don't need your shit."

Watch your tone asshole! You're losing him!

"You are right. I am sorry. But I don't need this shit either. I am totally frustrated. What are we supposed to do?"

"I am sure that Cooper and your mother will figure something out."

"They won't. They can't. They have totally shut down."

"So?"

"So you have to come get us."

"No. No I do not."

"What the hell are we supposed to do??"

"Then I guess big man, you are going to have to figure something out."

"How? We don't have a car. There isn't a bus or a cab or a train for miles. You picked this place. Tell me how are we supposed to get back?"

"Not my issue big man."

"Of course it is your issue!"

"This is the operator speaking. Please deposit eighty five cents for an additional three minutes."

"Damn it. Don't hang up. Don't hang up." I demanded frantically as I empty my pockets looking for additional change, but it was too late.

"Asshole."

"Young man, I would appreciate it if you would keep the profanity to a minimum please." corrected Mrs. Magoo, who had just served chocolate cake and apple pie ala mode to Christopher and Kevin.

"My apologies, ma'am." I said humbly as I joined my brothers at the counter.

"Sounds like you have some anger to work through young man." said Mrs. Magoo.

"With all due respect ma'am, you do not know the half of it."

"Here you go. Complements of the establishment." said Mrs. Magoo, as she slid a piece of chocolate cake and ice cream in front of me. "There isn't a problem in the world that can't be solved with a nice big slice of chocolate cake and a scoop of vanilla."

"Thank you. May we also get a pound of American cheese to take with us?

'Sure thing darlin'."

"What happened? What did he say?" asked Kevin once Mrs. Magoo was out of earshot.

"He's not coming back."

"Asshole."

"Keep in down."

"What are we supposed to do now?"

"I honestly do not know." I said taking a big bite of the moist cake.

"Gimme some money. I am gonna call Dad." demanded Kevin with his hand outstretched.

"You seriously think that he is going to come get us?"

"I don't know. It's worth a shot. It certainly beats walking. Now, fork over some money so I can call him."

I handed Kevin all of my change and he and Christopher got off of their stools and walked to the payphone. Mrs. Magoo appeared before me with the wrapped cheese and began to clear the counter.

"Who are they calling?" she asked.

"Doesn't really matter they are not going to get through. How much do we owe you?"

I settled the bill with Mrs. Magoo and left a small tip when Christopher and Kevin walked back looking completely dejected.

"How did it go?"

"She wouldn't let us speak to dad." said Christopher trying to hold back a tear.

"We both tried calling. She wouldn't put either of us through." said a visibly angry Kevin.

When Butch left the tiny house by the golden pond, he immediately moved in with his mistress and her three daughters, the youngest daughter who is Christopher's age happens to have the exact same coloring and complexion as Kevin. Mistress Judy, the she-wolf, who is quite content and adamant in keeping communication between Butch and his children to a bare minimum, is the only one who is allowed to answer the phone in their apartment. I am certain that he rarely gets any of his messages.

"What about Nana? Do you think she would come?" asked Christopher.

"In a New York minute. Except that she and Carrie are away on vacation someplace and I don't know where they are or how to get a hold of them."

The sound of the distant thunder was the sign that we needed to make our way back to Sunflower Cottage. On the way back we racked our brains trying to come up with names of people with big enough cars who would be willing to drive the two hours to pick us all up and not ask a lot of questions that would embarrass or humiliate Beatrice. We managed to reach the front door just as the skies opened up once more. Inside the music was playing loudly and Beatrice and Cooper were dancing the Madison in the living room. They had cigarettes in one hand and glasses of special lemonade in the other. They laughed and giggled louder with each misstep. Once Beatrice fell on the floor, I knew that I would be the one to make the grilled cheese.

On Wednesday we got a small break in the weather. The torrential downpours that plagued us for the last few days were replaced by a grey wet mist which was so thick it made it impossible to see the goat tribe that was nosily grazing as usual on the opposite side of the river. I noticed that the living room was in a state of shambles looking as though it had been tossed by a team of eager FBI agents as I left the safety of the loft bedrooms and came down the stairs. Both Beatrice and Uncle Cooper were unconscious. She was in what looked like a very uncomfortable position on the couch and Uncle Cooper was slumped in the green plaid chair. Between his nicotine stained fore and middle fingers was a cigarette butt which dangled above an overflowing ashtray, which was on the floor. There were glasses and plates with half eaten food on every flat surface. Six candles with different scents were slowly burning down on the maple buffet. The forest green plastic trash can that was normally kept in the kitchen was on its side next to a pile of broken glass by the television.

The kitchen was in worse shape if such a thing was possible. Every pot, pan and dish was out and about and covered with half cooked food. Two half gallons of milk were opened, sitting on opposite kitchen counters; they were both warm and one had a sour odor.

"What happened in here?" asked Christopher as he stood in the door way dressed in his pajamas shaking his head.

"Not sure. I'd pour you some juice but I don't think there is a clean glass."

Christopher just stood there with a look of shock and disgust on his face.

"Is Kevin still sleeping?"

"Yeah."

"Ok. Tell you what. Why don't you go in the living room and see if there is anything on television to watch? I'll straighten things up in here a little and then I'll make some pancakes for breakfast. Ok?"

"But..."

Speaking from experience, I knew that Beatrice and Cooper would not be up any time soon. "Don't worry. You will not wake them up. Promise. They are really tired."

I made sure that Christopher was plopped in the one clean living room chair and repositioned it in front of the television. It took some effort, but I was able to manipulate the rabbit ears just right ensuring that there was a clear signal for the one channel that was showing cartoons. It took the better part of an hour to put the kitchen back into some semblance of order so I could make some pancakes. Naturally the maple syrup was missing so I served them with the remaining grape jelly.

"No syrup?" asked Kevin who was sitting on the floor next to Christopher's chair.

"Nope."

"You sure?"

"Yup."

"We got any milk?"

"Nope."

"Damn."

"I'm telling!" Christopher said instinctively.

"Yeah. Good luck with that." shot back Kevin in a sarcastic tone that was quickly becoming an obviously shared family genetic trait.

After breakfast, I finished cleaning the kitchen. We got dressed in our shorts, t-shirts and zip up sweatshirts. I took ten dollars and the last of the change from the pocketbook lying on the floor next to the still unconscious Beatrice.

"Shouldn't we leave a note?" asked a concerned Christopher.

"Sure. Why don't you do it?" I said and then told him to meet us outside.

By the time we made the all too familiar three and half mile walk to Magoo's General Store, our sweatshirts were damp from the mist. The regular morning crowd over at the breakfast counter all turned in our direction as the shop bell on top of the door announced our entrance.

"Good morning boys." said Sylvia Magoo from behind the counter as she poured fresh coffee into the awaiting cups. Her silver white hair was tied up in a knot on her head. She made a point of giving everyone who walked into her store her undivided attention, even if it was with just a smile and a wave. "Nice to see you again. I'll be over there just as soon as I am done here."

"Thank you" we said in unison. "Just going to use the payphone again."

"You two look around, while I try to call Dad." I said confidently as I started dialing the payphone although I was very nervous about making the call. Throughout the weeks and months leading up to their separation, Butch was missing in action more than he was at home. He would "work late" or "have to help a friend out after work" which more than likely meant that he was drinking and playing cards at either the Italian American Club which I found more than a little ironic, since he didn't have a drop of Italian blood in him, the Legion or at the Moose Hall. I would often help Beatrice track him down via the telephone pretending to be someone other than his son. Thanks to the frequency of the calls, the numbers were still committed to my memory. The operator came on to tell me the amount of money that I needed to complete the call. Tired of fumbling through my pockets, I dumped the money on the counter so that I could quickly get at the quarters and dimes that I needed. The phone rang seven times before I gave up trying to reach him at the Legion. I hung up the receiver and the change fell loudly into the coin return. It had been months since I had even spoken to Butch. After he left, I went on one Saturday father time trip with him. I had such an awful time, I never went again.

Contrary to popular belief, I wasn't angry that my parents divorced. Quite the opposite...I was relieved. My parents were truly unhappy and in return that was making the rest of us miserable. Separating was the best thing that they could have done for everyone involved. I was just so pissed that he lived up to his promise. One night during a heated screaming match, he threatened Beatrice if she went through with the divorce, he would sell the store and she would never see another dime from him. And that is exactly what he did. He abandoned all financial responsibility for us. He couldn't help with the electric bill or give Beatrice money to buy groceries. Yet somehow he always seemed able to get his hands on the best of merchandise when the time called for it. He gave Carrie things like a new softball bat and a Panasonic SG-200 Funnygraph portable record player in space age groovy orange. Kevin got the latest hockey equipment and a new leather jacket. His new wife Judy and her daughters always seemed to have new bangles, rings and chokers. All of this made possible by a man without a job. I had long suspected back then that most of the items "fell off the back of a truck" adding grand theft and questionable integrity to my growing list of distain for my father.

While I dialed the Italian American Club, Kevin was busy stuffing Christopher's sweatshirt with candy, snack cakes, and jerky. Christopher's eyes always grew like saucers whenever he was confronted with any type of wrong doing.

"Shut up. Don't' say a word. We don't have any food left at home and this way I will make sure that you don't starve." Kevin said threateningly.

The phone was answered on the first ring by a familiar husky voice.

"Italian American. Who do you want to talk to? Chances are...he just left."

"Dad?"

"Mikey?"

"Yeah it's me."

"You can't be calling here, son."

"I know."

"Then you know, I have to go."

"Don't hang up."

"What??!!" Butch said in a tone that was a mixture frustration, anger and sadness.

"We need help."

"Where's your mother?"

"She's with us. We came up to Maine on a vacation. Fred knew a guy who said this place would be great. It's not. It's anything but."

"Who went?"

"Mom, Fred Uncle Coop, Me, Kevin, and Christopher."

"Where's your sister?"

"She went away someplace else with Nana Flossie."

"What's the problem?"

"They were all drinking before we got here. Then Mom and Fred got into a huge fight on the first day…and then he left us here. I called him but he says that he isn't coming back."

"What do you want me to do?"

"Will you come get us?"

"Look son, it's not my problem."

"Please! She and Coop haven't stopped partying. Christopher is freaking out. She has a black eye. Dad. I am in over my head here."

"If it was so bad, why didn't you call sooner?"

"We did! Kevin and Christopher called your apartment, but Judy wouldn't let them speak to you. "

"What the fuck?"

"I just can't drop everything and drive to Maine."

"PLEASE!"

After a long pause, Butch said that he would see what he could do. I gave him the address and then hung up. We filled a brown paper sack with a loaf of bread, a carton of eggs, maple syrup and a couple half gallons of milk. As soon as I paid for the groceries, we began our walk back.

Halfway back the sky opened up once more and water just seemed to pour down on us as though it were actually coming out of a fire hose. Ten minutes later, it was over as quickly as it started. We were soaked clear through when we finally arrived back at Sunflower Cottage. The only thing that we had on our minds when we opened the front door was getting out of the wet clothes. And then we heard the strong and powerful baritone singing voice of Uncle Cooper coming from behind the brightly painted yellow A-frame cottage. Shooting my brothers a look, we dropped the groceries and went around back to see Uncle Cooper standing on the dock in full performance mode. As soon as we made eye contact, he added some athletic high kicks and fantails and belted out the chorus, never once losing his perfect pitch or his balance for that matter.

When sober, Beatrice's younger brother was our favorite uncle. He was silly and funny and his laughter was infectious. I remember that we often had to beg him to stop because it actually hurt to laugh so hard. He taught us to use our imaginations and his own versions of nursery rhymes, which sometimes got us in trouble when we repeated them to my father's side of the family who were definitely much more subdued and stoic.

Hickory, dickory, dock.
The mouse ran up the clock.
The clock struck one,
The mouse shit.

Jack be nimble,
Jack be quick,
Jack jumped over the candlestick,
And screamed
Great balls of fire.

He taught us nonsense songs like:

After the ball was over,
Millie took out her glass eye.

Put her teeth in some water.
Hung out her wig to dry.
Unscrewed her wooden leg,
Leaned it against the wall.
Oh, what a sight was Millie,
After the ball.

As well as a couple of others that may be harmless in their intent when we learned them back in the day, but are certainly no longer considered to be politically correct by today's standards.

He had an eye for design and color and often used our house as his canvas. In those early days, Beatrice would sometimes put us to bed early because she and Cooper were going to work on a project. They would crack a few beers and turn the HiFi on low. We would fall asleep listening to an eclectic collection of music: a movie soundtrack or something from Frank, Barbra or Herb Albert and the Tijuana Brass. The next morning we would wake up and see our new purple bathroom or Kelly Green bedroom.

To this day, much to the distain of my wife and the embarrassment of my children, I cannot paint a room or a ceiling in my house without listening to Ethel Merman and the Gypsy soundtrack.

Cooper didn't have a family of his own. He was a confirmed bachelor and spent a lot of our childhood sleeping on the living room couch. He never really settled down in the same place for long periods of time, which Beatrice said started at a very young age. By the time he turned sixteen years old, Uncle Cooper was already weary of sharing the attic turned communal bedroom of his aunt's Victorian house which was located just over the railroad tracks on the West side of town with his brother, mother and Beatrice. Most days, he enjoyed the craziness of living with his aunt, uncle and seven cousins, but there were many days that he craved his privacy more. Most importantly, there were many days that he felt sorry for his mother. Nana Flossie worked long hours as a waitress since leaving her husband those many years ago, just scraping by and still had really nothing to show for it. He felt burdensome, when she had to work an extra shift so that she could get shoes to replace the ones that he had outgrown. Throw in his less than stellar academic achievements, at two different schools and his desire for stardom, Uncle Cooper decided that it was high time for him to take matters into his own hands. One late October afternoon, he boarded a greyhound bus headed to California and never looked back. Well at least for eight months.

Beatrice refused to talk about those days. When pushed however, she did admit that he tried to become a professional actor...that he actually found an agent named Harrison Putney to represent him. He made the rounds and was able to secure a couple of very small parts in two movies. Beatrice absolutely refused to share any details other than that the movies were considered to be blue...

They were sad?

...and that I needn't ever concern myself with it. She did tell me that Mr. Putney was able to get him some modeling jobs from time to time. Beatrice even managed to save a couple of those Physique Magazines where Cooper modeled men's underwear. She hid them in the bottom left drawer of her dresser underneath her jewelry box. To help make ends meet, he would dance at a club called the Pickled Onion which was on Sunset Boulevard. He did eventually come back east to finish high school but it was only after he made Nana Flossie promise to move out of the attic and get the family their own apartment.

Uncle Cooper made the pilgrimage out west in search of fame and stardom two more times.

Unfortunately, Uncle Cooper inherited his father's tolerance for alcohol. Zero. At a fairly young age, I classified the intensity of his drinking using an eight phase cycle.

Phase One: Sneaky Drinky Cooper. At this stage, he has completely forgotten any past indiscretions or incidences as a result of his drinking and has secretly convinced himself that he could handle alcohol, provided that he limit his consumption to just a couple of beers. He would stay away from any hard spirits and prying eyes. He would become a bit of recluse and keep to himself. If he had to interact with anyone, he would make sure that he would eat breath mints by the dozens in the hopes that it would disguise his breath.

Phase Two: Funny Cooper. Tired of the taste of breath mints and armed with a false sense of drinking accomplishment (*See I told you that I could hold my liquor!*) Cooper would add a boiler maker or three to his drinking repertoire. Tired of being trapped inside he would now seek out people in order to make them laugh. Be Silly Cooper. Be Entertaining Cooper.

Phase Three: Full On Performance Mode. He has now successfully made the transition to hard liquor. (*Of course I can handle it. What was I thinking?? I have missed you vodka!*) Without reason or any forewarning, Uncle Cooper would perform his cabaret act. It could be in the middle of an intense conversation or in the middle of the street. He wasn't particular about timing or location. Unfortunately, his act always involved some form of audience participation. He wasn't particular about who he chose to help him. He was agnostic that way. He might call on a family member, neighbor, or some poor unsuspecting passerby.

Phase Four: Speaking Ragtime And Gibberish. Sleep and meals have been replaced by additional consumption of hard liquor. When speaking with him, you always felt as though you were coming on the tail end of the conversation.

The stories, always from his colorful past were disjointed and didn't make much in the way of sense. At this particular stage, Uncle Cooper would put one of us on the phone with old friends or acquaintances that he knew from his days "in the business." It might have been a studio guard, a former make-up artist, Harrison Putney's widow or an actor who hasn't worked since his sitcom got cancelled in the nineteen sixties. As this phase intensifies, he might begin to have conversations with passing ghosts, aberrations, or just old memories.

Phase Five: Now You See Him, Now You Don't. The exact timing of this phase is the most difficult to predict as it is dictated by whatever fits his fancy. As the conventional population rises with the morning sun and heads out to work, they may discover that the automobile that was once parked in the driveway has now been replaced by a handwritten note with impeccable penmanship from Uncle Cooper explaining that something had come up and he felt the need to borrow the car and get into the city. Cooper never got a drivers license. For the owner of the missing car, they might have a slightly better than ten percent chance that the car would be returned without a scratch a few days later. Uncle Cooper would be returned as well with either a split lip or a black eye. The other ninety percent of the time, typically involved a call from the police asking where you wanted the wreckage towed. Uncle Cooper was usually pretty banged up and was sleeping in either the drunk tank or the lock down ward of a local hospital. Other times, Uncle Cooper was just gone. Sometimes he would pack a bag and leave a note, other times he would not. Eventually, Beatrice will get a postcard or a letter letting her know that he was fine and now living in Texas or Arizona and not to worry.

Phase Six: The Wounded And The Embarrassed. Uncle Cooper was been sober for a few days to a week's time, spending most of his time sleeping, apologizing to family and friends and consuming incredible amounts of sugar in the form of penny candy and snack cakes. He'd be relatively quiet and might have the trembles as a result of his self-detox.

Phase Seven: The Normal Uncle Cooper. The fun guy, that we all knew and loved. Silly, creative, and artistic. This phase might only last a few weeks, but it had been known to stretch out for a year at a time.

Phase Eight: The Dry Drunk. Cooper may no longer drink, but continued to behave in dysfunctional ways. He typically had poor impulse control and was very impatient. Cooper also got extremely cranky and short tempered. He was quick to complain and would yell a lot. He became a bit of a recluse. It was just a matter of time before he resumed drinking.

As he grew older, he seemed to try harder to stay in the Normal Uncle Cooper phase longer. Nana Flossie felt that he was getting his demons under control. Me, I thought that he was just getting older and he couldn't bounce back as quickly as when he was younger. Regardless the longer he spent in the Normal Uncle Cooper Phase, the better for us. However, as soon as he could no longer resist temptation and had that first drink, his progression of the first five phases may stretch out over a period of months. More than likely however, depending upon what was going on in his life; they could / would advance rather quickly.

"Who are you singing to Coop?" Kevin asked.

"My audience. The goats." slurred Uncle Cooper, as he gestured dramatically to the other side of rushing river.

"There aren't any goats." said Christopher.

"Humpf. Everyone's a critic." smiled Cooper. "Whoa." For a man as drunk as he was, Uncle Cooper had remarkable balance and steadied himself before he fell backwards into the water. Thanks to the monsoon like rains that had plagued the area since we arrived for vacation, the once tranquil waters of the river were at this point violently splashing and bubbling at an intense clip. The wooden dock turned impromptu stage was bouncing up and down looking more like a trampoline. It leaned towards the right with the push of the strong current and seemed like it was just a matter of time before it would break free of the pilings.

"You ok Coop?" I asked. "It doesn't look too safe."

"I'm fine Michael. Thank you very much for your concern. I have performed in much worse environments. Now, for my next number..."

"Isn't it time for intermission?" I asked trying to coax him off the dock which seemed to be rocking faster.

"No. I need to make sure that the audience gets their money's worth." Cooper said as he dramatically turned his back to us and faced the empty clearing where the goats once grazed. He spread his legs slightly apart as if he were a surfer getting ready to catch the next big wave. He closed his eyes, put his chin to his chest and channeled his inner Barbra. A few seconds later, he began to sing a heartfelt and soulful rendition of "People".

"Fuck this shit." muttered Kevin under his breath and he beckoned me to follow him to the end of the gangplank. Like a stealth ninja, Kevin was quickly on this stomach and leaning over the edge. A few seconds later, he came back up with the lynch pin that connected the gangplank to the dock in his right hand. With a shit-eating grim on his face, he nodded for me to do the same. It took me twice as long, but eventually I was able to do the same. And before Uncle Cooper could begin his second verse, the dock broke free and began to float away.

"Uncle Cooper!" screamed a frightened Christopher.

Once he realized what was happening, Uncle Cooper just smiled and said, "The show must go on kiddo! Never forget that!" And then he broke into an up-tempo song to mark the occasion. We could still hear him singing "Don't Rain On My Parade" as the dock disappeared around the river bend.

Christopher was really concerned about the missing Cooper and we tried to calm him down as we climbed the back stairs and entered the cabin. The living room itself looked a little less chaotic than when we'd left a few hours ago. It was obvious that someone made an effort to straighten things out, although a half hearted one. Beatrice was sitting on the couch with her chin resting on one of her knees; the other leg was on the coffee table.

No one is allowed to put their feet on the furniture. This is going to be bad.

Next to her on the side table was a glass of half emptied lemonade.

"I got your note." Beatrice said in a deliberate tone as though trying her best not slur her words. "I wished that you had woke me up instead. I was worried about you."

"We tried Mom." pleaded Christopher who was so very worried about getting into trouble.

"Did you have breakfast?"

"Yes. Mike made pancakes."

"Oh that was nice of him."

"They were really good. We were out of syrup so we had them with grape jelly."

"Did you save me any?"

"I don't think so."

"Why not?"

"Tell you what, why don't you guys go upstairs and change and I will make Mom some pancakes?" I said trying to defuse the situation which had the hallmark of very quickly spinning out of control.

Picking up on my cue, Kevin pulled Christopher by the hood of his sweatshirt and dragged him upstairs. I went into the front door and grabbed the grocery bags and began putting away the things that we lugged back from Magoo's. A few minutes later, Beatrice followed me into the kitchen clutching tightly onto her glass of special lemonade. She was obviously feeling no pain as she bounced off of the doorway like it was a bumper in a pinball machine. Beatrice had an unlit Kool hanging backwards from the side of her lips.

Shit! How much vodka did they bring on this trip?

"I expected more from you." Beatrice said sternly.

"That's funny; I expected more from you too."

"Watch the mouth! Regardless of how you are feeling, I am still your mother."

"Sorry." I said through gritted teeth as I poured the pancake flour into a mixing bowl.

"You can think what you want, but you will keep a civil tongue in your head when you are talking with me." she said as she crossed to the gas stove, turned on the burner and moved in closer to light her cigarette. "You only get one mother in this lifetime…"

"Ma!" I shouted and pulled her away from the stove. "Jesus Christ. You are going to burn the place down. You are trying to light the filter."

"Stop being so dramatic." she said collapsing on a kitchen stool. She took a big gulp of the lemonade and handed me her cigarette. "Here. You light it. I heard that you know how."

"You heard wrong." I said breaking the cigarette in half and throwing it into the trash. "I don't smoke. Never have. Never will." And I added water to the bowl and continued to mix the pancake batter.

"That's not what I heard."

"Then you heard wrong."

"What are you making?"

"Pancakes."

"What the hell for?"

"You said that you wanted some."

"No I didn't." she yelled.

"Ma. It's obvious that you are gunning for a fight. I am not going to give it to you." I said as calmly as I could as I cleared the counter and put everything in the sink. "You don't want any pancakes. That's perfectly fine by me. I'll make you something later if you want."

"You don't have to cook. That's my job."

"Ma. You haven't cooked all week."

"Who the hell do you think you are talking to?!!!!"

"You are right. I am wrong. I am sorry. It will not happen again. I am going upstairs to change my clothes and check on Christopher."

"I'm not finished talking to you…"

I left her in the kitchen and took the stairs two at a time until I reached the top. I closed the door behind me and locked us in. The sky opened up once more.

The next morning we were woken by the sound of a car horn blowing in the driveway. I stumbled to the window to see Butch leaning against the driver's side door of his teal late model Bonneville smoking a cigarette and honking the horn with his free hand.

"Dad?" I rubbed my eyes to make sure what I was seeing was real.

"Daddy's here?" Christopher said excitedly and jumped out of bed to see for himself.

"No shit." said Kevin. And he and Christopher ran outside to greet him.

I slowly walked down the staircase. I was somewhat relieved and happy that Uncle Cooper had made it back somehow and was pacing on the back deck smoking a cigarette and having an animated conversation with himself. From the look in his eyes, I could tell that he hadn't been to sleep yet. This meant that he would be unpredictable for the ride home assuming that my father would even let him in the car. He and Cooper had a tumultuous relationship at best…even when Cooper was sober. That meant that I needed a semi-functioning Beatrice to help keep him in check. I found Beatrice in a deep coma like sleep lying on her stomach on top of the sunflower quilt in the downstairs bedroom. Her mouth was slightly opened and the pillow she was using was covered in saliva. She had managed at some point last night to change into a nightgown which I took as a positive sign. However, her bare feet were caked in mud.

Unlike Uncle Cooper, whenever Beatrice consumed large amounts of vodka, she would eventually reach a point of saturation. I'd like to think her mother's instinct would eventually kick in and pull her back from the brink. Usually it was the tipping point and she would stop drinking, although temporary, we were all grateful for the break. However one of the side effects was the smell of cigarettes and cheap vodka would leak from every one of her pores and linger for days, no matter how often she showered. This morning was no exception.

"Mom. Mom." I said as I gently shook her shoulder praying that she would wake up in a civil mood.

"Wha? Mikey, leave me alone." she half moaned while trying to swat me away. "MMMM still sleeping."

"Mom. Wake up." I continued. "Dad's here."

"HmmmH?"

"Dad's here. He came to drive us home."

"Wha? What did you say?" she said trying to sit up and catch her bearings.

"Dad's here. He came to drive us home."

"You called your father?" she said shaking her head in. She reached for the half empty glass of special lemonade that was on the night stand and drained it with a trembling hand. "Oh my God. Why did you have to call him?"

"What else was I supposed to do?"

"Is she with him? Did he bring her? Tell me that he didn't bring the she-wolf!"

"I don't know…I don't think so."

"I can't…I can't…I can't let him see me like this."

"Too late." said Butch who was standing in the doorway with his arms crossed. "Jesus Christ Beatrice. You look like shit."

"You always knew how to flatter me, Butch." said Beatrice as she tried to stand up and stumbled to the dresser.

"Mikey, you have fifteen minutes to grab whatever you can and we are out of here."

"Cooper too?"

"Only if he can manage to keep his mouth shut. So help me God if he starts with his antics, I will dump him out on the side of the highway. Get hustling. I need a few minutes alone with your mother."

"Yes sir."

It was a long car ride back. Christopher and Kevin sat in the front with Butch and they talked about the goats, the dock, and the Red Sox. I sat in the back staring out the window and mentally taking inventory of everything that I was able to stuff into a couple of trash bags that I grabbed from the kitchen. If I had more time, I knew I could have certainly left Sunflower Cottage in much better shape, instead of looking like an unruly rock band had trashed the place. I felt guilty. I was also concerned that I missed a few things and I knew that there was no way in hell we would ever be going back to get them. Beatrice sat in the middle next to me. She was quiet and teary eyed since her private conversation with Butch and refused to look at me in the eye. Uncle Cooper sat next to her with his hands that Kevin had tied together with a small piece of rope resting in his lap. Kevin had also managed to cover Cooper's mouth with a piece of silver duct tape, ensuring a peaceful trip back.

Two days after we arrived back to the sanctuary of the tiny house by the golden pond, Beatrice checked herself into Sober Crossings, a thirty day rehabilitation center for alcohol and drug addiction.

And while the physical demands of the withdrawal took a terrible toll on her body, the nausea, the vomiting, the profuse sweating and alternating chills, it was nothing compared to the physiological discomfort she suffered. She felt a terrible anxiety and that each one of her nerves was raw, exposed, on fire, and ready to explode. No amount of psychiatric sessions or group therapy could possibly prepare her for the overwhelming tsunami size wave of crippling guilt that came crashing down upon her.

Less than fifteen days into her treatment, Fred came to the hospital for a visit. That afternoon, he helped Beatrice pack her suitcase and sign herself out of the hospital. Three days later they were married in a civil ceremony at town hall.

Calling Butch

With a freshly lit Kool and three quarters of a cold beer left, Beatrice sat in her perch with her feet on the windowsill. Cupping the yellow phone receiver between her left shoulder and ear she took a puff of her cigarette and a sip of her beer as she dialed an all too familiar telephone number with her right hand. After a couple of clicks, she was half relieved that she heard a busy signal and hung up the phone.

"Don't do it! Don't do it! Do not embarrass yourself!" Beatrice thought to herself.

She took another swig of her beer and stared out of the window at the blue grey house with black shutters and white trim that sat up on top of a small hill next door. The house was slightly larger and much more elaborate than the other modest houses that occupied the peninsula in this section of golden pond. Each room had hardwood floors, coffered ceilings, horse hair plastered walls...all of which were painted in various shades of white and were trimmed out in mahogany. All the interior doors had crystal door knobs and with the exception of the closets and bathroom, each room had a set of French doors with beveled glass. The living room offered a large flagstone fireplace with a thick heavy mantel and a panoramic view of the golden pond. From the kitchen window, her grandmother could survey the three houses at the bottom of the hill. Beatrice used to call her 'The Hawk On The Hill'...the tough old bird who knew everyone and everyone's business.

Beatrice wondered if her grandmother had an inkling of what was actually happening to her and her great grand-children. She also wondered if positions were reversed, how would this strong, formidable, and sometimes pain in the ass woman, who survived two world wars, the depression, buried three husbands and her only child would handle the situation that Beatrice found herself in.

With Carrie and me out at the movies with friends and Kevin and Christopher already in bed for the night, Beatrice was feeling a little sorry for herself, a little angry about her situation, and a little buzzed from her beers. Acknowledging to herself that this was never a good combination, she took another swig of her liquid courage, channeled her grandmother and redialed the phone.

Beatrice took another puff and was thankful that the line was no longer busy. After four rings, a woman answered the call with a breathy and sultry hello.

"It's Bea. Is he there?"

"Depends." the woman's voice became nasally and completely bitchy. "What do you want?"

"To speak with Butch."

"What for?"

"Judy." Beatrice said trying her best to control her temper. "I don't want to fight with you. I just need to talk with him. Tell him it's about his kids."

"I'll see if he is available."

Beatrice exhaled loudly trying to calm herself as she listened to the woman on the other end of the phone cup her hand over the receiver and yelled for Butch.

"Your soon to be ex is in the phone. How the hell should I know? She wouldn't fucking tell me. Did you give her this number??? I don't want her calling my house! Just get her off the goddamn phone!" in a tone that plainly showed she was making no effort to hide her hatred of Beatrice.

"What the hell is she so pissed off about? It's not like I was sleeping with her husband!!"

Beatrice heard the loud click of someone picking up the second line.

"What?" said Butch almost matching Judy's tonal hatred.

"Well that's real nice." replied Beatrice rather bitterly.

"What do you want Bea?"

"For starters, how about telling Judy to hang up!"

"Who the hell do you think you are?!" screamed Judy into the phone.

"I'm his wife! That's who!" Beatrice shouted back.

"Control your temper!"

"How the fuck did you get this number?! Ask her how the hell she got this number?"

"Will you please calm down?!!" Butch commanded.

"Are you kidding me? Don't you tell me calm down!"

"Yeah, calm down Judy." Beatrice said no longer caring that she was adding fuel to the fire.

"Don't start Bea."

"Listen to me you bitch! I'll..."

"Judy. Will you please shut the fuck up?" shouted Butch in a tone that had the same effect as a glass of cold water thrown into her face.

"I..."

"Judy. Please. Just hang up. I won't be long."

"See that you aren't." Judy said icily as she hung up.

"What has she got to be so upset about?" asked Beatrice.

"How did you get this number Beatrice?"

"Your sister, Patsy."

"You shouldn't have it." he said coldly.

"And if your children wanted to talk with you?"

"They know the arrangement. They can call my mother and she will get the message to me."

"And if it's an emergency?"

"Same deal."

"Let me get this straight. Your girlfriend doesn't want our kids to call you?"

"I never said that."

"That's what it sounded like."

"No. That's not how it is."

"Then how is it?"

"She simply does not want you to call."

"Honestly? Where does she get off? This, from the woman who has been having an affair with my husband for over a year? The same woman that you brought into our home to play house with while the kids and I were away at the beach on vacation?! A vacation, I might add that you said you were too busy with the store and couldn't get away."

"Bea..."

"You had sex in our bed. And while you were at work, you left her alone. Alone in my house! She went through our things. Touched my things! She rearranged the furniture and you didn't tell her to put it back the way it was."

"Do we need to rehash this again?"

"When we came home, I was so excited that the windows that you had been promising me for months on end to wash were finally cleaned. You stood there and lied to my face. You told me that you hired someone to clean the windows as a welcome home surprise. I guess the real surprise was on me."

"What do you want Bea?"

"I want to be able to pay the electric bill."

"What's stopping you?"

"Money."

"I just sent you a hundred bucks."

"We have four kids. How far do you think I can stretch a hundred bucks?"

"I'm not working."

"I know for a fact that you are working under the table for your brother."

"Prove it."

"What the hell are we supposed to do?"

"Ask your mother for help."

"I already have."

"Then what's the issue?"

"Aside from the fact that she shouldn't have too…the issue is that it is not enough!"

"There is nothing that I can do about it right now. I have to live too."

"You're choosing to ignore your own flesh and blood and are going to help that whore and her brats?"

"I'll send you some more when I have it."

"When will that be?"

"As soon as I can."

"What am I supposed to do with that?"

"Whatever you want to."

"That's not good enough."

"It's going to have to be."

"Do you want me to beg? Is that it?"

Silence.

"Each of the kids needs new sneakers."

"I just got finished telling you that I don't have any money."

"We both know that's a lie. If you are not going to give me the money directly the least you can do is make sure that they don't look like vagabonds."

"Fine. I'll get them when I have them on Saturday."

"About that. Michael doesn't want to go."

"Why the fuck not?"

"Why don't you call him and ask him? That is if Judy will let you use the phone."

"Cut the shit Bea. What's his problem?"

"He's pissed at you."

"Fine. Whatever. It's his loss."

"Really? That's the stance you are going to take?"

"Anything else?"

"What are you doing on Thursday night?"

"Why?"

"The athletic department is having their annual banquet. Carrie is going to get an achievement award. Can you make it?"

"What time?"

"Starts at six o'clock in the high school cafeteria."

"I'll see."

"It's a big moment for her. Do not disappoint her."

"I told you that I would see." Butch said quietly and curtly.

"Is this how it is going to be from now on?"

"I don't know what you are talking about?"

"Yes you do Butch. It's may be too late for us, don't screw it up with your children too. Good night."

Over the next several years, Beatrice and Butch had the same or a similar themed conversation. Each time he dug in and refused to pay Beatrice directly for any of the alimony and child support that he owed her. Since he worked under the table, there was no way for her or the state to attach his paycheck. And as soon as she got close to uncovering his employer, Butch left and found another job with a similar off the books pay envelope. Eventually, one by one each of us lost interest in Butch and at one point no one was speaking with him on a regular basis.

Butch had just married his fourth wife, when Carrie announced her engagement. Beatrice feeling nostalgic and more than a little drunk tracked him down through one of his brothers to tell him the good news. It was probably one of the most civil and friendly conversations the two had in years reminiscent of the ones they used to have when they both moved into the tiny house by the golden pond. They laughed and talked about the day their daughter was born. Towards the end of the call she begged him to try and make peace with his children. He had missed out on so much already and was going to miss out on even happier times with weddings and eventually grandchildren. He replied that he would see.

Years later, I had asked Beatrice if she was sorry that she divorced Butch. And to my surprise she said "Yes."

When pushed for an explanation she explained, "If I had the chance to do it all again, I would never have divorced your father...I simply would have had him killed instead. Don't look at me that way. It makes perfect sense. You all would have grieved in your own ways...but eventually you would have all gotten over it. The divorce just dragged on and on. We are still dealing with it and with him after thirty years. With the exception of Kevin, you kids still aren't speaking with him. Why would anyone in their right mind put themselves though that much heartache?"

Reality Check

Not It!

It was a typical Tuesday morning in the little house by the golden pond. Beatrice had risen at her normal time, showered, dressed and changed the sheets and flipped the mattresses in each of the bedrooms. She ignored the high pitch squeal and the small puddle of water coming from her trusted and faithful avocado green washer, which she had purchased in the scratch and dent section of a going out of business sale of the local appliance dealer that she always bought from. Beatrice never cared what it looked like, just as long as it worked. It was going into the basement. She knew that after eighteen years that it was probably on its last leg, but she didn't have the money or the heart to replace it. After all, it was certainly much more dependable and had more longevity than either of her husbands. So, she went upstairs, poured herself a fourth cup of coffee, sat on her perch, lit a Kool and dialed my office.

"Good Morning, Michael Rodgers office." said a young voice with a thick Boston accent on the other end of the receiver.

"Good Morning dear, would you please tell him that it is Mrs. Koufaso?"

I answered a couple of seconds later. "Ma. You can use your real name. Francesca knows who you are."

"You never know who else is listening and I do not want to get you in trouble."

"You are not going to get me in trouble. How is your morning going?"

I really enjoyed my morning conversations with my mother. She was feisty, quick-witted, upbeat and very entertaining. That morning, she filled me in on the latest gossip from her job behind the deli counter at the high end grocers. I learned about her coworker Joann's latest misadventures with her high maintenance daughter-in-law. Beatrice disclosed the long list of complaints this week from the real Mrs. Koufaso, her favorite customer who was never satisfied with anything that she bought at the store, yet somehow refused to shop anywhere else. And finally, Beatrice shared with me the latest stories about Kevin's sons, who coincidently have taken up right where he left off.

"God, I love them to death, but they are complete hellions." Beatrice said letting out a big belly laugh. "After all that your brother put me through; I used to pray he would end up with one just like him. God must have answered that prayer, because he gave him triplets!"

Before Beatrice could fill me in on the latest incident, she noticed a big brown delivery truck with familiar yellow logo coming down the hill and pulling into her stone dust driveway.

"Who is this?"

"Who is what, Ma?"

"Delivery truck. Oh, he is getting out....the new neighbor must have ordered something again from the shopping show. She must get a package every other week; I just wish that they would stop using my driveway…Oh crap. He is coming up the walk."

"Who is coming up the walk?"

"The delivery guy."

"Go see what he wants."

"You know I hate to answer the door. It's going to be bad news. It's always bad news. Maybe I can hide…" said Beatrice as she slid out of her chair and tried to look out the other kitchen window. "Ah crap. He saw me. Dammit."

The doorbell was original to the tiny house. It was weary and way past its prime, ready for retirement. Beatrice had always intended to fix or replace it, but it never seemed to make it too high up "the list" as there were always other more pressing repair priorities for her money. Once the button was pressed, it took a few minutes for the bell to kick in, as though you had disturbed its much needed slumber. It started off with the faintest of a hum, then became a much louder growl before eventually letting loose with a dinging and a ringing that always reminded Beatrice of the sound a railroad crossing gate.

"Let me call you right back."

She quickly hung up the phone and walked down the six stairs from her kitchen to the front door which she often left open to air out her home. When she saw the delivery guy, she needed to catch her breath.

He was a beautiful Korean man, who stood about five foot eight or five foot nine at the most. His golden muscular skin pushed hard against the restraints of his short sleeved brown uniform shirt and shorts. It was obvious to the casual observer that he needed the next size up, but was willing to sacrifice fit for the effect it was having on his female customers. His right bicep, which had an intricate barbed wired tattoo, bulged at full attention as he held a decent sized cardboard box under his arm. When he smiled she could see that he had perfectly straight bright white teeth and shiny black eyes that were the same color of his flawlessly styled hair, which was obviously filled with the latest styling products.

"Hello. May I help you?" Beatrice asked while trying to regain some form of composure.

"Good Morning. I have a delivery for a Mrs. MacMullen."

"That's me."

"Good deal." he smiled and handed Beatrice the package. "Would you mind signing for it please? I get in trouble if you don't."

"Can't have that." Beatrice smiled and flirted. She took the small electronic device from him and signed her name, doing her best not to squint and thus reveal that she desperately needed her glasses to see anything.

"Thank you ma'am. Have a great day." he said with a wink.

"I will. You see that you do too!" She smiled and watched him turn and saunter down her walkway towards his truck. She allowed herself to be momentarily transfixed by his equally muscular legs and firm bubble shaped buttocks.

"You damned fool." she thought to herself.

She laughed to herself and shook her head in disbelief as she watched the brown truck drive up over the hill. Beatrice then turned and walked up the stairs back into her kitchen. She placed the box with no return address on her yellow Formica counter and pulled a steak knife from her silverware drawer. She carefully sliced the packing tape along the top and opened the box. Sitting on top of the packing peanuts was a peach colored envelope with Beatrice's name written in blue fountain pen ink with a familiar handwriting. In it, she found the same color note card with embossed hummingbirds on the cover. She opened it and read:

> Dearest Bea-
>
> I still cannot believe that our dear Freddie has passed. Since you left the services so quickly; we never had much of an opportunity to discuss what you ultimately wanted. As you know, our dear Freddie had a complicated and often tumultuous relationship with each of his children, save one. I am sending these along to you as I am sure that you will ultimately know what to do with them.
>
> With much love,
> Felicity.

Half knowing what to expect, Beatrice quickly looked through the box and then dialed back my office.

"What did you get?"

"That bitch just sent me his ashes!"

Beatrice was thankful that later that night, Carrie had already scheduled a family barbeque at her house to celebrate her eldest daughter's birthday. After dinner and before cake and presents, Beatrice, Carrie, Christopher and I gathered around the family computer to Skype with Kevin.

"...so she just sent them to you?" asked Kevin, still unclear that he heard correctly.

"Yes. What the hell am I supposed to do with them?" asked Beatrice as she shook her head. "Why don't one of you take them?"

Simultaneously we all put our fingers on our noses and said, "Not it!"

"Not fair. You know that there is a lag when you call me." complained Kevin as his image flickered.

"Can't help it if there is a small delay in the connection, Kev!" I razzed.

"You can't break with tradition Kevin." Carrie teased.

"All kidding aside, Carrie doesn't one of your friends own a barn? Couldn't we dump the ashes in one of the stalls?" I asked almost sounding serious.

"I wouldn't do that to those helpless animals." said Carrie, sincerely concerned with the welfare of the stable animals.

"Well, Ok. Do we know anyone with zoo access?" I asked half joking, but mostly serious. "I still think it's fitting that we put him someplace where animals can shit on him."

"Why can't we just put him out with Wednesday morning trash and be done with it?" Kevin questioned.

"We need to decide on something. I don't want them coming back at me." Beatrice said.

"What about the dump? It has a nice circle of life moment, don't you think? "

"Just named a superfund site." Christopher responded matter-of-factly, while taking a swig of his beer. "We'd never get near it. And before you ask, yes, I did look into it."

"What's a little more toxic waste?" Beatrice joked.

"I know, right?" said Carrie.

"There's got to be another dump somewhere."

"What if we divide him up and mail him to people we don't like?" I asked.

"Are there enough ashes?" Christopher questioned.

"What if we left him in the men's room at a Royalty Burger?"

"I like it Michael. It's kind of poetic."

"No. Be that as it may, they just offered a small settlement, which we are, taking." said Christopher.

"Really?" Kevin asked genuinely surprised. "I didn't know that was still going on."

"Could have floored me. But according to their outside counsel, they just want the matter closed and off the books."

"Looks like we have to scratch Royalty Burger." stated Carrie.

"I say we flush him." said Kevin.

"No! We all have septic systems and do not need the bad juju." Beatrice commanded.

"Then someplace that's hooked up to town sewage." Carrie decided.

"Like A Royalty Burger?" I joked.

"Exactly." Kevin said.

"No Royalty Burger." Christopher stated vehemently.

"Killjoy." Kevin and I would have said simultaneously, if not for the bad connection lag.

"All kidding aside, doesn't one of his kids want them?" I asked.

"I talked to Libby and she said no." said Beatrice.

"Not even LJ?" Carrie asked.

"She's nowhere to be found."

"Figures."

"Did she try the police station? There's a better than fifty percent chance that she could be there." said Christopher sarcastically.

"What are you going to do, Mom?" asked Carrie.

"Royalty Burger! Royalty Burger! Royalty Burger!" chanted Kevin.

"Here we go again." said Christopher and everyone in the room laughed.

"Guys, we have to go do cake." said Carrie taking control of the situation. "We are getting nowhere fast with this. Let's think about it and circle back in a couple days. Ok? Mom would you help with the candles and the ice cream?" she asked as she and Beatrice left the room.

"Ok by me. Catch you later. Wish I could be there." said Kevin feigning sincerity.

"No you don't." I smirked.

"You got me there." said Kevin. "Later losers."

He signed off.

"Not too productive." said Christopher taking the last swig of his beer.

"Did you really think it would be?" I asked.

"Not really."

"Where are the ashes now?"

"They're in the trunk. Mom insisted we bring them just in case."

"Hmmm." I said as I finished off the last of my scotch. "What do you say we put them on Carrie's mantel and see how long it takes before she notices?"

"Works for me."

Three days later, Christopher and I received a phone call from an irate Carrie, where she ripped each of us a new one. That same afternoon, she mailed the ashes to an unsuspecting Kevin.

Reality Check

The Magical Fairy Land

Carrie and I live less than fifteen miles away from one another. Our children attend rival schools, which we actually consider to be a bit of a blessing. We cheer passionately for both sides and regardless of the final score, the family wins. We each have three children, she has two girls and a boy and I have the opposite. Each of our kids is a couple of months apart in age and the youngest actually share the same birthday. All of our children are very active so coordinating a combined families event or get together usually takes a truly herculean effort. Trying to pull one off in a very short time period is almost next to impossible. Through sheer will and determination and a lot of finagling we were able to navigate around a soccer game, a cheerleader car wash, a drum line rehearsal, a basketball practice, two sleepovers, a birthday party, a CCD Community Service activity, and a trip to the library to meet friends to allegedly work on a class project to steal a few hours to visit and clean the place where Fred lived.

Fred won a small parcel of land from Bobby Big Brass Ones in a poker game shortly after he divorced his first wife Libby.

"It ain't much." Bobby explained to Fred as he signed over the deed. "But a fella with your skills might be able to make something outta it."

To the rest of the poker players, it appeared that Bobby was pulling a fast one. However to Fred, his fortune had just changed thanks in part to a straight flush queen high. He was now the proud owner of a little slice of heaven up country – number 24 Oak Ridge Terrace. The potential was limitless. The parcel was just shy of quarter of an acre located in a small rural town about an hour's drive west on Route Sixteen from Portsmouth to the heart of New Hampshire's lake region. Once he turned off the highway, he took a series of lefts and rights to eventually reach the partially cleared level plot which sat two dirt roads away from Sun Shadow Lake.

Sun Shadow Lake was barely a mile and half long and almost as wide. It is considered to be a shallow lake, meaning the average depth was about seven feet although it did go as low as sixteen feet in some spots. It is classified as a warm water fishery by the state and has what appears to be an endless supply of largemouth bass, chain pickerel, horned pout, and white perch. The modest houses and cabins that surround the lake are owned mostly by locals. A couple more elaborate residences are second summer homes owned by wealthy Bostonians looking to get away for the summer. Almost each home had some sort of boat access or dock used for anchoring their watercraft. It's not uncommon to see children diving or jumping off of the docks and into the water on a hot summer's day looking to cool off. At the northern most tip of the lake there is a small beach with a gravel ramp for town residents with permits to launch their boats.

Of course, the only way Fred could see Sun Shadow Lake from number 24 Oak Ridge Terrace was if he managed to climb up one of the one hundred foot pine trees that border the property.

In the years that followed his introduction to the family living in the little house by the golden pond, Fred spun yarns about the majestic beauty of his land up in the north country. His stories were a lot like him, loud, colorfully flamboyant, and inclusive. He would uncover nuggets of interest from his audience and find a way to spin them into his tall tales. For example, he knew of Beatrice's love for flowers so he would spend what seem like hours describing the flora and fauna that grew in abundance around his plot. Each time he told his story, the rarity and the majesty of the flowers became more elaborate. He described fields of yellow Lady Slippers, Dame's Rockets, and orange Hawkweed. He knew that Carrie loved to spend hours picking blueberries with Nana Flossie so naturally there were blueberries and of course strawberries and grapes that happened to miraculously grow in the wild there. For Kevin he produced a broken arrowhead from the Penacook Abenaki People, "the Indian tribe" that first lived there. His friend Grandfather Ashwood was the tribe's shaman and was looking forward to meeting Kevin.

Fred never referred to the Penacook Abenaki People as Native Americans.

He knew the quickest way to win Beatrice's heart was through her children so he continued to press the issue. During homework sessions where we would sit around the dining room table under the wagon wheel chandelier, Fred would sometime join us. He would borrow Christopher's crayons and construction paper which naturally upset Christopher.

"Do you know how many crayons of mine that he broke??? Everyone knows that you are supposed to sharpen them before you put them in the box. He never sharpened. And he never put them back in the right order."

"Are you medicated yet?"

While Christopher would draw pictures of his stuffed animals and toys, Fred would draw different versions of the house that he planned to build. And if he was lucky enough maybe one day retire in with Beatrice. Each version was a variation of the same theme, a modified Cape Cod Style home with two dormers on the front, a one car garage underneath with a wrap around farmer's porch and a large swing. Somewhere on the property depending upon zoning regulations, he will also have a free standing barn / workshop where he could fix his cars and maybe build furniture. He had lots of experience repairing the furniture that he had broken over the years. The color of the house would change continuously in an effort to please the person to whom he was speaking.

Like every project he started, Fred would spend an inordinate amount of time researching. He would go to the library and take out books.

Sometimes he would actually return them.

He would buy trade journals, or walk onto jobsites and ask questions. He would stake out bars, saloons, or other waterholes where tradesmen might throw back a couple after a tough day. He would buy them drinks, play pool or darts and all the while pumping them for information on whatever subject matter he was researching at the time. He would learn the electrical code and hound electricians to explain the proper gage wire he should use with a forty amp breaker and why. He would question which manufacturer they preferred and made them explain why. He learned their negotiation tactics and where could he get the product cheaper. He would pepper his unsuspecting subject matter expert with all sorts of if / then scenarios looking for worse and best case scenarios. He even figured out a mathematical formula to calculate the breakeven point for him to complete the work himself or when it was more cost effective to sub the job out. Once he felt as though he had enough, he would then move on to the next trade.

He once was arrested for inciting a bar fight at Rusty's Log Cabin between a pair of inebriated cousins over which was the better material to use to insulate the garage door Polyurethane or Polystyrene. It may have cost him fifty bucks for the fine and seven stitches, but the answer was Polyurethane.

After each research project was finished, he would break out Christopher's crayons and draw out what he learned. He also made lists of potential materials and the quantities that he needed as well as where he could buy them. He kept everything in a business accordion file which Beatrice kept in the dining room hutch next to her bill basket. Additionally he would purchase a sample or two so he knew exactly what he was looking for when it came time to make the big purchase.

This became a bone of contention for Beatrice during the time he lived in the little house by the golden pond. Between the samples, his hobbies and his other get rich projects; Fred made very little contribution to basic household staples like groceries or the electric bill. Fred felt that even though he was in love with Beatrice, it wasn't his responsibility to pay for her four children. Support from Butch was also non-existent. He sent Beatrice a hundred dollars three weeks after he first moved out. When she was finally able to track him down to question the amount, Butch explained that was the best that he could do. He needed money to live too. Besides, Fred was there, why should he pay to have some other man live in his house? It was the last time that she ever received money from her first husband.

We were all lured to number 24 Oak Ridge Terrace under the pretense of a family waterskiing trip. All we needed to do was to help with a little bit of the yard clean up, while

Fred did a quick tune up on the outboard motor for his boat. It seemed like a fair trade off and Beatrice only needed to threaten us twice with bodily harm.

We all piled into his silver grey battered Pontiac with the missing muffler and began what seemed to be a never ending journey to No Where, New Hampshire. With Christopher trapped between him and Beatrice in the front seat, Carrie, Kevin and I fought for the much coveted seat next to the one working window in the back. Between the smell of mold and chain smoking, fresh air was a precious commodity on that trip. Fred explained that he bought his boat shortly after he won the property. It was a Larson's fourteen foot all American Runabout boat with a thirty five horse power Johnson Javelin engine. The hull was aqua and the captain's chairs and bench seat were covered in white vinyl. He apologized that he only had one set of water skis; however he was quick to point out that he had a couple of inner tubes that he could tow behind the boat.

It seemed like it took three years for us to finally reach number 24 Oak Ridge Terrace. We all heard the loud squeal as Fred turned the steering wheel all the way to the right to enter his dirt driveway from the dirt road.

"I just adjusted those belts last week." Fred announced. "I am going to have to take a quick gander at them before we head back home."

Crap. We are never getting home.

Kevin and I jumped out of the car and raced to the nearest tree to relieve ourselves, all the while looking for additional Indian artifacts from the Penacook Abenaki People.

"Not too far!" yelled Beatrice.

"They'll be fine. It's not like they can get into any trouble here."

"You have met them?"

"Haw! Haw!" Fred belly laughed. "So what do you think? Beautiful isn't it?"

"It's quite lovely." Beatrice replied trying to think of something positive to say about the densely populated collection of trees and buzzing mosquitoes. "It certainly is majestic up here."

He gave us all the grand tour of this property, making sure that we walked from one end of the lot to the other. He was proud to point out where he had staked out the perimeter of the house and where his barn would be built. Once finished, he gave Carrie, Kevin and I our instructions to pick up any twigs or branches that were in the outline of his house. If we saw any stray stink trees, we were to pull them up by the roots. He showed us where we were to dump our debris and then he went back to his dirty Pontiac and removed his tool box from the dented trunk and began to work on the outboard motor.

Beatrice and Christopher armed with a couple bottles of Windex and a roll of paper towels were responsible for trying to return the dirty vinyl seats back to a color that was in the white spectrum. Christopher was a trooper and tried not to succumb to the terror brought on by the collection of spider webs and Daddy Long Legs that made the boat their home.

On one of what seemed like numerous trips to the dump pile, we caught Kevin carving his initials into a tree with a pocket knife we assumed he "lifted" from Mrs. Card's Shoppe.

Mrs. Card's Shoppe was a small family run store in the center of the only shopping plaza in the center of our home town. The shopping center had four stores in the front, a pharmacy, a jeweler, a grocery and Mrs. Card's Shoppe. The back stores had a sandwich shop, a hardware store, a bakery and a shoe store. These stores were bookended by banks. Mrs. Card's Shoppe sold a little bit of everything: school supplies, candy, small toys, greeting cards, wrapping paper, and home décor items. It was also the only local place where residents could purchase Sillisculpts, a very popular resin statuette with comical and sometimes considered racy for the times sayings, like "I love you this much", "World's Best Mom", "Black is Beautiful", and "Bitch a little…you'll feel better." Every day after school let out the store was filled with a swarm of junior high students looking to score some candy or some other snack before they walked home.

In those carefree days, Kevin was a bit of a behavior handful in school. The more that he was compared to Carrie and I, the more that he would act out.

"Why can't you be more like your sister and brother?"

As punishment, Kevin spent a lot of time in the vice principal's office and before long he was on a first name basis with Mr. Hawkes. Most days, his exhausted teachers would keep him after school just long enough to miss the bus so that he would have to walk the five miles home. Kevin didn't really mind. He actually liked the walk. It also meant that he could spend some more time with his friends that lived outside of our neighborhood. In those days, Beatrice rarely allowed us off the block. He and his buddies would also stop off at Mrs. Card's on the way home. Most days, they would see who could shoplift the best stuff. Kevin was the most daring of them all naturally. However, most of the items he took like candy or matchbox cars were earmarked for Christopher.

When Beatrice found his secret stash, she went thermo nuclear. Rarely had we seen her that mad before. She yelled. She screamed. She hit Kevin a couple of times with the wooden spoon. She yelled some more. She screamed and she cried wanting to know what was wrong with him and when was the precise moment that she failed him as a mother. She screamed some more before dragging him into the car. They drove to Mrs. Card's Shoppe where Kevin had to apologize to Mr. and Mrs. Card. He had to return everything that he took and make an accounting of any items that he no longer had like gum and candy. Beatrice insisted that he work off his debts. So every Saturday morning in the months of April and May, Kevin reported for work at Mrs. Card's Shoppe. Under the watchful eye of Mr. Card, he had to sweep floors, empty trash, clean the bathroom and unload the truck. Mr. Card found that he eventually enjoyed Kevin's company and offered to keep him on board for minimum wage after his debts were paid off, provided that Kevin swore never to take anything from the store again and to also help keep an eye out for would be thieves on his frequent after school visits. Mr. Card's daughter Rachel was also extremely happy that Kevin agreed to stay. It would be several years later before he discovered that Kevin also took Rachel's virginity.

It seemed like hours later, before Fred who was covered in grease and oil announced that the outboard motor was fixed and we were going to be able to put the boat in the water. We all offered to help as he carefully attached the trailer to the boat hitch on the back of the silver Pontiac. And before we knew it, we actually backed the car down the ramp and launched the boat.

Beatrice did explain later that she was very nervous and half suspected that the boat would spring a hole or two. It only took eight or nine tries before the motor grumbled to life and we took off to the middle of the lake.

Beatrice made sure that each of us was snuggled tightly in our orange life preservers even though they were dirty and smelled of mold.

"I don't want to hear it. Hold your nose. You wear it or you can watch us from the shore."

"But Ma..."

"If you but Ma me one more time..."

By the time we reached the center of the lake, Fred slowed the boat down to an idle. Kevin won the toss to water ski first. He sat on the edge of the boat as Fred showed him how to put on the skis before jumping into the water. He handed Kevin the nylon yellow tow line and told him to remember to bend his knees and to hold on tight. After a false start, Kevin was up and skiing on the second try. And as his confidence grew, Kevin tried a couple of tricks as he skimmed across the surface of the water.

More than once, Fred cut across the wake of his waves trying to shake Kevin free, which made him all the more determined to hang on harder and laugh even louder.

Eventually, it was time to switch it up. Much to his disappointment, Kevin had to trade places with Carrie. Christopher squealed as Fred lifted Kevin out of the water with one arm. While Kevin transferred the skis to Carrie, Fred tied an old rope from a clothesline to one of the inner tubes, which was covered in patches.

"Don't worry sport. They'll hold."

"Freddie? Are you sure that you should pull them both at the same time?" Beatrice asked nervously as Carrie and I got into the water.

"Oh, yeah. They'll be fine sweetie." He said trying to reassure her." The rope for the inner tube is twice as long as the one for the skis. They'll never cross. Besides, I am pulling them both from different sides of the boat."

True to his word, the boat raced forward and before long Carrie was up on her skis with the first try. This was no real surprise to me. As a side note, Carrie received the bulk of the athletic genes in our family. She was the only freshmen in the history of our high school to make the varsity team for field hockey, basketball and softball in the same year. A record, I am happy to announce, that she still holds. I sat there on my patchwork quilted inner tube as she and the boat raced away. And then just like that with a hard jerk tug, I was off. Carrie was side sliding and skiing across the wakes of the boat, while I hung on for dear life, the centrifugal force pulled my fat cheeks past my ears giving me the appearance of a Cheshire cat.

Aside from the occasional water bug in the mouth, I eventually came to enjoy the sensation. So naturally it was short lived as the former clothes line rope gave way with a loud snap. I skidded across the water for a couple of feet before coming to a stop just as one of the larger patches gave way. I tried to signal to the boat, but they just kept racing off into the direction of the setting sun. To this day, I swear that I saw Kevin waving good bye as they disappeared from my view.

Once the air was finally out of the inner tube, it didn't take long for me to swim to shore. With the holey inner tube wrapped across my shoulders and chest, I followed the edge of the lake dragging my black and orange life preserver behind me until I eventually made it to the town ramp. A frantic Beatrice with tears rolling down her face raced towards me and ensnared me in an uncharacteristically tight embrace.

"Oh my God! Oh my God! Oh my God! I thought I lost you!"

"Ma. I can't breathe!"

"I don't care! I don't care!"

"Ma! Cut it out! I'm fine." I shouted trying in vain to break free.

Christopher came running over as well and threw his arms around both of us.

"Come on. Knock it off!"

"You missed it. There was this really loud noise and then all this black smoke started coming out of the motor...and then...and then there were flames."

"No suh."

"Yes suh! And then…"

"There were a couple of flames. The motor caught on fire."

"What?"

"See I told you he'd be ok Sweetie." shouted Fred who was standing chest deep in the water trying to maneuver the boat towards the ramp. "Why don't you get out here and help me sport?"

"Sure."

"Right after we noticed that you were missing, the engine started to smoke. Freddie thinks it was either the electrical harness or the battery voltage regulator that caught fire. Thank God he had a fire extinguisher and that it actually worked."

"Yeah. Otherwise we wouldn't be alive."

"It wasn't like that." Beatrice corrected Christopher. We weren't going to die. I will admit that it was a little intense especially when I couldn't find you." She went in for another hug.

"Ma!"

"Freddie insisted that we row the boat here."

"Yeah. It took forever."

"Hey loser! Come help us." shouted Carrie from the boat.

"You better go. I am so glad you are ok." smiled Beatrice as she got another hug in.

With relatively no effort, we were able to maneuver the boat on to its trailer and eventually returned it to its final resting place at number 24 Oak Ridge Terrace. Beatrice insisted on heading home straight away, only making one stop for the perfect fried clams. We eventually pulled into the driveway of the little house by the golden pond shortly after midnight.

To the untrained eye, our traveling back to number 24 Oak Ridge Terrace caravan style would seem logical and made perfect sense…a group of three cars wanting to make sure that they did not lose their way. To anyone who knew us and our family would be quick to uncover that it was merely a ploy to keep tabs on one another making sure that no one "accidently" wandered off and got "lost".

We barely pulled into the dirt driveway and parked behind the twenty two foot yellow dumpster that I ordered before the doors swung open and six of Beatrice's nine grandchildren piled out.

"Eww! This is sooo gross."

"Someone actually lived here?"

"What's that smell? Do you smell that?"

"Oh my God! I don't have any service? How am I supposed to survive up here without any cell service? Mother. You told me that we would have service. That's it. We need to go back. Right now!"

"Drama Queen."

"I am not!"

"You most certainly are too!"

"I am not!"

"You are too!"

"Dad! Make him stop!"

I slowly opened up my car door and stood up resting my elbow on the roof of our minivan. I pulled the rims on my sunglasses away from my eyes to rest on my nose so that I could take in the splendor of this magical fairy land. Across the paved road were a mixture of older and newer homes, each immaculate in their own way and all having direct access to Sun Shadow Lake. And thanks to the thoughtful deforesting of their lots, we had a partial view of the lake from the driveway.

The lot next door was recently sold according to Christopher. It was almost the same size as this one. However it was higher up and with potentially better partial views of the lake. On the flipside, it also looked down on Fred's home. The owners were in the process of building a new home with the help of Goodinson Construction, at least that is what we all assumed thanks to the red, white, and blue wooden yard sign that was staked in front of it. The house had most of the sheathing up with holes for the window and doors cut out. The rafters were up and awaiting a roof. It had a stone chimney and it reminded me of one of the many drawings that he did while at our dining room table. I couldn't help but wonder if Fred actually shared one of his designs.

While each of his designs may have changed over the years and months, he always remained consistent with his plans for the basement. The house would stand in the center of his property. It would have a poured foundation with a one car garage underneath which would be on the left side accommodating his existing dirt driveway. It would also have a six panel steel door and ten basement slider windows. He felt the natural light would help him save on electrical costs. He was true to his design. The yellow paint on the wooden garage door was cracked and peeling and the window panels all appeared to be painted black. There was an aluminum storm door which was missing both screens in front of the six panel wooden door, which I had padlocked on my first trip up here. To the right of the door was a cracked lantern light which was hanging from a couple of exposed electrical wires.

After all his plans and designs, he never got around to adding the main floor and second story. Instead he chose to cover the foundation with a flat roof which was covered in tar paper and blue tarps that were in various forms of disrepair and nailed in place. In the back left side corner stood what we later confirmed to be a surplus light pole, made of aluminum, which he jury-rigged as a connector and a chimney for a wood burning stove.

The perimeter of the property was literally littered with hundreds of garbage bags some were clear, some green and some were black. All were filled with empty soda and beer cans. Some of the bags were tied up tightly, others were overflowing and in some cases it appeared as though he just started new piles. Most of the cans were marked return for deposit. So here laid the dilemma, knowing that he never recycled a day in his life when he lived with us, adding to the fact that the state of New Hampshire doesn't have any bottle bill laws, we could only assume that this was yet another abandoned get rich quick scheme.

There were two sheds, both in need of a good paint job and filled to the brim with "stuff". Opposite of the house stood two campers that were separated by a screen house. In the back corner of the lot sat what was left of Bea's Traveling Kitchen with two cracked front windows, a busted headlight and a couple of flat tires. Next to that was his American Runabout aqua colored boat, the ruined remains of a golf cart, several motorcycle parts and pieces and what may have once been a go-cart. Peppered throughout were boxes, plastic bins, and storage containers that we knew we would eventually have to go through. And hanging from every tree surrounding his homestead were strings of Christmas lights and holiday decorations of all different shapes, sizes, seasons, and colors.

"Your description did not do this place justice Chief." my wife Holly said as she snuck up behind me.

"Isn't it everything I said and more?"

"All I can say is thank God I picked up a shitload of disinfectant wipes and sanitizer. When was the last time we all had tetanus shots?"

"I was just asking John the same thing." said Carrie.

"Where is…"

"He is dealing with the eldest. I am sure you heard her melt down over lack of cell service out here. There are some days that I just want to take that phone and shove it up her ass. I was never that high maintenance."

"Hahahaha. Oh. You are being serious. Really? Do you not remember anything from our childhood?"

"I have chosen to block most of it from my memory."

"That's healthy."

"Doctor Rudnick seemed to think it was ok." Carrie added. "And for the official record, I was never that bad."

"I suppose your perspective can change with age."

"What a pig sty. This is quintessential Fred." said Christopher coming up the driveway loaded with bags and pulling his camera from its case. "You didn't mention that he was living in a land fill."

"I've seen cleaner dumps." remarked Holly. "Where is Beatrice?"

"We parked on the street. She insisted on unloading the food and all the other shit that she had to bring with her immediately."

Taking her cue, my wife yells to all of the children, "Kids. Kids. Come on. Let's help Nana Bea unpack her stuff."

"Long trip?"

"Next time we have to come up here, one of you is taking her. I almost tossed her out the window a couple of times." said Christopher looking through his camera lens and snapping pictures.

"That bad?" asked Carrie.

"She's nervous, excited, interested, not interested, overwhelmed, and angry. She ran the whole gambit the ride up here. She may have to go home with one of you."

Simultaneously, Carrie and I put one finger on our noses and say "Not it!"

"Real mature you guys." said Christopher with true disgust as he took our picture.

"Christopher. Christopher." shouted Beatrice as she was coming up the driveway surrounded by six of her grandchildren and her son-in-law and daughter-in-law. Each was carrying a grey plastic bag from a well known large box store chain. They were filled with potato chips, pretzels, napkins, paper towels, contractor bags, and rubber gloves. The two oldest boys were pulling matching orange coolers that were filled with waters, sports drinks, fruit and submarine sandwiches. "I'd like you to take a picture of me with all of my grand babies."

"Grandmother. We are not babies."

"Granddaughter," smiled Beatrice, "You are and will always be my babies, babies. And that is what makes you special. Now put that phone away and come stand next to me. On the count of three, everyone say Drop Dead Fred. One, Two, Three."

"Drop Dead Fred!"

"John? Would you do me a favor please?" asked Beatrice.

"Sure Bea. What do you need?"

"Would you please check out the roof on that house? I would like to know how much weight it can support."

"Sure. Why?"

"I thought it might be a good place for us to eat our lunch."

"Really?"

"John, after everything that he put us through, if I can't dance on the man's grave, the least I can do his have a picnic on the place where he died."

"That's pretty twisted, Bea. Alright, who has the key?"

"Here you go." I said as I handed him the key. "Wait until you see the inside."

"Hard to imagine it being worse than this."

"It's pretty rank. We shouldn't let any of the kids inside, until we have a chance to check it out."

"Makes sense. Chris you are with me."

"Nana Bea. Did you know that your husband lived in a junk yard?" asked Carrie's oldest.

"Unfortunately, yes."

"Is it true he used to suck his thumb?" asked Carrie's youngest.

"Yes."

"Why?"

"Because your grandmother was too much woman for him." I chided.

"Michael. Go to your room." Beatrice snapped. "I don't know why he sucked his thumb. To be perfectly honest with you Jonah, it never occurred me to ask. But it was only at night when he was asleep. He used to put his whole thumb in and rub his nose with his index finger...like this." Beatrice exaggerated the motion of sucking her thumb and all of her grandchildren laughed.

Turning to Carrie, Beatrice and Holly, I asked "Where do you want to begin?"

"I think that we sort whatever we can." started Carrie. "Anything that we can salvage that could be sold should go in one pile; anything anybody wants to take home in another pile and everything else we toss in the dumpster."

"Ok. Let's also keep the kids out of the campers and sheds too. No telling what sort of critters are living in there now." suggested Holly.

Making sure that everyone had a pair of gloves on, Beatrice and Holly directed the boys to start putting all of the cans into one large pile next to the dumpster. I am pretty sure that there was talk about trying to make a mountain of cans that they could climb and eventually jump off of. The rest of the crew began going though the boxes and plastic tubs that were scattered about the property. Each was filled to the brim with random items. Some had things like stuffed animals, books and puzzles. Others were filled with baby clothes, soaps, mismatched dishes, baking pans, Halloween decorations, old National Geographic Magazines from the Nineteen seventies and Archie Comic Books. Any items that were wet, damp or covered in mold and mildew were immediately tossed into the dumpster. The others were sorted by purpose and function placed in neat piles closest to the road.

Carrie and I checked out the larger camper first. The lovely avocado, orange, goldenrod, and earth tones color pallet was straight out of the nineteen seventies. The floor and the furnishings were still in fairly decent shape. It smelt a little musty but that was to be expected. It was apparent from the dirty dishes in the sink and the half filled trash barrel that someone had been living in there not too terribly long ago. The cabinets were stocked with dishes and women's clothing. The bathroom toilet hadn't been flushed in a long while. The exterior was a little dirty from sitting under the pine trees, but there weren't any visible signs of rust. A quick rinse from a power washer and it would be good as new. Carrie measured the camper to be about thirty six feet.

The fabric screen house was not salvageable due to all of the holes in the netting. He had strung hot pepper miniature lights from the ceiling that were attached to a long yellow extension cord that went down one wall and out through a hole that he had cut in the bottom. The Astroturf rug appeared to be in decent shape and we might be able to get a couple dollars for the resin couches and lounge chairs that were also inside. We unplugged the lights and tossed the structure into the dumpster.

Next to the screen house was the smaller slide in style camper which was made to fit on the back of a pickup truck. The four leg supports kept it off the ground and remarkably level considering the terrain. It was an older model that was also in decent shape and looked like it could easily accommodate three sleepers. We didn't recognize the brand name, but Carrie was certain that with a little research she could market it to the right buyer.

The door of the first shed was off one of the hinges which made it slightly difficult to open. Pushing against the onslaught of material inside didn't make it any easier to enter.

"This has all the makings of a bad reality television show." said Carrie as we pushed our way into the shed.

The inside was pure chaos. The floor was carpeted in beige shag that was stained from excessive use and what looked like several accidents involving coffee and dropped cigarettes. There were several boxes of vinyl records and old forty-fives, fishing poles and bait boxes, a bicycle built for two, radios, old speakers and miles of wire. There were turn tables and eight-track tapes in one corner. One wall on the other side of the room was covered in floor to ceiling book cases that were also overflowing. There were two sewing machines in various states of repair, glass jars filled with colorful buttons, crayons and marbles. There were tubs of acrylic paint, brushes, artist pallets, loft boxes, sketch pads and charcoal. In the center of the room was a potbellied stove that was surrounded by padded beach chairs, metal and wooden baseball bats, hockey goalie equipment, school books and at least three incomplete sets of encyclopedias. With help from the kids, about half of the material made it directly to the dumpster. The other half joined the sorted by function piles.

The other shed was two stories of similar pandemonium. It must have served as his tool shed. In it we found hammers, chain saws, socket wrenches, roofing shingles, assorted plumbing and electrical fixtures. He had a box of coffee carafes that he salvaged from old coffee makers and tons of coffee cans and old baby food jars that were filled with screws, nails, nuts and bolts. There were swimming pool noodles, oars, life preservers, rakes and hoes. One box contained nothing but combination locks, while another was filled with index cards, elastics and match books. Still another was filled with rusty bicycle chains and pedal pieces. On the plus side there weren't any apparent signs of furry creatures living in any of the things that we looked at…so far.

On one of our many trips to the almost filled dumpster we heard the creaking of the garage door struggling to move on its tracks. The springs and cable system were obviously broken, however John was eventually able to open it fully. Jamming a piece of two by four on each side, he propped the heavy door open. Fresh air and natural light filled the space and everyone with the exception of Beatrice was curious for a tour.

"Wanna see how your worse half lived?" I asked Beatrice as I took her by the elbow and escorted her towards the covered foundation house.

"No. No I really don't think that I want to."

"Come on Ma. Let's see if they left a chalk line where he died."

"It wasn't a homicide, you damn fool."

"So no chalk line?"

"No. You know he died on the toilet."

"Be a hell of a chalk line."

"Will you knock it off?!?!?!"

Beatrice let out a small gasp as we crossed the threshold into his home. Truth be told, she expected to see more of the same filth that she witnessed outside. Instead she was sincerely amazed how Spartan he kept his residence. With the exception of the bathroom and the utility room, there were no other interior walls or doors. He strategically had hung sheets or used furniture pieces to add definition to each of his "rooms". It consisted of a kitchen which ran along the back of the foundation. He had hung some stock beige laminate and oak cabinets that were very popular in the early nineteen eighties. The counter was also a laminate that was made to look like butcher-block. Considering its age, it had the normal wear and tear. He had a white range with coil elements and an apartment sized refrigerator. Beatrice couldn't help but notice the maple dining set with captain chairs was almost an exact replica of what she had in her house. He had a plaid table runner and a vase with some artificial daisies in the middle of the table.

He made his bedroom in the garage area, and defined his space by hanging sheets from the ceiling. His bedroom consisted of a king sized water bed frame with what looked like an air mattress in place of a water one. He had two mismatching night stands each with three drawers. Sitting on one was an alarm clock and a wedding picture of him and Beatrice. On the other was a picture of his children taken on what we assumed was their last Thanksgiving together, a small table lamp and a change jar. Between his two large armoires and the sheet, he had stacked piles of laminated veneer lumber which almost reached the ceiling. We assumed, and it is always dangerous making assumptions with anything that Fred did, that this material he was stockpiling to eventually begin construction upstairs.

The living room floor was covered in brown carpet remnants. He had a teal green pullout coach and a couple of reclining chairs, end tables with fake tiffany style lamps and a massive coffee table with a neat assortment of magazines that faced a large flat panel television set that sat upon an old walnut television console. Like each of the other rooms, he had bric-a-brac decorations that he had obviously found from

Goodwill Stores or recycling centers arranged throughout. Christopher was sitting at the roll top desk quietly shuffling papers and meticulously searching through drawers and the adjoining matching file cabinet.

"Find anything interesting honey?" Beatrice asked her youngest son.

"He was surprisingly organized here. Found some information on bank accounts and it looks like he had another life insurance policy. I'm going to have to wait until Monday to see if it is up to date."

"Been in the bathroom of death yet?" I asked.

Before he could answer and before Beatrice could dope slap me upside the head we heard a husky "Hello in there" coming from the doorway.

Chief Huckleberry Wentworth was in his late forties and stood about six foot three inches tall. He was in full uniform and he had his right hand strategically resting on his holstered service revolver. He needed to duck his head as he entered the foundation home.

"Hello Chief." I said crossing to him with my hand outstretched. "It's certainly nice to see you again sir." I took a few minutes to introduce everyone who was in the "house."

He gave an all clear into the walkie-talkie that was attached to his right breast pocket and smiled. "Neighbors had called in some activity, so I wanted to stop by and make sure things were alright."

"I appreciate that sir."

"Please, I told you to call me Huck."

"We've been trying to take an inventory and see what we are actually dealing with here."

"I don't envy you. He was certainly a character."

"You don't know the half of it." Beatrice added.

"Ha. Ha. I am sure that I don't."

"We'll probably only be here for another couple of hours or so. It looks like I am going to need another dumpster."

"More than likely. Have you been approached by Donny Goodinson yet?" the Chief asked as we headed back outside.

"No."

"He owns the place next door. He had been trying to buy Fred out for years. You might want to give him a call and see if you can work out a deal."

"Thanks. We'll certainly do that."

"In the meantime, do you folks have any plans for that slide in camper?" he asked as he nodded in the direction of the camper.

"Nope. You interested?"

"Well don't know for sure. Been kicking around the idea with the Mrs."

"Tell you what. Why don't you go take a look at it? If you interested, tell me what you think is a fair price and it's yours."

"I certainly appreciate that."

"Hey and if there is anything else that catches your eye, just let me know."

A few minutes later we agreed on a price and in less than twenty minutes, Chief Wentworth was back with his pickup truck and his bother-in-law, who was interested in the other camper. Carrie thought that it was best that we leave all negotiations to her and before long the yard was filled with neighbors and other passersby interested in our impromptu yard sale.

We all jumped in and assumed different roles. John, who also happened to be a licensed contractor, handled any questions related to tools. He even sold the dividing wall lumber to one of the neighbors for a far price. Christopher quickly checked for ownership papers, vehicle titles and wrote up bill of sales for Beatrice to sign immediately. Holly and I sold the lawn furniture and the records. No price was too low. We didn't dicker with anyone as we knew that anything that was left over was something that we were going to have to lift or dispose of.

Even the kids were a fantastic help. The girls were guiding people through the maze of items and the boys did a lot of lugging and lifting items back into people's cars when they weren't building their mountain of cans.

At one point a young woman with an adorable two year old girl on her hip made her way into the house. Both were dressed in threadbare clothing and had their dirty hair pulled back into high pony tails. She explained to Beatrice that she was a neighbor of Fred's. She had four small children and that he had helped her out a few times after her husband had passed away. She was embarrassed but needed to ask if she could have whatever foodstuffs were left in his cabinets.

Beatrice's heart nearly broke into a million pieces as she helped the poor woman fill up a couple of plastic bins of baked beans, soups, ramen, and condiments. When Beatrice noticed that the woman was loading up the expired canned macaroni, she stopped her, saying that in good consciousness she couldn't let her feed her children that. The freezer was filled with pocket pizzas and hamburger which also went into a bin. Beatrice even went into the bathroom of death looking for shampoo, conditioner, soap and laundry detergent so that she could pass it along.

With her bins and bags filled, Beatrice summoned four of her grandsons to help lug everything to the poor woman's car. And before the woman could say another word of humbled thanks, Beatrice grabbed her and hugged her tight.

"I know that it may not seem like it now, but I promise you everything is going to be alright." Beatrice whispered into her ear.

When they finished with the embrace, Beatrice shoved three hundred dollars into the young mother's hand. It was the money that Carrie negotiated for the aqua blue boat and trailer.

"I can't..."

"Yes you can. Now go take care of your babies."

"Ma..." I began.

"Not another word out of you. It was the right thing to do. By the way, you'll be disappointed to know that there wasn't a chalk line in the bathroom. Now go see if you can sell those stackable washer and dryer he has in there."

The yard sale ended almost as quickly as it began. We were able to sell much of the inventory and a majority of what we couldn't, made its way into the dumpster, but there was certainly a lot more cleanup that needed to happen. We regrouped on the roof of Fred's house where Beatrice had laid out the picnic lunch she had brought. She raised her can of Fresca to her family and thanked them for giving up their day to help her.

"We still have a lot to clean up." Christopher added.

"No. We have done enough for today." Beatrice corrected.

"Are we going to have to come back up here Nana?"

"Not if I can help it kiddo." Carrie replied. "I just got off the phone with a Mr. Donny Goodinson."

"How come you have cell service?"

"Because I am the mother and I have a better plan than you do."

"I knew it. Daaaaaaaaaaaaaaad!"

"She's kidding Paige. Let it go." John said as if he has had the same type of conversation a million times.

"Donny made me what I think is a fair offer to take the property as is. Cash. If you are ok with it Mom, I think we should take it and be done here."

"Done." said Beatrice.

"Hey Carrie, I found a souvenir that I just know you are going to want to keep and treasure forever." I said as I tossed her a TV Guide magazine which landed in her lap.

"What is it?"

"It's the TV Guide Fred was reading in the bathroom when he dropped dead. See, I think he died on a Wednesday because it's stuck open to that date."

Carrie instinctively stood up and the TV guide dropped to the roof. "Ewww. You loser! I don't' want that. It's disgusting."

"Come on. I know you want a memento. You loved him so." I said standing up and holding the TV Guide.

"No. You idiot! Keep that thing away from me."

I began to chase her around the roof trying to tag her with the TV Guide. "You know you want it. He lovvvvved you."

"Cut it out!" Carrie screamed as she tossed it into the dumpster.

We packed up and as John was locking up the house, I asked Holly to take a picture of Christopher, Carrie, Beatrice and me in front of the tree where Kevin had carved his initials years ago. Just as Holly snapped the picture, I told Beatrice the story of Kevin and his stolen pen knife.

"He did what???? Kevin!!!!!"

The Chicken Little Syndrome

Even though it was the hottest and most humid August on record, a cold front had blown in between the neighbors who shared the peninsula on the golden pond. George had spent most of that spring inebriated. The plastered plasterer! He missed too many days of work, resulting in him losing his standing with the union thus negating any chance of filing an unemployment claim with the state. With little to no money coming into the house and two growing boys to feed, Vivian transformed more than half of their lawn into a lavish vegetable garden. She planted parsley, peppers, cabbages, and celery, asparagus and watercress and lettuces, corn, squashes, egg plant, carrots, green and yellow wax beans, cantaloupes and tomatoes. As a young girl, her grandmother taught Vivian the art of canning and making preserves. With a little hard work now, she knew that she would at least be able to keep her family fed through the long winter months ahead.

She drove George back and forth to the union hall each day in the hopes that he might pick up some day labor work. And as soon as they came down over the hill and parked the dented green RAM pickup truck on their stone dust driveway, she sent Farmer George out to tend to their crops. While he was responsible for weeding, hoeing, feeding and watering their sizeable family vegetable patch, she took care of the family of ducks that set up residence in the cove behind their house. She had no intention of roasting one for dinner any time soon, however, she did not have a problem harvesting the dozens of eggs that the wildfowl abandoned by the shore.

Vivian kept George on a short leash that hot summer. On more than one occasion after the children and Vivian were fast asleep, he would sneak out across the way and have a couple of pops with his old friend and new neighbor Fred. One particular evening, Aunt Maura was also over and all four were in a rare and jovial mood. They were all snickering, smoking, and drinking beers on the back deck that overlooked the golden pond. Fred was merciless in his teasing of George's new agricultural career and it wasn't long before the conversation evolved into discussing the size of his zucchini. With the beers and the innuendos flowing at breakneck speed, Beatrice ever the instigator convinced Maura and Fred to go across the yard and steal the biggest zucchinis that they could find. Stumbling down the backstairs, the pair set off on their mission navigating by the little light thrown from the flame of Fred's Zippo. From their spot on the deck George and Beatrice could hear Maura's cackles and Fred's loud guffaws that were quickly followed by equally loud shushes and then by more laughter and snickering. Intrigued by the noises and the progress of their cat burglar comrades, Beatrice and George went down the stairs and tiptoed across the small front lawn, maneuvering around the pots of red inpatients and Martha Washington Geraniums trying to catch a better glimpse of the zucchini napping.

Maura and Fred threw their arms straight up in victory, tightly grasping massive zucchini's in each hand.

"We did it! Success" they shouted simultaneously.

Beatrice shushed them, and in a loud stage whisper, commanded that they get out of there before they wake up Vivian.

"Ok." Maura whisper-shouted back. She turned much too quickly for someone with that amount of alcohol in her system and bumped into Fred, catching him unaware. His footing gave way and before you know it, both fell over ironically squishing a mound of squash.

The pair roared with laughter which seemed to echo all around the golden pond. The floodlights attached to George's front porch snapped on revealing the tangled mess that was Maura and Fred and that only got them laughing all the harder. The wooden screen door squeaked open and out stepped an angry Vivian who was trying to keep her cotton robe closed tightly around herself.

"You have got to be f-ing kidding me!" shouted Vivian obviously angry and exasperated. "You two, get the hell out of my garden. Now! Or so help me I will have the police down here so fast, it will make your goddamn heads spin! George? George, don't think that I can't see you cowering over there with her. You have exactly one minute to get your ass over here and in this house or you can find yourself another place to live!"

"Looks like, the party is over Bea." whispered George sheepishly as he swayed back and forth trying to keep his balance as he crossed the yards to his home.

"Viv. I'm sorry." Beatrice tried to apologize.

"Go to hell Bea!" shouted Vivian who slammed the doors and shut off the lights as soon as George entered the house.

The next morning, Vivian arose early, poured herself a cup of tea and went outside to inspect the damage done to her garden. She found that the damaged squash plant had been staked and tied into place. The four purloined zucchinis had been returned and meticulously scotch taped to the stalk along with an apology note written on pink card stock in Beatrice's familiar handwriting. After reading the note, Vivian glared at the little house by the golden pond. She ripped the note into several small pieces and threw them in the flower bed of marigolds and yellow mums that made up the boarder of our property line.

Over the next few days, Beatrice made several attempts to apologize in person to Vivian. She knocked on the door, called her on the phone, tried desperately to wave her down each time Vivian drove George back and forth to find work. To make matters worse, George was not allowed to acknowledge Beatrice and Vivian kept her boys inside the house as well.

Ultimately it was Fred who brokered the peace two weeks later with a bouquet of Black Eyed Susan's, a heartfelt apology, and the promise of a combined family outing to Salem Willows for a skee-ball tournament and then a trip to The Great Wall, his favorite Chinese restaurant. His treat. Thanks to the loose change that he collected in a four by four square Christmas tin which he kept on his dresser, which ultimately became Kevin's own private ATM.

No matter how much we begged for popcorn, fried dough, or some other such snack, our requests fell on deaf ears. We were told repeatedly that we needed to save our appetites for the feast of Chinese cuisine that was to follow. Fred would then go into detail describing the succulent pork strips, the plump dumplings, the fluffy egg foo young, the moist chicken wings and spare ribs, and the tangy bite from spiced cabbage and other fillers that made up the moo shu pork with scallion pancakes. With our mouths watering and our bellies growling simultaneously, it didn't take long for us to lose interest in the contest. As soon as George was officially declared the high scorer, we cashed in our winning tickets for the assorted prizes that more than likely would never be in our house beyond next Wednesday's trash pickup. The summer sun was a couple hours away from setting and we loaded up into the battered gray Pontiac and made our way through the maze of streets that separated Salem and the City of Lynn, with George, Vivian and the boys following in hot pursuit.

The Great Wall Chinese restaurant was in a two-story brick commercial structure with a double storefront located on the northeast corner of Gorsuch and Kennedy Avenues which was not too far from Fred's old apartment on Clinton Street. It was located in what most people who do not live in the area would refer to as a sketchy section of the city. Regardless, it was one of his favorite haunts. Over the years and hundreds of visits sometimes as much as three times a week, Fred struck up a fun rapport and a friendship with the owners Bobby and Sammy Li. He truly enjoyed their company and loved hearing their stories of growing up in New York's Chinatown as he sat at the bar in the Tiki Torch Lounge, eating egg rolls and pounding down Mai Tai's and Headhunters as if they were going out of style. During most of his visits, Fred would close the place and make his way home somehow.

"Oh no." sighed Fred genuinely disappointed at the sight of his favorite restaurant boarded up. He parked the Pontiac as quickly as he could and jumped out to assess the situation. The red and yellow neon tube signage was broken and the dragon logo was covered in black soot. Even to the untrained eye, it was pretty obvious that there had been a significant fire. The families gathered around him as he stood there in front of the graffiti covered door shaking his head in disbelief. Beatrice put her arm around her husband and gave him an affectionate squeeze.

"Aww, Man!"

"Now, where are we gonna eat?"

"I'm starving."

"Figures."

"Look guys." said Vivian trying to gain some control of the situation. "If we don't feed them soon, we are going to have a mutiny on our hands. I was looking forward to the Chinese as much as you Fred, but what do you say we grab a bite next door?"

Vivian was referring to the Royalty Burger franchise that shared the same building as The Great Wall. The lights were on and it appeared that they were open for business. "If you close your eyes Fred, I bet the chicken sandwich tastes just like Peking Duck."

Fred let out a half hearted smile.

"Come on Bea; let's get everyone off the street. Not sure we are all that safe out here." quipped Vivian who held the door in an effort to shoo everyone inside quicker. Then just as the last of the stragglers entered the fast food restaurant, she noticed the sign that has been scotched tapped to the door and rolled her eyes. Written in bold purple letters and with a penmanship that would surely get the author six whacks on the knuckles with a ruler from Sister Margaret Anne that said 'Open During Renovation.'

Of course I wasn't too sure it was going to be much safer in there!

The families crowded in front the two overweight women dressed in the red, orange, and brown polyester smocks who were taking orders at the registers. For each Royal Kid Together Banquet Meal, Double Patricia Burger with onions, loaded baked potato, and jester sized chocolate shake ordered, the women slowly and methodically punched a correlating button on the register and then repeated each item into a microphone which came out of the greasy red Formica counter. Fast food here was an oxymoron.

The florescent overhead bulbs, the ones that were actually working gave off an eerie yellow glow in the dining room area which was in a state of disrepair. One section was cordoned off with masking tape and another purple lettered sign that said 'Closed'. Some of the brown and mosaic beige colored carpet squares were dirty beyond recognition and others were just missing. The same could be said about the two by two drop ceiling tiles above our heads. Although some seemed a little more saturated with water stains than others. Most of the napkin dispensers and salt and pepper shakers were empty, which Beatrice tried to overlook. However she was most insistent that the ladies supply her with a clean hot soapy wet towel so that she could wipe down some of the tables and chairs in an attempt to make them less sticky.

To an army of starving children the fast food seemed to take forever to arrive. It was eventually delivered to the table by the order takers, who shuffled their feet across the dirty carpet, as well by Joaquin, the shift manager, a Hispanic man who stood about five foot nine inches. He had a swimmer's body and wore black trousers, a yellow shirt and red tie. Vivian later estimated that Joaquin couldn't have been more than twenty years old based on the acne pock marks on his face and the wisps of black hair that were slowly growing over his lip.

"Folks," began Joaquin in a thick Spanish accent, "Welcome to Royalty Burger. My name is Joaquin and I am the shift manager tonight. I wanted to apologize on behalf of the company for your food taking so long."

"I told you it took forever!"

"Where are my onion rings?"

"Did he say his name was Jo?"

"Finally. I'm starving!"

"As you can see, we are undergoing some repairs. Tonight is the first night we have been able to open since the accident next door."

"What happened?" asked Fred.

"I am not one hundred percent sure. There was a grease fire in the kitchen about three weeks ago."

"Do you know if anyone was hurt?" asked Fred with genuine concern.

"No. Thankfully, I do not think so. The smoke and water damage was quite severe."

"How about Bobby and Sammy...the owners? Do you know if they are ok?" Fred grilled poor Joaquin.

"I have never met them. From what I was told the fire started after hours. They lost everything."

"I smell an arson investigation." whispered Vivian to Beatrice.

"Don't even joke about something like that, Viv." snapped Beatrice trying desperately not to break out laughing.

"Do you know how to get a hold of them? The owners?" pushed Fred.

"No. I am sorry. I do not." apologized Joaquin.

"Maybe someone left a contact number out back?" Fred pushed harder.

"I do not think so. But I can see that you are upset about this. So I will tell you what I will do. I have already added more French fries and onion rings to your order. When you are finished eating, I will make sure that everyone gets a My Lady, The Queen sundae—on the house."

"Are you kidding?"

"That's awesome!"

"I love the sundaes here!"

"Do you think that I can get a fruit cup instead?"

"Thank you. What did you say your name was again?" asked Fred.

"Joaquin."

"Wha?"

"Joaquin."

"Thank you Joaquin. That is very generous of you." said Fred very sincerely and shaking Joaquin's hand. "Do you think you might be able to check out back and see if anyone left some contact information for Sammy and Bobby?"

"I do not think that there is anything back there, but I will be happy to check for you, if you insist."

Before Fred could answer, a very small piece of the fiberglass ceiling tile gave way and landed on his head with a loud wet slap. Everyone around the table immediately began to laugh hysterically. Fred looked directly at Beatrice. He smiled and winked. He then grabbed his head and fell to the floor.

"Aw man." panicked Joaquin.

An ambulance ride and several hours later, Beatrice squinted at her watch as she desperately tried to read the numbers on the tiny silver dial face. She nervously continued to pace the hall outside of the emergency room of Lynn City Hospital. She sat down on the green vinyl couch with the duck tapped patches. She crossed her legs and kicked her foot as she mindlessly flipped through a stack of very old magazines. Vivian and George had taken the kids back and made sure that they were tucked away in their small bedrooms in the tiny house by the golden pond. She knew that despite their recent fight, Vivian would make sure that we were well cared for until she got home.

Just as she picked up another magazine, Beatrice was approached by a lovely young Chinese woman, who is wearing blue scrubs and a white laboratory coat. She stood just under five feet tall and her hair was the most amazing shade of black, which looked like spilt ink under the harsh hospital lighting. She had it cut in a long shag complete with graduated sides and progressive layers which went way past the stethoscope that she had wrapped around her neck. She introduced herself as Doctor Helene Mantineo, third year emergency room resident at the hospital. Beatrice could tell that the young doctor had a normally high voice that she had spent a lot of time training to sound deeper in an effort for people to take her more seriously.

"I've reviewed your husband's films and they do not reveal anything out of the ordinary. His lab results have come back normal as well. I can't see anything that is any real concern here. So I am going to release him. However, I am going to refer you to a Neurologist."

"A brain doctor? Is that necessary, Doctor?"

"As I said, I am sure that it is nothing. But it's better to be safe than sorry. The discharge nurse will give you a list of recommendations. For now, I am going to recommend that you take him home and get a good night's rest."

"Should he sleep Doctor? I have always heard that if you have a concussion, the last thing that you should do is sleep."

"That's true...if you have a concussion. Which, by the way, your husband does not have. To be perfectly honest with you Mrs. McMullen, I can't find anything medically wrong with him. However, since he continues to complain about dizziness and a headache, I thought that the referral makes sense and would give him some peace of mind. He should be just fine. I promise.

"Thank you Doctor." said a grateful Beatrice.

"No problem, Mrs. McMullen."

Less than an hour or so later, Beatrice found herself driving the dented grey Pontiac with the missing muffler through the streets of Lynn headed back to her home on the pond.

"How are you feeling Freddie?"

"Told them I had a headache and that I was dizzy. I was really surprised that they didn't admit me for observation." complained Fred as he tried in vain to free his wrist from his patient ID bracelet. "Damn I need scissors."

"I spoke to your doctor. She said that there was nothing wrong with you."

"The kid? Who are you going to believe sweetie?" he replied while desperately searching the messy glove compartment looking for something sharp.

"Well, you of course. I am just thankful that you are coming home with me."

"There is no way that place should have been opened tonight. I have half a mind...Pissah! Found it!" He said as he produced a screwdriver and immediately wove it between his wrist the patient identification bracelet and began to turn it counter clockwise. "I could have been killed, right there and then. Did you get the piece that whacked me on the head?"

"It's in my pocketbook, just like you asked."

"Good. We are gonna show them. They are going to pay me for the pain and suffering that they inflicted."

"Pain and suffering? It was a very wet piece of fiberglass; it couldn't have been any heavier than a wet facecloth."

"It hit me square on the head. I have witnesses. It shouldn't have happened." he said paying more attention to the twisted identification band that was now beginning to cut off circulation.

"You are right. It shouldn't have. But..."

Before Beatrice could finish her train of thought Fred shouted "Got ya! You son of a bitch!" as identification band snapped setting his wrist free.

"Really?"

"Sweetie, I was hit in the head. The place had no business being open. It wasn't safe. All I know is that I feel dizzy and that I have a head ache because of it. What would have happened if it hit one of the kids? Would we even be having this conversation?"

Recognizing that this was the beginning of what had the potential to be a much longer argument; Beatrice did something that she rarely did in her lifetime. It was certainly something that she never did during her first marriage; she decided to keep her opinions to herself and kept her mouth shut. She kept her mouth shut the next morning when Fred called out sick to work. She didn't say anything when he filed a short term disability claim with his union representative later that morning. She kept her mouth shut as he called each of the neurologists on the referral list trying to figure out which one would give him the answers that he sought. She silently hoped that after the visit to Doctor Leonard Maxwell's office, who could not find anything medically wrong with her husband that this 'adventure' would come to an end. Still she bit her tongue when they visited three more doctors on the list each ending with a similar result. Even though he pleaded that he was forced to chew aspirins like they were breath mints and that he now developed a slight ringing in his ears. She didn't say anything when he asked her to screen all of his calls and to make sure that when the human resources representative from the plant called, Beatrice was to always say that he was sleeping and he would have to call her back. When they met with Nicholas Orphanos a legal referral of a friend of a friend who would be more than happy to wave his usual retainer and work on contingency for a larger percentage of the settlement, Beatrice spoke up.

"Mr. Orphanos..."

"Please call me Nick." smiled the handsome man in the blue pinstriped three piece suit with the dark eyes, a full mustache and tight black curls that almost resembled an afro from behind his large dark walnut stained desk.

"Nick. I am not sure I understand."

"What's not to understand sweetie?" interjected Fred. "Instead of paying his fee now, we only have to pay him when we win the case. Like interest on a credit card."

"I understand that!" snapped Beatrice as she adjusted herself in her rather uncomfortable burnt orange faux leather barrel chair. "What I mean is, how do you have a case? We have seen up team number of doctors over the last two and half weeks and not one of them thinks that there is anything wrong with you."

"Mrs. McMullen," began Nick as he leaned forward. "From the way that your husband has described the situation, there is no doubt in my mind that we have a case. There are safety violations. Negligence. And yes, medical documentation can only strengthen our argument."

"But every doctor he has seen so far hasn't found anything wrong with him."

"Then you haven't been seeing the right doctors." Nick smiled revealing a chipped upper right tooth.

"Excuse me?"

Nick handed Fred a business card. "I want to go see this guy. Doctor Markos Angelopoulos. He is the best. Hey Angie? Can you see if Doctor Angelopoulos has an opening today for Mr. McMullen? Thank you darling. You go see him and he will get you straightened out. In the meantime, I'll draft up a letter to Royalty Burger and let them know that you now have representation."

"This Doctor Angelopoulos...he's Greek?" asked Fred.

"But of course."

"How long will this case take?" asked Beatrice.

"To be up front with you, I am not sure. It could go either way. Royalty Burger has deep pockets. They may want to fight it or they may just consider it a nuisance and will want to write a check to make it go away. Why do you ask?"

"He's out of work right now. His boss called this morning and he seemed really upset that Freddie wasn't there."

"Sweetie, Nick doesn't need to know..."

"I most certainly do. I care about my clients and their families. That's what makes me so good." Nick stood up and began to usher Beatrice and Fred out of his office. "I'm not going to lie to you. The longer that you are out of work, the better our case looks. Go see my guy and let me get this letter out this afternoon. I will call you in a couple of days to follow up. We are going to make these sons of bitches pay through the nose."

"Thanks Nick. We appreciate your help." said Fred as he vigorously shook Nick's hand. "I'll go see him now and we'll just have to tighten our belts a little on the home front."

Doctor Angelopoulos had a suite of offices on the second floor in a professional building off of the Lynnway. Thanks again to his intimate knowledge of the area; it took Fred barely twenty minutes to cross the city and make his three o'clock appointment. After an initial intake with Doctor Angelopoulos, a team of nurses and assistants put Fred through a complete battery of physical and physiological tests. One assistant even interviewed Beatrice, questioning and probing for information regarding her husband's moods, eating and sleeping habits.

Eventually the couple came face to face with Doctor Angelopoulos once again in one of the exam rooms. Beatrice was infatuated by the good doctor's rugged good looks, square jaw, olive skin, piercing Paul Newman eyes and a thick head of hair that was little longer than it should have been and was the color of cream cheese frosting.

"So give it to us straight, Doc." demanded Fred trying to gain some control over the situation.

"Mr. McMullen, Mrs. McMullen." Beatrice thought that the doctor's deep husky voice was velvety. "First of all thank you for bringing the medical records from the hospital with you today. It certainly saves us some time because I can now look at the entire picture. I happen to agree with the findings of...Doctor Mantineo was it?"

"A baby." Fred stated trying to diminish her standing and expertise.

"I have no point of reference on her age. Regardless, Mr. McMullen, there doesn't seem to be a physical reason for your dizziness and ringing in your ears."

"Well that's certainly good news." said Beatrice trying to lighten the mood.

"However, the tests that we conducted seem to indicate that you have something called "manic-depressive illness."

"What?" asked Fred who clearly did not understand a thing the doctor was saying.

"It is classified as a mood or affective disorder. It is characterized by extreme swings in mood. You've admitted that you have had some mood swings. Tremendous highs that may last for three or four days or even weeks at a time. And then most certainly followed by severe bouts of depression or exhaustion."

"Freddie that seems true honey."

"While we don't know what causes bipolar disorder, we believe it has a biological basis. As for the cause, we are still learning a lot about this disease. There have been remarkable strides in this area of science and with the right treatment; you can lead a very successful and fulfilling life."

"Could the accident have caused this?" asked Fred still trying to wrap his head around the conversation.

"It may have acerbated the situation, as for the cause, I will let the lawyers argue that one. The takeaway here is that the accident forced you to seek treatment and we now have a diagnosis."

"So how do we treat this, Doctor Angelopoulos?" Beatrice asked.

"There are several prescription therapies out there. I would like to try a regiment of mood stabilizers. In the right combination Methamphetamine and Benzodiazepine have shown great promise in leveling out moods." explained Doctor Angelopoulos as he handed Beatrice a written prescription for both. "Unfortunately, this is not an exact science. It may take a couple of weeks to get the mix right. So until then, I will want to see you Mr. McMullen every couple of weeks. Would that be ok?"

"Sure thing doc." he said while shaking the doctor's hand. "Let's give this stuff a whirl. You'll make sure that your girl gets a copy of your report to Nick Orphanos' office?"

"Promise. It was a pleasure meeting you both. I will have my assistant call to set up your next appointment. Have a great day."

After stopping at his favorite pharmacy to fill his prescriptions, Beatrice and Fred swung by the corner of Gorsuch and Kennedy Avenues and saw that the Royal Burger now had a closed indefinitely sign hanging on the front door. He tried stopping several passersby to get some information, but most of the people he tried talking with, gave him a funny look and crossed the street to avoid coming into contact with him. Feeling a little upset by the situation, Fred drove around until he found a working payphone and abruptly dialed his attorney.

Back on the home front, Fred was true to his word about tightening his belt. He insisted that Beatrice start using powdered milk as a way to save money. Since the sugar shortage had caused an increase in the prices of our beloved breakfast cereals, he also insisted that we break off our long term relationships with the Captain, the Sugar Frosted Tiger and the Fruity Toucan. In their place, we were now expected to spend our mornings with thirty two ounce clear plastic bags of puffed rice and puffed wheat cereal that had no color, less taste and no free toy surprises inside. Of course, once he discovered that we went through ten pounds of sugar in an effort to make the Styrofoam tasting substitutes more palatable, coupled with the new ant problem as a result of some messy sugar application on Kevin's part, Beatrice was allowed to bring back our delicious friends.

Still missing work and burning through his sick and vacation time, Fred tried to keep busy by working on some small projects around the house or put some additional touches on Bea's Traveling Kitchen. Unfortunately, he was still not able to set the levels right for his medication and spent several hours "zoning out" or eventually going to take a nap. Often too tired to eat or just not hungry enough for a full meal at the dining room table, he often asked that Beatrice serve him a can of soup and some saltines on a tray in the bedroom. The only time that he left the bedroom was to either use the bathroom or check in with Nick Orphanos.

Beatrice used to enjoy her morning rituals. The only time you were allowed to sleep past seven thirty was if you were sick...very sick. Other than that, you were up and dressed. Breakfast dishes were cleared from the table and put into the sink before we left the house to go play up the block with our friends. She would then wash and put away the dishes. Sweep and vacuum the floors. Dust. Bleach the bathroom and make the beds. On Tuesdays, she would flip the mattresses and change the sheets. Thursdays were for heavy dusting and polishing. Wednesdays and Fridays were laundry days. Most days her routine chores were done by nine thirty and she was ready for whatever the day would bring.

Fred's bedroom confinement had lasted several days and totally threw off Beatrice's routine. Not being able to vacuum or change the sheets in her own bed which were now soup stained and full of cracker crumbs was making her more than a little cranky. Sitting in her perch, drinking a beer and smoking her Kools, Beatrice complained / talked to Aunt Maura on the telephone. When that conversation was finished, she opened another beer and tried unsuccessfully to reach one of the Bettys. When the phone rang, she picked it up within one ring in the hopes that it would be a friendly sympathetic ear. Unfortunately, it was Charlie Wilcox, Fred's union representative at the plant. Beatrice had remembered Charlie from last year's Christmas party. He was a kind and fair older gentleman who wasn't always happy about being a union leader, especially when he had to deliver bad news.

"I hate to be the bringer of bad news here Bea." said Charlie in a three pack a day voice. "I just got a heads up from human resources that Freddie's short term disability claim is going to be denied. If he doesn't show up with a doctor's note clearing him for work on Monday, they are going to let him go."

"Charlie is there anything that you can do? He's been in bed since Sunday." pleaded Beatrice.

"I wish that there was. I have called in every favor and tried everything that I can. But they are not budging. Tell the big lug to get back here. People miss him and his crazy stories."

"Thanks Charlie. I'll make sure that he knows."

"Bea, I truly wish that I had better news." he said softly as he could in a voice that still sounded as though he were gargling with rocks. "Try and have a good night."

Beatrice hung up the receiver and wiped a tear of frustration from her eye. She pulled on the string of the overhead lamp so that she could see the number in her personal phonebook which she kept on a small shelf below the counter. She briskly dialed Nick Orphanos, who was sympathetic to her plight. He reported that he had a couple of calls with the lawyer from Royalty Burger but they were not at the settlement stages yet. It may stretch out a few more weeks. Her next call was to Doctor Angelopoulos' office and explained the situation to his assistant. She asked for the note and for the doctor to call her back as soon as possible. Just as she hung up the phone, Fred bellowed from the other room asking for Beatrice to bring him something cold to drink. She poured him a big glass of milk made from the powder he insisted that everyone drink and walked to her bedroom. She returned to the kitchen shortly after and with her hands resting on the countertop she hung her head down and cried a little. When I asked her what was wrong, she shook her head no, exhaled loudly and said, "Fred would like to have chicken noodle soup for dinner." She opened the knotty pine door to the cabinet where she kept her canned goods and searched for some chicken noodle soup. Not being able to find any, she decided that he will have to settle for vegetable beef instead. She took out her smallest aluminum pot, poured in the soup, a can of water and placed the pot on the front burner to heat. She asked me to keep an eye on the soup as she went on the back deck to make sure that she could still see Kevin who was using the row boat to hunt frogs.

Seeing how upset my mother was, I took a page from Carrie's book. During the courtship of Beatrice and Fred, Carrie's distain for Fred was immediate and immense. On one of his visits, Carrie had taken the liberty of baking some double chocolate laxative stuffed brownies and served them to Fred for dessert. She then locked herself in the tiny house's only bathroom for the next few hours with her transistor radio feigning a much needed bubble bath. By the time the brownies kicked in, the only recourse he had was to high tail it into his car and up over the hill. To this day, we were not exactly sure just where and when he actually crapped in his pants.

I opened up the middle cabinet door where Beatrice kept our Winter Frost White Corelle plates and bowls. It was the top shelf where Fred stored his medicine. I calmly and methodically took a few pills out of the Methamphetamine bottle and made sure to replace the bottle exactly as I had found it. Next, I crushed the pale yellow pills with a spoon and added them to his simmering soup. Then I grabbed the teakwood serving tray from the dining room buffet and placed it on the kitchen counter. I placed a white Corelle bowl on the right hand side of the tray leaving just enough room for a folded napkin and soup spoon. I even went as far as to open a fresh sleeve of Ritz crackers and applied butter to half a dozen or so and arranged them on a small plate next to his awaiting soup bowl.

Once she screamed a couple of times for Kevin to make sure that he put his lifejacket back on and promise that the boat would not under any circumstances leave the cove, Beatrice came back into the kitchen.

"Thank you baby." she smiled and kissed me on the forehead. She stirred the soup a couple of times, shut off the burner and poured the contents into the bowl.

"Wish me luck." Beatrice smiled and winked at me as she took the tray to her husband.

Within the hour, the hush toned argument that Fred and Beatrice were having exploded into a huge scream fest. Fred insisted that she needed to support him; arguing that the payoff could be worth a lot of money. Beatrice was sympathetic; however it could be months maybe even years before it settled and it cannot be at the cost of his job. Once the profanities started to fly, it was just a matter of time before his dinner tray went flying as well. As soon as I heard the crash, I grabbed up a confused and frightened Christopher and took him outside. Shortly after, a dressed Fred shoved the white aluminum storm door so hard; it almost came of the hinges. He made his way down the two front stairs and almost ran down the front walkway to his car. He was screaming and swearing almost incoherently. Beatrice was right behind him, matching his intensity and saltiness almost word for word.

Once he was behind the wheel, he demanded that Beatrice back the fuck away and slammed the car into reverse almost backing into Vivian's garden. He shot up over the hill flipping the bird out the driver side window as the car zoomed out of sight.

She stood in the driveway shaking her head for just a minute. She took a deep breath. Straightened her shoulders and said, "Come on you two. What say you help me flip my mattress and vacuum?"

Reality Check

Family Therapy

"I only have time for a quick one. I have to get back and help finish the kid's Halloween costumes." said Carrie as she took off her jacket and squeezed into the tight booth that Christopher and I occupied in the back of the restaurant.

"I hate Halloween." added Christopher.

"You need to let that go." I added.

"What? It's a pointless made up holiday. It's just an excuse for people to drink too much and for women to dress slutty."

"What's the issue with that?" asked Kevin via FaceTime.

"Hey Kev. Shit!" said Carrie as she accidently knocked over the cell phone with Kevin's face on it which was resting against the salt shaker.

"Where did everyone go?" asked a confused Kevin.

"Sorry." Carrie quickly apologized as she repositioned the phone so that it was now also being supported by the beige ceramic ramekin that held the multicolored packets of sugar substitute. "Better?"

"Much. Thanks." said Kevin as he took another swig of his morning coffee from behind his desk in his office in Japan.

"Come on Christopher. Are you telling me that you never had fun?" Carrie asked as she scanned her text messages. "Where the hell is the waitress? It's been a hell of a day."

"You each took turns dragging me around the neighborhood going from house to house…."

"Isn't that the point of trick or treat?" I interjected. "More houses typically mean more candy."

"You used to tell your friends that you were stuck with me and then you would try and ditch me and run off."

"That isn't true." insisted Carrie half feigning interest as she reviewed her email.

"It most certainly is!"

"Yeah. He is right. I did try to ditch him." admitted Kevin.

"You have to agree that you had the best costumes in the neighborhood." Carrie reminded him.

"That's right. You were a bottle of ketchup one year…a refrigerator…the sales rep in the leisure suit…" I rambled off, still quite proud of the costumes that I made.

"They were all home made. People used to make fun of me. All I wanted was to get a costume from the department store like everyone else in the neighborhood."

"We were on a tight budget. Besides, your costumes were so much more creative and imaginative. They were just better." I said almost angrily. "How many kids can say they got to dress up as Oscar the Grouch?"

"I got to walk around in a dirty trash can."

"I washed it out first." claimed Kevin.

"No you didn't. It really smelled!"

"Oh crap. You're right. I didn't. I was such a shit."

"What about the year that I dressed you as a vampire? You looked great." I added trying to put a positive spin on it.

"Sure. Until I realized that the Vaseline you put in my hair didn't come out."

"In my defense, it was before they invented hair gel. Besides, you looked great."

"It took two weeks for it to wash out. I looked like I had dirty hair. Diane Saxon tortured me. She told everyone on the playground that we were too poor to buy shampoo."

"She was always a pain in the ass. And needy." Kevin added matter-of-factly.

"Wait a minute." I asked. "Did you sleep with her?"

"Twice in high school." Kevin said nonchalantly.

"Are you telling me, that in your entire life, you never had any fun on Halloween?" asked Carrie as she desperately tried to change the subject and make eye contact with a passing waitress.

"There was the one time that Mom bought me a dozen eggs."

"Wait a minute. Mom bought you a dozen eggs? You?" Kevin asked not believing what he had heard.

"Yeah. All of us actually." I added.

"She never bought me a dozen eggs to throw on Halloween." complained Kevin.

"That's because she knew that you would just take them from the refrigerator." I added. "Besides she wanted to make up for that stupid therapy session we had to go to! You do remember therapy, Kevin."

"How could I forget? They were going to kick me out of school unless I attended a few sessions. It's not my fault that the therapist wanted to meet all of you." Kevin said.

"That was the session that you skipped out on." Christopher jokingly snapped.

"Dude, how many times do I have to explain it to you? It was Halloween. McKenzie Moran was going to let me touch her boobies if I beat up her next door neighbor." said Kevin with a smug grin on his face.

"McKenzie Moran. Oh my God. I haven't heard that name in a dog's age." I stated. "I always thought that she was either going to end up in a trailer park or with a Washington Senator."

"Better." Kevin chimed in. "Her husband is a plastic surgeon."

"We shouldn't have had to go." Carrie said as she texted a couple of quick messages.

"It was junior high school. I was acting out." Kevin explained.

'When weren't you acting out?" Carrie questioned.

"Excuse me," Christopher said politely to a waitress who at that moment just happened to pass by our table. "Would you mind sending our waitress over?"

As the waitress agreed and left, Christopher faced Carrie and smiled victoriously. Carrie's only response was scowl and to shoot Christopher the look mothers use in public when they do not want to scream but immediately want their children to fall into line. Christopher was slightly frightened when he realized how much his sister resembled Beatrice at that moment.

"True." Kevin admitted.

"You still should have been there." I said.

"Dude. Boobies. Enough said." Kevin smirked.

"Oh God. What was her name again?" Christopher asked.

"Doctor Rula Minkle." I said without missing a beat.

"How the hell did you remember that?" Kevin questioned.

"Because, he is fucking Rain Man." Christopher added.

"It was a weird name. How could you forget it? Say it with me. Ruuuula Mink-le. Remember? She had that long disco afro and wore earth shoes."

"You're not right. There is something terribly wrong with you." Kevin said.

"You're just catching on to that?" Christopher asked.

"I still can't believe Beatrice made us go to that session." I said still in disbelief about an event that happened over thirty years ago.

"I remember Mom finally giving up on you and she and Fred dragged us to Doctor Minkle's office. We were a few minutes l…" Carrie stopped midsentence as soon as a perky twenty something girl with a low cut v-neck jersey with a Storming Norma's logo embroidered over her left breast approached the table.

"Hello folks. My name is Tiffany and I will be taking care of you this…" began the girl with bleached blonde hair, a nose hoop, and fresh cigarette breath.

"Hello Tiffany. I don't mean to be rude. But we've been waiting a bit and we are all extremely parched." interrupted Carrie.

"I'm sorry for the delay. We've been slammed tonight." Tiffany halfheartedly apologized.

"Oh I get it. It's been a rough day for a lot of us. Look we will try and make it simple for you. May we please have three extra dry Sapphire Martinis? Straight up. Also, be a dear and please check with the bartender to see if she has any blue cheese stuffed olives. And we will also take an order of vegan nachos, when you get the chance. Thank you."

"A little witchy there, sis?" I stated just as soon as an obviously disgruntled Tiffany was out of earshot.

"Really? I don't think…"

"Oh you were." Christopher agreed.

"Always said you could make a platoon sergeant cry." Kevin piled on.

"Ok. Ok. I get it. Stop ganging up. It's been a bad day and I am trying to juggle too much as usual. If it will make you all feel better, when she gets back to the table, I will give Tiffany a heartfelt apology. And Michael, you can ease your embarrassment by leaving her a generous tip. So where was I? Right. We were late getting to Doctor Minkle's office."

"Rain Man? What color was the office?" snickered Kevin.

"Peach."

"It's uncanny." said Christopher.

"How do we know he is not full of shit?" asked Kevin.

"He's not. He's got a photographic memory." Christopher said.

"Then why is he always losing his keys?" Carrie piled on.

"Har. Har." I said rather sarcastically.

"I remember that we got in there and Doctor Minkle had some very stoic interns who were going to observe and take notes of the session." Christopher said. "Very robot like."

"Yah. Yah. There were three of them. Right? I just remember Mom not being too thrilled about it." said Carrie excited that she was able to remember a detail.

"I just think that she was more worried about them psychoanalyzing Fred." Christopher laughed.

"We had to sit at that kiddy table. There was a big log of clay." Carrie pushed herself to remember.

"Right. Right." Christopher agreed. "Doctor Minkle wanted to see how well we worked together so she asked us to use the clay to make our family. So you…"

"I cut the block in half and told Michael to use one half to make Fred." Carrie laughed out loud. "And then you and I would do everyone else."

"Except when we finished, Doctor Minkle pointed out that Dad was missing." Christopher said.

"Oh my God. You should have seen your face Christopher. I thought that you were going cry."

"Give me a break. I was in the fourth grade." Christopher shot back defensively. "We forgot Dad. It was a pretty big deal."

"I tried to fix it for you, didn't I?" I reminded him.

"Fix it?" Christopher said mockingly. "You grabbed a chunk of clay out of Fred and made Dad!!"

"Why have I never heard this story?" Kevin laughed.

"The white coat and clipboard brigade went crazy. They couldn't move their pencils fast enough." I laughed. "But that wasn't the worst of it. Our illustrious step-monster, who the night before finished off all of the hot dogs and beans and later copped to having two generous servings of turkey chili for lunch, let loose with the Mount Vesuvius of back-end blowouts!"

"No. No." said Kevin in disbelief as the rest of us burst into uncontrollable laughter.

"Kevin…it was so bad…and so long! It was as if time stood still and everything was moving in slow motion. I swear it must have gone on for fifteen minutes!"

"And the smell…" said Christopher who was a shade of red from laughing so hard.

"It was so gross." Carrie jumped in.

"I thought that he shit himself." Christopher finished.

"Stop. Stop." begged Carrie who was holding her stomach and had tears rolling down her face. "It hurts to laugh this hard."

"What happened next?!" asked Kevin who was enjoying us laugh just as much as he was enjoying the story.

"We just sat there as if nothing happened. It wasn't the first time that we were trapped in a Fred made wind tunnel.

The white coat and clipboard brigade totally lost it." I snorted. "One actually screamed like a five year old girl."

"It was like watching the Three Stooges, as they bumped into each other trying to get out of the office looking for fresh air." Christopher howled.

"Doctor Rula Minkle turned a slight shade of green and hers eyes were watering. You could tell that she was trying her hardest to hold her composure, but was on the verge of letting go. She strongly suggested that given the circumstances, she thought it would be best if we rescheduled." I said doing my imitation of Doctor Minkle.

"Mom was so pissed she yelled at Fred all the way home." Carrie giggled.

"Not before we stopped off at the store so she could buy the eggs for us."

"She was trying to buy our silence."

"That fart was anything but silent!" Carrie half screamed and we all continued to laugh.

We eventually calmed ourselves and wiped the tears from our eyes. As Tiffany approached our table with a tray of martinis, her sticky shoes squeaked and tooted with each step.

We all laughed even harder.

New Tenants

When Beatrice and Butch were first married, they scoured the local newspaper classifieds each Friday evening looking for the newest apartment listings that could accommodate their growing family. During the week, Beatrice and one or both of the Bettys loaded up the baby carriages and walked the neighborhoods that they felt were most desirable and advantageous for young families, not to mention affordable looking for those places without curtains hanging in the windows. Lack of curtains always meant one or two things back then to Beatrice. It was either laundry day or there was a vacant apartment. It took a bit, but she eventually found their next home.

Compared to the cramped apartment on the first floor of a very busy main road, 19 Pearsall Place was a palatial mansion. It was a two story duplex style townhouse home nestled in a quiet residential neighborhood. The first floor had maple hardwood floors throughout the living room, dining room, and kitchen. Upstairs there were two decent sized bedrooms that were separated by a recently refurbished full bathroom and linen closet. There was a washer and a dryer hookup in the basement, which meant once they could afford it, Beatrice would no longer have to drag Carrie, me and the dirty clothes to the laundromat. All of these things checked off the right boxes on her list. However, what excited her more than anything else was the fact that there was a beautiful side yard with a patio made of blue stone pavers and a raised vegetable garden. Plus the backyard was completely fenced in, which meant that Carrie and I could run, play to our heart's content, and most importantly, be safe.

Sure we would need to share a bedroom, but we were toddlers at the time and it really didn't matter at that point. Beatrice was convinced that she and Butch would have saved enough to buy a larger home, preferably close to one or both of her friends, by the time we were older. That fantasy ended when Kevin arrived fifteen months later.

Each of Beatrice's children was beautiful at birth. Carrie and I were both round, plump, pink, and fair skinned. When we were born, we each had long thick black curls that the nurses loved to style differently each morning before we left the nursery. Both of us, according to Beatrice were easy text book style deliveries. Kevin, not so much. He was three weeks early when he decided to make his presence known. Beatrice barely had time to wash and iron clothes, polish our white shoes, and stock the refrigerator before heading off to the hospital. Kevin's birth was as difficult as it was long, lasting almost three times as long as ours. When the nurses handed Beatrice her new son, she knew that there was something magical about Kevin. He was lean and wiry. He had the same coloring as one of Butch's older sisters, olive skin, light brown hair, hazel green eyes and a smile that could melt hearts and light up a room at the same time. It was love at first sight. If she tried hard enough, Beatrice could eventually find a way to make the living arrangements work.

Two years later, the once palatial two-family home was bursting at the seams for this young family of five. The three of us shared a bedroom which made things difficult as we, no matter how hard Beatrice tried, were on different sleeping schedules. Although she kept an immaculately clean home, each corner and crevasse was filled with the normal day to day items needed to care and entertain three very active and very rambunctious young children. On rainy days, the house was downright claustrophobic.

There were some days where Beatrice would like nothing better than to lock herself in the bathroom and have a good cry or at the very least take a solitary pee. But fear of what we might get into quickly struck those thoughts from her mind. Each of us seemed to have an endless supply of energy that we needed to burn off. None more so, than Kevin. You see, the fenced in back yard no longer offered the peace of mind Beatrice had originally thought it would when they first arrived. Kevin was a fast baby. He was also a climber. She would turn her back for a split second and poof he was gone. She would find him scaling the fence like a Navy Seal on a search and rescue mission. A few times she barely grabbed him before he reached the top. Beatrice also too often found herself at the doctor's office or emergency room seeking treatments for the injuries Kevin sustained from falling off of the refrigerator or jumping down the stairs. Simultaneously, I proved myself to be a bit of a Houdini managing to unlock every door, window, and deadbolt and making a run for it. While she long suspected it, it would be many years later before Beatrice could actually prove that it was Carrie the instigator who was encouraging our exhausting and sometimes dangerous behavior.

Each night, after we were bathed and put to bed, Beatrice would wash the dishes, clean the kitchen, and straighten out the house before taking twenty minutes to melt into a lukewarm bath.

We had a very small hot water heater.

Butch was working two jobs back then so that they could make ends meet. Some nights, she was so exhausted she could barely wait up for my father to come home. So when Butch approached her with the idea of getting a pet, it was no wonder that Beatrice made him sleep on the couch.

The cloudy morning that Beatrice's paternal grandmother showed up for a surprise visit, the house was in total bedlam. In the middle of the night, Carrie went into the freezer and liberated a half gallon of chocolate ice cream, which she took back to the our bedroom along with three spoons. As much as we were able to eat, an equal amount of chocolate ice cream seemed to make its way on the pillows, blankets, sheets, furniture, and toys. Somewhere between trips up and down the basement stairs to check on her laundry and scrubbing down everything in the our room with Pine Sol, Kevin had somehow managed to bite the finger off of Carrie's beloved Bozo the Clown doll and there was no consoling her. Beatrice answered her front door while balancing a waling Carrie on her right hip.

"Am I catching you at a bad time dear?" asked the woman in the Dongle tweed custom tailored suit and pearls clutching her matching gloves and black alligator handbag.

Slightly taken back by the sight of her grandmother standing on her front stoop, Beatrice panic slightly because she knew her house wasn't in any condition to receive company, especially someone who was as fastidious as her grandmother.

"What the hell is she doing here? She never comes by unannounced." Beatrice screamed to herself.

"No. No. It's just been one of those mornings. Come on in Gammie."

Beatrice's grandmother was Judith Simonson, who insisted that her grandchildren call her Gammie. She was a handsome woman of German decent who had married three times. She had divorced her first, buried her second, and was living comfortably with her third. With each marriage, Judith traded up financially. She had just come from the hairdresser where she had a blue rinse added to her substantially thick grey hair before it was set and blown out in her traditional style. She had long manicured fingers with bright red nail polish. On her right hand she always wore her three karat yellow diamond ring which was a gift from husband number two and on her left, a platinum wedding band set which included a pair of matching one karat round diamonds.

"Please make yourself comfortable. Just let me get the kids settled and we can have a nice visit." said Beatrice trying desperately not to show the panic in her voice and kissing her grandmother on the cheek. "Can I make you some tea? Coffee?"

"No thank you dear. Take your time." Gammie half smiled as she walked around the small living room admiring the family photos on the wall. "I don't see a picture of your father dear?"

"Excuse me?" Beatrice shouted from the kitchen.

"I said, I don't see any pictures of your father." Gammie shouted back as she admired a black and white picture of herself, Flossie and baby Beatrice that was taken in the rose garden at her house. She didn't notice Beatrice who entered carrying a tray.

"That's because I don't have any." said Beatrice with a sadness in her voice as she put the tray with the mismatched jelly glasses filled with lemonade on the coffee table. She signaled her grandmother to sit. "He wasn't around much and when he was, you certainly didn't want any pictures."

"I know dear." said Gammie with a little sadness in her voice as she took Beatrice's wrist. "My son was a drunk. I am truly sorry that he wasn't a better father to you and your brothers. I had such high expectations for him. I should have done more."

"I am not really sure what more you could have done." said Beatrice as she handed her grandmother a glass of lemonade and passed the cookie plate. "The kids should be all set for a little bit."

"Oh, no thank you." she said as she refused the cookies. "As a mother, you always feel as though there was something more that you can do."

"I'm glad that you came by, although I am afraid that you haven't caught us at our best today."

"Don't worry about it. That's why I am here."

"Oh?"

"I've evicted my tenants that live in the house at the bottom of the hill and I want you and your family to come move in."

Beatrice stared at her grandmother in disbelief.

Back in the early nineteen twenties, Judith had a passionate love affair with a married man named Conrad C. Walsh who was a real estate developer with a very successful architectural firm in Boston. The affair was quite scandalous for the times especially when Conrad left his wife, children, and his sophisticated upscale Beacon Hill address and moved in with Judith and her young son into a real estate project that he had spent the better part of the prior year working on in a very rural town with a beautiful golden pond on the North Shore.

The project consisted of a private road on a peninsula which he named after himself. It had a beautiful house that sat on top of a small hill that had panoramic views of the golden pond. The house he designed with Judith had a flagstone fireplace; coffered ceilings and mahogany board and batten walls. Below, he also built three small homes that hugged the shores of the golden pond. Built into a portion of the hill was a building that he referred to as the towers. It had a three stall garage below. The main floor had a two car garage and a workroom and above was a small four room apartment designed specifically for visitors and guests. Across the dirt road was a fifteen by fifteen shed that had the same architectural details and color as the main house and was used as a kennel for their three German Shepherd puppies.

When Conrad's divorce was final, he married Judith in a small simple sunset ceremony on their cement patio dock by the golden pond.

"Don't look so shocked dear."

"I…I…" said Beatrice still trying to comprehend what she had just heard.

"I want you to move into the house at the bottom of the hill, Beatrice. I couldn't find a way to help my only child, but I will be damned if I am going to sit back and not help his children."

"I don't know what to say?"

"What is there to say? It's the same house that your parents lived in when they first got married. It needs some work, I am not denying that. However, it is at least twice the size of this place and it has three bedrooms."

"Three?"

"It's right on the pond so there are plenty of things to keep your children busy."

"I…I…"

"Of course, you will have to pay a very small amount of rent to help pay for the property taxes. In addition, your husband will need to do some handyman work around my house and yard as well. Nothing too strenuous or difficult: mowing the lawn, gardening, washing and replacing the storm windows and screens that type of stuff. After a couple of years if it all works out, I'll sign the property over to you."

"I can't believe…I don't know what to say."

"You say, thank you."

"Thank you. I am going to have to talk with Butch."

"What's there to talk about dear? I have already put everything in motion. Give your notice here. You can move in next month."

"I can't make this decision without talking to my husband."

"Sure you can."

"No, I really can't. This is a big decision."

"Darling girl, let me give you some advice. You come from a long line of strong women on both sides of your family. Many of us were stronger then the men we married. I am sure that is the case with you and your husband. Sometimes you just need to take the bull by the horns and make a decision that you know in your heart is best long term for you and your family. Do you understand what I am saying to you dear?"

"I think so. But…"

"No buts. You just need to answer a very simple question. Do you want to take advantage of this wonderful and very generous opportunity or am I going to have to find other more appreciative tenants?"

The day after Carrie took her fourth consecutive first prize win in the Most Creative category in the annual WSSC Doll Carriage Parade thanks to the creativity and imagination of Uncle Cooper, Beatrice and Butch packed the last of their boxes into the sky blue Chevy Impala and drove to their new lives in the tiny house next to the golden pond.

The War To End All Wars

As she sat patiently at the four way intersection in her older model year dandelion yellow Volkswagen Super Beetle waiting for the traffic light to turn green, Beatrice stared at her reflection in the mirror that was attached to the driver's side visor and wondered just exactly when she got so old.

Accepting that there was very little chance of her fairy godmother finally showing up at this moment in time, Beatrice ran her fingers through her black hair and then flipped the visor back up against the round roof of her car in disgust. She then turned up the radio, hoping to be distracted by the latest top forty hit. As soon as the light turned green, she shifted into first, released the clutch and off she drove. Beatrice was on her way home from another intense meeting with her social worker Loretta Hazelwood.

Even though she had been going for what seemed like years, Beatrice always worked herself up into such a state of panic each time she was summoned to the local Aid to Families with Dependent Children office. She hated to explain herself and her actions in mind numbing detail as if she were guilty of some heinous crime. While she had long ago accepted the fact that Loretta Hazelwood was probably a nice woman who was simply carrying out the duties of her job to the best of her abilities, Beatrice often felt exhausted and emotionally violated each time she left Loretta. She used to say that she had less invasive cervical cancer screenings!

Beatrice used this windshield time to decompress and work all of her frustrations out before arriving at home. She would talk to herself, replay conversations that she has had over the last few weeks, but this time she would be much more forceful, witty, or pithier. This time, she would have the winning argument. Sometimes she would let her imagination run crazy and redesign the living room pretending that she had an army of craftsmen and an unlimited budget like those television shows that were starting to pop up. Most times however, she would just sing. In high school she sang alto and was the secretary of the choral society. Thanks to the cigarettes and the coffee she didn't have much of voice or the singing range she once had, but it felt good, well after a couple of deep coughs.

Eventually, she down shifted into third gear as she turned onto the half paved road that was named after her grandmother's second husband. As she slowly drove down the hill and into her stone dust driveway, Beatrice couldn't help but notice that summer was coming to a close. The tops of the maple and elm trees that surrounded the golden pond were in the beginning process of changing colors. It would still be several weeks before they were a blazed in magnificent red hues of a ripe watermelon, the bright yellow of a lemon and the orange of a succulent peach.

The end of the summer also symbolized the beginning of the fall birthday season for three of Beatrice's children. First on deck was Christopher, who was turning eleven. It was such a tough age for a boy and she was at a complete loss as to what to get him for a present.

"Hello?" she shouted as she entered the tiny house. "I'm back. Is anyone home?"

A quick zip through each of the rooms answered Beatrice's question. No one was home, which meant that we were more than likely up in the neighborhood at a friend's house. With the usual dread, she quickly flipped through the stack of mail that I left on the countertop. She put the bills that needed to be paid into her bill basket not wanting to think about how she was going to pay them and dumped the advertisements into the trash. Her heart leapt when she saw the postcard from Cooper at the bottom of the pile.

"Sis.

Money took me as far as El Paso, so it looks like I will be staying here for a while. Renting a room from a nice retired Mexican couple and working at a local café. I am sober and aim to stay that way. Tell Momma that I will call her soon.

Love, Cooper."

Beatrice smiled, lit a Kool, and sat in her perch and starred at her brother's handwriting for a few minutes. She missed her younger brother immensely. She was truly happy and relieved to learn that he was safe after not hearing from him these last few weeks. Make no bones about it; she still wanted to kill him. Cooper put everyone through a complete shit show before he disappeared and she was still trying to pick up some of the pieces.

This last performance was totally out of character. Sure he had been on drinking binges before, that wasn't the point. This last binge, there was something off...something not quite right with her brother. She didn't know what exactly set him off other than he had been binge drinking for about a month solid, which made him much more uninhibited, sloppy, and careless. In drunks past, Cooper would call Beatrice at all hours of the night talking ragtime about their childhood or people that he met over the years or his failed dreams or lost lovers. Sure it was equally frustrating and exhausting for Beatrice, but it was a small price to pay because she knew that he was relatively safe. After a few days, he would typically arrive by cab or sometimes via a stranger at her tiny house by the golden pond and sleep it off. He would take a few days to sober up and then try and rebuild / repair his relationship with Nana Flossie. This time was different. He didn't check in. And when Beatrice was able to track him down, Cooper was cold, curt, and distant.

She had seen him hit rock bottom before, but this last time was a new all time low. She could excuse the car accident, the small kitchen fire, even falling out of his apartment window on the second floor. He was drunk. Not in his right mind. It was a miracle that he emerged from each of those incidents without as much as a scratch or a bruise. What she couldn't excuse...couldn't forgive was the night that he stumbled into The Cottage, the family restaurant that Nana Flossie had worked at for as long as I can remember and began singing and dancing in the middle of the dining room during a busy dinner push. When the owner, Artie Papadopoulos with the help of Flossie tried to reason with Cooper and get him to leave quietly, Cooper responded with a violent shove which sent Artie ass over teacup crashing into a family table of six knocking food and guests to the floor. Flossie stood there shaking, crying and utterly humiliated, when the police arrived and cuffed her son. She wouldn't look him in the eye when they dragged him from the turmoil he created kicking and screaming some sort of guttural gibberish. It was Beatrice who bailed her brother out of jail the next day. Luckily Artie wanted to put the incident behind him and refused to press charges. That afternoon, Cooper emptied out his bank account, packed a suitcase and left town.

With a big exhale, Beatrice began to punch the familiar number into the telephone keypad. She still wasn't comfortable with the new phone that Fred had installed and missed the ease and the muscle memory familiarity of the dial. A couple rings and Nana Flossie picked up on the other end.

"Hello?"

"Hello Momma."

"Is that you Beatrice?"

"Yes Momma."

"Where have you been? I have been trying to call you for hours?"

"Sorry. I had an appointment."

"How was your meeting at the Welfare office this morning?"

"Who told you I went to the Welfare office?"

"Carrie."

I'm going to kill her!

"Oh?"

"You mustn't be mad at her. I must have called right after you left. I wanted to talk to you about Christopher's birthday before I had to go to my hair appointment. Now that I am back, I wished to God I never went. "

"Sorry to have missed you. What happened?"

"He's maimed me that's all."

"What?"

"I don't want to talk about it. The more I talk about it, the worse I feel. Let's just say that I'm never leaving my house again."

"What happened?"

"Nothing, dear. I just need to get my mind off of it. Tell me about you. How did you make out this morning?" Nana Flossie said trying to be as pleasant as possible.

"Fine. Fine. It wasn't any real big deal. Fairly routine. I just hate going down there, that's all."

"Well, what is it that you don't care for? What do you talk about? I have never been inside an office like that, Beatrice."

"Momma…"

"I am asking because I am genuinely interested, dear."

"It's nothing special. I sit with my social worker at her desk which is in the middle of a very busy office. We talk for about an hour. I just hate the way it makes me feel. Like I have done something wrong. It's humiliating. That's all."

"I don't know why you don't just go get a job and put all that nonsense behind you. When I left your father, I didn't get the chance to accept welfare. I went right to work."

Beatrice bit her tongue and refused to take the bait today. When it came to the subject of child rearing and the importance of the mother being home, Beatrice and her mother had polar opposite points of view. Over the years the pair has had some very heated conversations on the subject. More times than not, it resulted in a mutual cooling off period that often lasted several days. While both women shared an intense and complicated mother and daughter bond built on love and respect, it was fairly obvious to family members that there were times when the pair just didn't like one another.

"I am tired talking about me Momma. What happened today at your appointment?" asked Beatrice desperately trying to change the subject.

"I can't…I can't talk about it. I am just so upset." replied Flossie who was close to tears.

"Will you please tell me what happened?!!!"

"I can barely talk about it." Flossie replied dramatically. "I have been going to Mr. Ernie's Beauty Bar for years."

"Even before Mr. Ernie bought it from….what was his name again?"

"Louie."

"That's right. Mr. Louie."

"You know that I have a regularly standing weekly appointment for a wash and a set. And every month or so, I get a little color."

"An Apricot Rinse."

"Exactly. I haven't made any changes…"

"Has to be at least eleven years, since before Christopher was born."

"Yes. But not today! Mr. Ernie is getting a little too full of himself lately. Putting on airs…redecorating the beauty parlor. A little too fancy for Redstone Square, if you ask me. This morning was complete chaos. His normal receptionist Joanie was out sick today so naturally the phones were ringing off the hook. Mr. Erne was trying to answer them, wait on customers, and overseeing the person trying to hang the new and very expensive wallpaper in the bathroom. Not to mention cutting hair. He was trying to juggle too many things. I should have just gone home."

"It sounds like he had his hands full."

"On top of that he was also training the new shampoo girl. Lovely looking little thing…straight out of the vocational school. Had the most beautiful green eyes that I have ever seen on any one in my entire life. Her name was Heather. Didn't you want to name Carrie, Heather?"

"Yes. But I got tired of you saying 'Come hither, Heather.' So I dropped it."

"Oh, you know that I was only teasing you. Besides Carrie is such a stronger name. Don't you think so? I think so."

"Yes, Momma. So what happened?"

"Well Heather", continued Flossie, "Must have gotten confused with all the turmoil. And instead of using my apricot rinse, she decided to use mahogany instead!"

"What?"

"Yes. The little twit put a mahogany rinse in my hair!"

"Oh my God. What did you do?"

"What could I do?" shouted Flossie as she began to cry. "Mr. Fancy pants Ernie starts screaming and carrying on like a complete lunatic. The next thing you know he is swearing like a sailor and throwing his hair brushes. Heather breaks down in tears and quits on the spot. I am trying to hold it together as he makes this special shampoo in the hopes that it will rinse the color out. But that hardly worked. After about an hour or so, he decided to call it quits. He eventually wants to strip out the color, but my hair is so thin and brittle from the repeated washing that we need to give it a rest for a week or so...otherwise it could fall out. Can you believe it? I am sick to my stomach. I have never been a brunette in my life!"

Beatrice's heart broke for her mother. Flossie was always so fastidious about her appearance. "Oh Momma, I am so sorry. What are you going to do?"

"Not much I can do. I cannot let normal people see me like this. Not so soon after the troubles with your brother. They'll think that I have gone off the deep end! I have some vacation time due me, so I have already made arrangements to take the week off from work. I'll stay in. Be a recluse like Howard Hughes. If I have to go out, I will wear a hat and pray to God that I don't bump into anyone that I know!"

"I'll save the postcard for later!"

"Is there anything that I can do for you Momma?" Beatrice asked.

"Just say a prayer that I don't lose my hair. Let's talk about happier things. What do you have planned for Christopher's birthday?"

"I don't know yet Momma."

"Well, I think that we should do something special for him."

"That would be nice. What do you have in mind?"

"The circus is in town and I thought that it would be a nice night out for everyone. So I bought tickets for Tuesday night."

"Momma, that sounds like a great time. Thank you. When you say everyone…"

"Yes. I bought one for your husband."

"He has a name. His name is Fred, Momma."

"I bought him a ticket Beatrice. What more do you want from me?"

For the next few minutes, mother and daughter made all the necessary plans and arrangements and said their goodbyes. Beatrice hung up the phone, thankful that Flossie wanted to do something special for Christopher's birthday, hoping for it to be a throwback to happier times. She lit another cigarette and stared out her window looking at the house on the hill that once belonged to her grandmother. It had been four years since Gammie passed. The house sold twice. Once to a very unhappy couple who thought that the golden pond would help add some much needed tranquility to their lives and again three months ago to Joshua and Ellen Sutcliff. While her new recently transplanted from Southern California neighbors were extremely nice and accommodating, it was sometimes hard for Beatrice to see other people enjoying her grandmother's home. Beatrice felt nostalgic. She remembered the grand birthday parties that they used to have back in the day for Christopher.

Christopher shared his birthday with Great Uncle Walter, who was married to Gammie's sister Rosemary and for some forgotten reason everyone called him Chief. Even though the boys were seventy years apart, Uncle Chief made it quite clear that he had no intention of sharing his birthday with a 'Little Whippersnapper'. Gammie felt that it was a true blessing and as such needed to be celebrated. So, she used it as an excuse and as a catalyst for a combined annual family celebration, which became bigger and more elaborate with each passing year. The two yards were covered in streamers, banners, balloons, and other festive birthday decorations. There were dedicated stations set up for desserts, appetizers, chips and dips, salads of every description and of course the triple grill section which was usually manned by Butch and a couple of neighborhood friends. They cooked hot dogs, hamburgers, chicken, steak tips and kielbasa until the heat became too unbearable or until the men needed a little down time in order to sober up. Scattered about were trash cans filled with ice and cold water that served as giant coolers for cans of beer and soda. Naturally there was a well stocked bar just in case someone needed something with a little kick.

Beatrice used to make certain that there were plenty of activities for the kids, face painting, a small traveling petting zoo and pony rides. And of course there were fishing poles and life jackets for anyone provided they were accompanied by an adult who wanted to take the row boats or canoes out on the pond.

They were long, fun packed days filled with music, laughter, jokes, and stories told by aunts, uncles, cousins, and distant relatives from all sides of the families. Neighbors and close friends were encouraged to bring their families and a dish to share. The more the merrier. There was music and cake and presents and the day typically ended with an elaborate fireworks display shooting off of the dock and into the golden pond.

The parties stopped shortly after Gammie suffered her second stroke, which left the right side of her body paralyzed. She didn't feel too blessed after that. Christopher was forced to become accustomed to a much more low key immediate family celebration, which he will tell us to this day was a rough and very difficult adjustment. Excited with anticipation,

Beatrice decided to go meet the school bus to give Christopher the good news.

Aside from Beatrice's threat of skinning us alive if we made any mention of Nana Flossie's new hair color, it was one of those far and few occasions where we looked like every other family enjoying our time at "The Greatest Show On Earth." Between the high wire acts and the monkeys riding motorcycles, Fred opened up his usually locked wallet and plied each of us with popcorn, programs and other assorted treats. He strategically positioned himself between Beatrice and Nana Flossie making sure that he divided his time equally between both women. He did his best to ooze charm and shamelessly and harmlessly flirt with both. Every now and then he turned his attention to us, making sure that we had enough to eat and that we were enjoying ourselves. The show in our row was almost as entertaining as Princess Pricilla Bellini and her astonishing acrobatic polar bears.

When the show ended and most of the audience simultaneously headed towards the exits in the back, Fred left us in our seats and navigated the crowd heading in the opposite direction towards the stage floor, where the roustabouts were busy preparing for the next show.

"What is he a salmon?" Nana Flossie questioned Beatrice. "Beatrice, what is he doing?"

"I don't know Momma."

"Why is he doing that?"

"I honestly do not know. I have learned that sometimes with him, it's just easier to ask after the fact."

"That's no way to live."

"I know Momma."

We watched as he talked intently with one of the crewmen, who threw his hands up and shook his head no before finally walking away. Looking dejected, Fred eventually made his way back to our seats.

"What was that all about Freddie?" asked Beatrice.

"I offered that guy half a C-note, to let Christopher hold a monkey. I guess fifty bucks doesn't go as far as it used to. Come on we don't want to miss our train."

"How did you meet your husband?" asked Fred as he paid the train conductor for our tickets home.

"Oh, that's a long story; no one is really interested in hearing about that." half flirted Nana Flossie as she used her compact mirror to make sure that her dark hair was fully covered under her burgundy wool felt flapper style Cloche hat.

"Momma, you look fine. Nothing is showing." Beatrice reassured her mother as she cupped her hand on Flossie's. "Go one and tell the story."

"It really isn't much of a story." Flossie began. "Back when I was in school."

"When exactly was that Nana?" I asked.

"Never mind you. During the summer months, my sister Elsie and I used to work at a restaurant called Duke's Dew Drop Inn. It was a small place directly across the pond. Gosh it went out of business a long time ago, but I am sure that you can still see the building from your mother's bedroom window."

"It's a sandwich shop now." Kevin added.

"Well it was a million years ago Kevin, so I am sure it has changed several times. Anyway, my father used to drop us off and pick us up on his way to and from work."

"What did he do for work?" asked Christopher.

"He worked for the railroad. He used to drive big trains like this one here." Beatrice added.

"Back in those days, Gammie and her husband used to travel a lot. And sometimes they would leave Jack to fend for himself."

"Really?" asked Carrie.

"Darling, your grandfather Jack was quite a ballplayer when he was younger. I like to think you got that from him. He played a lot of summer baseball so he wasn't able to travel that much. But Gammie made sure that he had plenty of food and she made arrangements for him to have all of his meals at Dukes."

"That sounds cool." said Kevin.

"He used to row his boat across the pond a couple of times a day."

"What did he look like, Nana?" Carrie asked.

"Ooo, he was movie star handsome. He looked like a sheik that stepped off the silver screen. Skin was tanned and golden. The first time I laid eyes on him he was dressed in white linen pants and shirt. He also had on a sleeveless white cable knit tennis sweater with a wide crew neck and a hunter green and blue v-shaped band. They were very fashionable back then. His hair was the color of coal and I lost myself in his eyes. They were the perfect combination of corn flower and sapphire."

"He sounds like he was a good looking fella." Fred added trying his best to keep part of the conversation.

"He was." blushed Flossie. "I knew he would be trouble the minute I met him. I married him that fall."

"Was it true you used to live in our house?" I asked.

"Yes. Your mother and your uncles Joe and Cooper were born there."

"Wow." said Christopher who was having trouble wrapping his head around the concept.

"What line of work was Jack in?" asked Fred.

"Oh, this and that. He played professional baseball for a couple of years."

"For what team?" Carrie asked.

"What position?" I asked.

"Pitcher."

"Does he have a rookie card?" Kevin chimed in.

"Nothing like that honey. Back then he was minor league ball. The equivalent of a double A team."

"Oh." replied a disappointed Kevin.

"He did very well. He got a lot of playing time. He just never got the chance to play in the majors."

"Why not Nana? Wasn't he good enough?" asked Christopher.

"He was my handsome boy. He was very gifted that way. He just liked to drink more." said a sad Flossie. "So after he washed out, your great grandmother decided that he needed to get back up on his feet quickly and the best way to do that was be his own man. So she bought him a business and we all move to Salem, a couple of streets from Dead Horse Beach."

"What type of business was it?" asked Fred.

"A liquor store."

Fred tried very hard to suppress his laughter.

"Believe me. The irony is not lost on me either."

Beatrice smiled and just shook her head.

"He would come home late every night, with presents for me and the kids."

"That sounds nice." said Fred.

"It was. I just would have preferred that he remembered to buy milk and bread every now and then."

"I remember that he used to wake us up to show us what he bought us." Beatrice said fondly. "Do you remember the time we had the lobster races in the kitchen?"

"Lobster races?" I asked looking for more clarification.

"My dad knew that I liked lobster so he would bring them home all the time. Joe, Cooper, and I used to race them on the kitchen floor to see whose was faster before we cooked them."

"We didn't have money for the electric, but we certainly had money for lobster."

"Oh Momma."

Sensing that the conversation was getting a little heavy, I asked, "How long did you live in Salem?"

"Not too long. As you can imagine, your grandfather consumed most of the profits. One August night, he had come home from work feeling no pain. It was a mess. So after he passed out, I packed up the kids and we left."

"When was this?" Fred asked.

"Nineteen forty eight."

"You left him? Wow. That was pretty ballsy for a woman for that time." said a genuinely impressed Fred. "Excuse me. I meant to say that was pretty impressive. You never heard about a woman leaving her husband back then."

"Thank you. It took us three different cabs to get us to my sister Elsie's house."

"Where did you live?" asked Christopher.

"That's just it Christopher. We had no place to go, so Nana split us up to go stay with other relatives while she figured out what she was going to do." said Beatrice trying to mask a condescending tone.

"Who did you stay with Mom?" asked Kevin.

"My Uncle Henry and his wife Maude."

"Have we met them?" asked Christopher.

"No honey. They weren't too nice to Mommy growing up."

"What would you have had me do Beatrice? We couldn't stay with him. He was dangerous." snapped Nana Flossie in a loud stage whisper.

"Anything was better than where I ended up. They treated me like I was the hired help."

"There is nothing wrong with children helping out around the house."

"I was barely seven and she had me doing the laundry."

"Why am I just finding out about this now?" asked Flossie.

"You left me with them for over a year. I begged you. I begged you to take me with you."

"Beatrice, I didn't want to break us up, but there wasn't any place for you. Thank God, I had a big family. I can't tell you how many couches I slept on or how many double shifts I pulled so that I could send money for you kids. What little I had left, I saved so that I might be able to afford an apartment. I still managed to make sure that we got the chance to spend Sunday afternoons together. I am sorry that I was such a rotten mother. I was just doing the best that I could with what I had." said a tearful Nana Flossie. "I just needed to make sure that you and your brothers were safe."

"Fuck! I walked right into that one! When will I learn?"

Beatrice reached for Flossie's hands and took them in her own. "Momma, I am sorry. Let's not do this. Let's not fight. Let's call a truce. We were having such a nice time thanks to you and Freddie. Let's not end on a sad note. Ok? I'm sorry. I love you very much."

"I love you too dear."

The women hugged for a long time until the train pulled into our station. We quickly disembarked and one by one said our thank you's, kissed Nana Flossie good bye, and took our seats in Bea's Traveling Kitchen, which Fred had taken to driving full time since his beloved grey Pontiac with the missing muffler shit the bed. Fred carefully backed the truck out of the parking space as Beatrice and Nana Flossie said their goodbyes.

"Honestly. A mail truck?" said Nana Flossie as she rolled her eyes.

"Don't start Momma." replied Beatrice half smiling. "It's only a truck...an ugly truck grant you. But it makes him happy."

"What's he done to make you happy, Beatrice?"

"Momma..." before Beatrice could finish her thought, there was a loud grinding noise coming from the engine of the truck.

"Oh my goodness." said Flossie.

"That doesn't sound good." said Beatrice as both women walked over to the truck. Fred had already jumped out and opened the engine hood and began tinkering.

"Try it again!" he yelled to me. "Did you try it?"

"Yes."

"Are you sure?"

"Yes. It's not working."

"Damn. I thought that would work."

"Freddie, what's wrong?" Beatrice questioned.

"Anything that I can do to help?" asked Nana Flossie.

"Nah." Fred replied closing the engine hood loudly. "Wish there was. It's the transmission."

"That sounds serious." said a concerned Nana Flossie.

"Not really. I've noticed that it had been slipping for the last couple of weeks. And when I took it in for an estimate, the guy wanted an outrageous amount of money to fix it. It's nothing that I can't handle. Besides it will give me a chance to show the boys how to do some repair work. They should know how to do these things."

"Well, I am parked over here. We will be a little tight, but I think we can manage." said Nana Flossie asserting control over the situation.

"Oh. No thank you, Flossie. We are all set. We can still get home."

"How? Fred, you just said that your transmission was broken."

"Well it is. The car won't go forward, but it still works in reverse."

"You're not going to drive all the way home in reverse?!!"

"Oh, yeah. We'll be fine. Come on Bea, hop in." said Fred as he hopped in the truck. "Thanks Floss. We had a swell time tonight."

"Beatrice! You can't be serious."

Beatrice hugged her mother tightly. "We'll be fine. I promise. Thank you for a wonderful time tonight."

"Beatrice, you can't be serious. You're going to get yourselves killed."

"Momma, we will be fine."

"Beatrice, I am begging you. Let me at least take the kids with me and I can follow you. Kids! Kids! Come get in my car."

"Stay where you are!" Beatrice ordered. "We will be fine Momma. I promise you. Thank you again for a wonderful time. I love you."

"Beatrice. Please."

"I will call you in the morning, Momma." said Beatrice as she took her spot in the truck. "Bye."

And we backed our way down the street.

The ride home from the train station was nerve-racking as Fred maneuvered the neon turquoise blue former mail truck backwards through various side roads in an attempt to avoid any potential contact with a passing patrol car. He tried to convince us that the situation wasn't all that dire and that he had it all under control. Between the reverse auxiliary lighting that he installed last week and the yellow glow coming from the revolving safety utility light that he mounted on the roof, he claimed to have had plenty of light, provided he shut off the front headlights.

"I just need an hour or so with the transmission tomorrow morning and everything will be right as rain." He said trying to convince us.

Each of us could see that Beatrice was stressed and anxious from the way that she rocked back and forth in her seat, letting out loud gasps with each swerve of the wheel. It seemed quite possible to me that she could throw an aneurysm at any moment. Trying to relax his wife, Fred pushed his eight-track tape of *The Best Of Benny Hill* into the stereo system and blared the music as loud as he could. Before the second verse of *Ernie (The Fastest Milkman In The West)* could play, Beatrice ejected the tape and tossed it out her window. From the look on her face, Fred knew better than to say anything. We finished the rest of the ride in relative silence until we reached our road and backed down the hill into our stone dust driveway. We quickly exited the truck and made a bee line for the safety of our house. Beatrice stayed outside with Fred because as she put it, she needed to discuss something with him.

It was one of those rare times in their marriage where the pair actually fought without any alcohol being involved. The screaming match went on for exactly eight minutes before a red-faced Fred shouted "I don't need any more of your shit! I am tired of you and this whole fucking mess!"

"The only fucking mess around here is you!!!" Beatrice shot back.

"Fuck you!"

"No. Fuck you!"

With the vein clearly showing on his forehead, Fred took an angry step towards Beatrice.

"Go ahead Freddie." screamed Beatrice matching his ferocity and intensity. "I fucking dare you!"

"Ah. You're not fucking worth it!" he spat. "I'm outta here."

"Good. Go!"

With that, he hopped back into the truck, backed up the hill and sped away. Once his flashing yellow light disappeared completely from her view, Beatrice dropped to her knees. She embedded her palms into her eyes hoping that the pressure would hold back the tears that she refused to shed for him. Beatrice stayed there for the next several minutes taking some deep cleansing breaths desperately trying to keep her heart from beating out of her chest. Eventually, she stood up and calmly entered the house and did something that she never did. She locked the front door.

Back in those days, it wasn't uncommon to be awoken by Beatrice screaming or the sound of breaking glass. Tonight was different. It was Carrie who was screaming. "Leave him alone you fat piece of shit!"

I rolled out of my bed, put on a t-shirt and rushed up the basement stairs taking two at a time. As I stood in the mahogany stained door frame that led from the kitchen into the living room, my brain seemed to have a difficult time processing all of the information that was in front of me. The usually immaculately clean colonial multi-colored oval hand braided rug was now littered with the remains of shattered glass, pottery, and picture frames. A familiar wrought iron patio chair that usually sat on the deck just off of the living room was now inside and toppled on its back, its right front leg was no longer straight. The room had the chill of a cold night wind which entered the now chaotic space freely and no longer inhibited by the former pair of double hung windows which once faced the deck. There were shards of glass that resembled the broken teeth of a jack-o-lantern where the window panes used to be, each clinging to their frames refusing to yield. What was left of the battered and broken honey pine colored louvered shutters that once offered some decorative privacy clung to hinges that were barely attached to the window molding. The early American tea cart that Beatrice methodically rubbed each Saturday morning with Old English Furniture polish no long held its place in front of the windows. It was also tipped on its side; a deep gouge now ran across its once pristine surface. In the center of the living room stood Fred who had Kevin by the throat with his right hand, lifting him slightly off the ground.

Kevin's eyes bulged and flashed with panic as his face turned red and he gasped for breath. Carrie tried desperately to pry Fred's herculean grip from our brother's throat.

"Where's your fucking smart mouth now, tough guy?" Fred barked in a tone totally devoid of reason.

"No. No. No. Not my Kevin! Stop Freddie! For God's sake stop!" screamed Beatrice as she frantically yanked on Fred's left wrist with both of her hands desperately trying to stop the serrated knife in his hand from getting any closer to her son's throat.

"Let go! Let go of him!" screamed Christopher with tears rolling down his face pounding both of his fists into Fred's back.

Instinctively, and with a most uncharacteristic athleticism, I dove at Fred, taking him out at the knees, sending him crashing onto the coffee table, which collapsed and splintered under his sudden weight. Kevin, now free, dropped to his hands and knees gasping and coughing as he tried desperately to regain his breath.

While on his back, Fred flailed and wildly kicked his feet managing to catch me square in the jaw igniting fireworks of pain. "Shit!" I shouted as a rolled onto my side holding my throbbing jaw.

Using a speed that you wouldn't think was possible for a man of his girth; Fred rose quickly to his feet, just as Carrie pounced on his back locking her arms as tight as she could around his large neck…trying her best to put him in a choke hold.

"Get the fuck offa me!" he shouted through gritted teeth as he dug his fingernails deep into Carrie's arms. From the look on her face we could see that Carrie was in a tremendous amount of pain but she refused to give him the satisfaction of screaming out. Instead, she squeezed harder. Fred tried twisting his shoulders back and forth like a spastic agitator in a washing machine, hoping that the momentum would set him free. No such luck. Carrie more determined than ever, squeezed even harder. It was getting difficult for him to breathe and Fred's normal wheezing was even more pronounced.

"You fucking little bitch."

Once he realized that he didn't have the leverage, he changed tactics and began to charge backwards slamming Carrie hard into the corner of the mahogany molding of the broken windows.

"Aaaaaaarrrrrg!" screamed Carrie as the pain in her shoulder made her release her grip and fall off his back.

With a vindictive determination, Fred picked Carrie up off the floor by her tee shirt and shorts and threw her out the broken windows making sure that she cut her arms and legs on the protruding broken glass.

"I hate you! I hate you! I hate you!" screamed Christopher swinging the broken leg of the coffee table at Fred unwavering in his desire to bat clean up. Fred merely responded with a backhand which sent Christopher flying backwards over the tea cart and into one of the end tables that flanked the couch.

"Christopher!!!! No!!!!!!!!!!!!!!!!!" screamed Beatrice frantically.

Kevin and I simultaneously circled Fred. Each of us doing our best to ignore pain of walking on broken glass in our bare feet...hoping to find an opening that would allow us to inflict some pain of our own.

"You tough guys think you can handle this?" sneered Fred intensely. "Come on you pussies. I'll show you what's for!"

With that Fred threw a left hook and connected with Kevin's nose, which immediately erupted with blood. A dazed and confused Kevin dropped to his knees, just as Fred followed up with overpowering right cross which knocked Kevin flat to the floor. My right fist made contact with Fred's left eye, but it did little to slow him down. Instead he promptly returned the blow with repeated jabs to my face and stomach. I didn't last long.

We heard the distant sirens as Beatrice lunged at Fred's face. Before she could connect, he grabbed her by the wrists and held her arms up over her head.

"Get the fuck out of here you bastard." she spat squirming in vain to free herself.

"Make me." he roared back.

"What do you want? Just tell me what you want and get the fuck out of here and leave us alone."

"I want some respect."

"You have to earn it!!!!"

"I do, damn it!"

"How? By coming in here in the middle of the night and beating on me and my kids? By destroying my house? That make you feel like a big man, asshole? Is that how you earn respect?"

"I want some acknowledgement of all the work that I do around here!"

"Work around here? Are you kidding me??? When was the last time you actually did anything around here?"

"I shouldn't have to put up with all the shit I get from you and those bastards of yours. Who the fuck do you think you are? Locking me out of my own house?"

"This isn't your house asshole. It's mine!" Beatrice screeched just as she managed to knee Fred in the crotch with a ferocity that surprised even her. Fred let her go and instinctively covered his genitalia hoping for some relief, just as Beatrice with her hands clasped together hit him in his chin with all of her might. He spat blood and a tooth on her hardwood floor.

Both cried out in pain as the sounds of the sirens got louder.

"My tooth. You Bitc..."

"No. No more!" Beatrice commanded in a defiant tone as she picked up the serrated knife that he had dropped earlier. "You will not talk to me like that anymore!"

Coughing, Fred crawled to the doorway that led to the living room and used the frame to steady himself as he stood up. The police sirens grew louder still.

"I'm gonna..."

"You are going to do nothing but get the hell out of here and leave me and my kids alone!" Beatrice growled pointing the knife at her husband in a voice hoarse from screaming. "I don't want to see or hear from you ever again. Do you understand me?"

"Who the hell do you think you are?" Fred swore as he took a step towards her.

"Look what you have done. Everything you touch turns to shit!"

Fred stopped in his tracks and glared at Beatrice with a look of pure hatred. He opened his mouth to say something, but Beatrice quickly cut him off.

"I'm not afraid of you Fred. You can't hurt me anymore than you already have. Look what you have done. Look."

His facial expression relaxed slightly in its intensity as he shook his head in disbelief. With a tear in his eye, Fred gave Beatrice one last look hoping that he might be able to somehow salvage the situation. When he finally realized that there was no recovering from this, Fred waved dismissively at Beatrice and left.

The knife that Beatrice had been holding white knuckled in her hand dropped to the ground. Her whole world went black and she collapsed on the floor.

Here Come The Judge. Here Come The Judge

Friday afternoon Fred had a standing four fifteen appointment with Doctor Penney Matthews, DDS at the newly refurbished offices of Smiles of Perfection Dental Practice in Peabody, Massachusetts. Doctor Matthews had been working on Fred's long neglected mouth for the past several months. Today was the day that she was going to begin his second root canal, just as soon as she cleared some debris from the hole left by his missing posterior bicuspid. She had just tested his gum line with her periodontal probe and mouth mirror to confirm that the Novocain had worked its numbing magic and asked her assistant Tess to administer the nitrous oxide. Just as Fred had finished his sixth inhale of the gas and a euphoric and relaxed feeling took hold of his large frame, four police officers entered the small office, read him his rights as they cuffed him and quietly escorted him from the premises. The police officers swiftly exited the front lobby of the office building with Fred where they were met by an additional pair of officers standing at the ready outside of their cruiser. Clearly they were expecting Fred to put up more of a fight. Instead, he just quietly got into the back seat of the police car and they all drove away with the sirens off.

Because the officers took so long to process his paperwork, Fred was not able to have his bail posted and spent the weekend as a guest of the Peabody Police Department. First thing Monday morning, Fred and his court appointed attorney Charles Hargreaves were standing in front of his honorable William C. Niewenhouse impatiently waiting for his arraignment to begin. To their right stood Jerry Cloutier, an assistant prosecutor from the Essex County District Attorney's office. We all sat in the row behind him. Beatrice made sure that we were all dressed in our Sunday best, blazers, ties and penny loafers for the boys. It was one of those rare times outside a funeral that Beatrice and Carrie were both wearing dresses. Kevin was fidgety and pulling on the collar of his dress shirt indicating that it and the tie were way too tight for his liking. With one fluid motion, Beatrice loudly snapped her fingers and used her index finger to point at Kevin. Even though she wore a pair of big black sunglasses in an attempt to hide her black eye, everyone in the row could feel the death stare. Kevin quietly sunk back in his chair.

I was truly disheartened when I learned that the reality of district court was nothing at all like the dramatic and glamorous court room dramas as portrayed on television by shows like Petrocelli or Kate McShane. Once the bailiff announced the docket and the list of charges, the prosecutor, read from a yellow legal pad and outlined the events of Fred's late night visit. He gave a very clinical interpretation of the events only stumbling over his words once or twice. Something that I am sure that Anne Meara as Kate McShane would never do! At first I thought that perhaps it was part of some grand and elaborate plan of the prosecutor to feign incompetence to lull the defense into a false sense of security. And then I realized that the prosecutor was just having trouble reading his own handwriting.

When it was his turn, the defense attorney gave a similar performance while countering each of the prosecutor's points which prompted Judge Niewenhouse who was leaning on his elbows, to take off his glasses and massage the bridge of his nose.

"Thank you." said the very tired Judge talking into his hands. "Thank you, gentlemen. Good job. It seems that we have polar opposite views of the facts of this case. How unusual. In cases like this, I usually like to hear from the defendant. Mr. McMullen, why don't you tell me what happened in your own words, sir."

"Excuse me, sir." replied Fred sounding extremely professional.

"The story. In your own words. Tell me what happened that night."

"The night?"

"Why are we here Mr. McMullen?"

"Well Judge, I am not sure why we are here. Beatrice, that's my wife, and I had a bit of a disagreement after spending a great night with the kids at the circus. You ever been to the circus, Judge?'

"Each and every day, sir."

Fred stopped for a second stared at Judge Niewenhouse and then once he understood the judge's comment replied, "That's pretty funny, sir."

"Thank you. You may continue."

"So we get home from a great time. The kids go into the house to get ready for bed and Beatrice and I stay outside to have a quick cigarette. And that's when she lets into me."

"What was she upset about?"

"You know, I honestly don't know. Sometimes she can get a little picky."

"You don't remember what it was about?"

"No sir. It couldn't have been too important."

"So then what happened next?"

"Nothing…really sir. She went into the house and I decided that I probably should give her some time to cool down so I went for a drive."

"Where did you go?"

"Nowhere special sir. I just figured that I needed to give her some space. She is a wonderful person with a lot on her plate. Sometimes the stress just gets to her."

"So you have this disagreement about something and you decide to give her some space and go for a drive. So then what happened next?"

"Well, I get back a few hours later and discover that Beatrice has accidently locked the front door. We live in such a great neighborhood that we never lock the door."

"Except that night."

"Except that night. Right. So I went around back to see if the side door was opened. And that was locked too."

"So what did you do?"

"I took out my keys to unlock the door, but I dropped them."

"You dropped them?"

"Yes sir."

"Well, why didn't you simply pick them up?" asked the curious Judge.

"That's not always that easy, Judge."

"Why not?"

"I have arthritis in both of my hands." explained Fred as he held up hands making sure to bend each of his finger tips so that they resembled enormous backscratchers. "Most days they don't bother me, but this night, they were really acting up."

"This night? The night in question?"

"Yes, Judge."

"So then what happened?"

"Well I couldn't pick the keys up. I tried to knock on the door, but there wasn't any answer. I tried waiting for a little bit, but I needed to use the bathroom pretty badly. So I tried knocking a little louder."

"And then what happened?"

"Well, when she didn't answer the door, I thought that there might be something terribly wrong."

"Something terribly wrong? Like what?"

"I am not sure Judge. It was just a feeling. Have you ever gotten one of those feelings?

"No, Mr. McMullen, I cannot say that I have. So then what happened?"

"Well, I was worried about my wife's safety, so I threw one of our patio chairs through the window."

"You threw a chair through the window? May I assume you checked to see if the window was locked?"

"No sir...I mean yes sir. Of course sir. We just replaced a lot of the windows."

"So what happened next?"

"Well as you can imagine, Beatrice was pretty upset."

"Naturally. But you were relieved to see that she was fine."

"Yes, Judge."

"Then what happened?"

"She was pretty steamed about the window. And then she started yelling, so I thought it would be best if I left."

"Why is that, Mr. McMullen?"

"Well, her yelling woke the kids up, you see and I don't think that it's right to argue in front of the children. So I left."

"You just left?"

"Yes sir."

"And then what happened?"

"I found myself here, sir."

"That's quite a story, Mr. McMullen."

"Gospel truth, Judge." said Fred as he held up his right hand.

Judge Niewenhouse folded his hands together and shook his head. "Clearly Mr. McMullen there is more to your story. However, I am loathe to waste this courts time on domestic disputes. Therefore…"

"Excuse me, sir." said Beatrice softly as she stood up. "Excuse me your honor."

"And you are…"

"Beatrice McMullen, your honor. And these are my children…" she waved us up out of our seats. "I realize that you have a very important job to do. And…" Beatrice cleared her throat and prayed that the Judge did not see her knees knock. "And I hate to take time away from your day. However, I was hoping that I might be able to show you some photographs."

"Photographs of what, Mrs. McMullen?"

"From that night, sir."

"Your honor, I have to object."

"You should Mr. Hargreaves. But I am going to overrule you. Mr. Cloutier, have you seen these photographs?"

"No, your honor. I have not."

"Hmm. Curious. Mrs. McMullen, would you please bring them to me?"

Beatrice removed a manila envelope from her purse. Her heart raced as she entered the gallery and crossed what felt like over a mile to Judge Niewenhouse.

"Please don't trip. Please don't trip!" Beatrice prayed to herself.

"Here you go sir." Beatrice said almost completely tongue-tied.

"Thank you." said Judge Niewenhouse as he took the envelope. After opening it, he carefully poured a dozen or so Polaroid pictures onto his desk. His eyes light up as he studied each picture.

Beatrice was extremely pissed when Butch first bought that Polaroid Swinger Camera for Carrie. She thought it was too extravagant of a gift outside of Christmas. She knew deep down that Butch was just trying to buy his daughter's affections so soon after their separation. Nonetheless, that night she was thankful that it was there when the paramedics revived her. She snapped pictures of the damage done to the house and more importantly she snapped pictures of the damage done to us. She took shots of the Carrie being loaded into the ambulance, of the doctors splinting Christopher's arm, stitching Carrie's leg and arms and of the bruises left on my face and on Kevin's throat. These were images that she would never forget, but wanted photographic proof just in case.

"These are pretty disturbing photographs Mrs. McMullen." said Judge Niewenhouse as he looked up.

"It was worse to have been there your honor." said Beatrice as she took off her sunglasses revealing that her right eye was purple and swollen shut.

"Wow. Alright. Let the record show that I find that there …"

"Excuse me again your honor."

"What is it now Mrs. McMullen?"

"I don't want to press charges."

"What?"

"I don't want to press charges."

"May I ask why?"

"I don't want to."

"Well, what is it exactly you do want, Mrs. McMullen?" asked Judge Niewenhouse who was obviously getting angry.

"I want…I want you to make him leave us alone."

"Excuse me?"

"Locking him up would kill him. I don't want that. Even after all he has done, I know that I don't want that. But I can't be around him anymore. It's just not good. It's not healthy. I don't want him near me. I don't want him near my children. I don't want him near my home. If you can get him to agree to that, then I won't press any charges."

The Judge gave Beatrice a look of disbelief and turned his attention to Fred. "Mr. McMullen, while I am sure that I do not understand your wife's decision, I need to ask you if this is something that you feel as though you can abide by."

Fred stood there for a few minutes dumfounded before he said, "Ok. But I will need to stop over to get my things."

"Perhaps, I am not making myself clear here sir. You are ordered to stay away."

Pointing to a pair of large matching orange duffel bags that Kevin and I held up, Beatrice said "I brought most of your clothes. I have washed them, pressed them and folded them. Just let me know where you end up and I will send you the rest of your things."

"This is a very generous offer Mr. McMullen. I want you to think long and hard before you answer. Are you willing to stay away?"

All eyes were on Fred who stood quietly like a deer in the headlights. After what seemed like an eternity, he sheepishly answered "Yes."

"Good answer."

"Officer, would you please make sure that Mr. McMullen stays here until Mrs. McMullen and her children leave the courthouse? So unless either of you has any further business here to discuss involving this case…"

"No your honor. Thank you your honor." smiled Beatrice.

"Good luck Mrs. McMullen. Case dismissed."

Reality Check

LJ Lawyers Up

Christopher was pushing his late model Honda Accord as fast as he could, taking each turn through the familiar New Hampshire roads at slightly over the speed limit. My last meeting of the day ran over resulting in a late start. Once you add in traffic as a result of construction on a key back road and an accident on the opposite side of the highway causing a lag due to rubbernecking onlookers it meant that we were ten minutes late for our meeting at the office of Louisa A. Nickels Attorney and Counselor at Law. With each sharp turn, Beatrice who was in the back seat blessed herself with the sign of the cross and said a short novena, while I tried my best to listen to a pointless conference call which was cutting in and out on my cell phone.

A couple of months had passed since our adventure at number 24 Oak Ridge Terrace. Carrie had negotiated for the better part of three weeks with Donny Goodinson before finally agreeing to a sum that left both parties feeling somewhat comfortable. Luckily, Christopher had found the deed among all of Fred's papers and with the help of Francis from Louisa's office; we were all overjoyed to hear that the deed had come back clean and that the sale could go through as scheduled.

With a light screech, Christopher pulled into the only parking space available outside of the two-story building which housed her humble law offices.

"Thank you Mario Andretti." snapped Beatrice as she freed herself from the backseat.

"If we left when we were supposed to..." snapped Christopher.

"I get it. It's all my fault. I've already apologized fifteen times on the way up! You need to let it go." I snapped. "Let's just get upstairs and get this thing started."

"You two go ahead of me. I need a cigarette." explained Beatrice as she swooped her signature Kool into her mouth.

"Ma. We don't have time."

"Christopher. I have been trapped in the backseat of that race car for over fifty minutes. I saw my life flash before my eyes on three separate occasions. And it wasn't pretty. My nerves are shot. I am having a few drags to center myself before I go inside. As I see it, you can both stand here and keep me company, or you can go upstairs, make apologies and get the meeting started. Which is it going to be?"

Christopher and I opened the door and went up the stairs leading to Louisa's office.

"I thought so." muttered Beatrice as she searched the bottom of her pocketbook and eventually found her red disposable butane lighter. Cupping her hands to protect the flame, she tried a few times before the empty lighter gave off its final flame which was just enough to light her smoke. She took a long satisfying pull before eventually releasing the blue grey smoke. Simultaneously, all of the tension in her body seemed to release. She took another puff and checked out her reflection in the passenger side window of her son's car. She was wearing a navy and white horizontal striped shirt with a boat collar, matching blue pedal pusher pants and her signature bright white Keds Champion canvas sneakers. Her round tortoise shell sunglasses complemented her face and she was slightly embarrassed that she so admired the haircut MaryAnn gave her this morning thanks to a last minute cancelation. She took another puff and smiled at the small gold studs in her ears.

Growing up in the predominately Irish neighborhood with her aunts, uncles and cousins, it was made very clear to her at an early age that only certain types of girls pierced their ears. Still, it didn't stop her from wanting them. She went so far as to save her babysitting money so that she could buy a self-piercing set when she first started high school. Unfortunately, her "self-mutilation" plans were foiled when one of her jealous cousins ratted her out to Nana Flossie. There was hell to pay that night. So on Beatrice's fortieth birthday I surprised her with a trip to the mall to get her ears pierced. She could still hear Nana Flossie's voice repeating in her head "Cheap. Cheap. Cheap."

Before she could take another drag, she was approached by a beautiful older woman with poker straight hair that was dyed in shades of indigo, eggplant, and violet. It was pulled back into a high pony tail with face framing bangs. The woman was wearing an impeccably tailored blue Chanel suit and red high heels. She had a white silk power blouse and an all too familiar silver fork necklace with each of the tines delicately hammered so that they now curled outward.

"How are you Lou?" asked Beatrice.

"Sorry I am late hon. It's been a hell of day and court ran late."

"No worries. We just got here ourselves. Traffic."

"Hey. Can I bum one of those from you?"

"Sure thing." responded Beatrice as she pulled her cigarette pack out and handed it to Louisa. "Lighter bit the dust so you are going to have to light it old school."

Beatrice handed her cigarette to Louisa who took it and touched the tip of her own cigarette. Louisa loudly exhaled.

"OOOOOOOh menthol." Louisa said with great satisfaction. "God, I needed this. Do you remember when smoking was glamorous? We'd all be sitting around a large dining table…stuffed from an incredible meal. And then people would begin to light up? I loved the after dinner smoke."

"For me it was the first one with the morning coffee." reminisced Beatrice.

"And everyone had all the smoking accessories. I had inherited a fourteen carat gold cigarette case from my grandmother. It was striped with double inlay silver circles." Louisa said laughing. "Gosh I thought I was really something. So naturally I had to have a lighter made by Alluma."

"Alluma?"

"It was made by a Swiss company that specialized in high end luxurious lighters. All the stars had them. Mine, had this wonderful golden lacquered lizard finish. It was very chichi."

"Sounds it. What happened to them?"

"When I gave cigarettes up the first time, I meticulously wrapped them both in tissue paper and put them in a velvet lined wooden box for safe keeping."

"The first time?" Beatrice asked with an exhale.

"It's been a long drawn out battle. I am happy to say that I only smoke now, when I am stressed. Which lately, seems to be all the time."

Both women laughed.

"Have you ever tried to quit?"

"Oh yeah." replied Beatrice. "Back when the kids were in high school, I thought I should stop. But I knew that my will power was for shit. So I went to that Mad Lithuanian in Boston to get hypnotized."

"Did it work?"

"Yeah. I think it did. From day one, I didn't have any cravings for the nicotine at all. But what drove me crazy were my hands. Maybe it was muscle memory...I don't know. But all of a sudden I became hyper aware of what my hands were doing now that I wasn't puffing away. I really tried to find things to do with them that didn't involve shoveling food into my mouth. It was the worst part."

"Any mood swings? I was a bear."

"I didn't think so at first. But after a month, each of my kids bought me a carton of cigarettes. Think they were trying to tell me something?"

Again both woman burst into laughter.

"Ever think about quitting again?" asked Louisa.

"Nah." replied Beatrice shaking her head no. "It's the only thing in my life that I can control."

"I hear you sister."

"Lou, I have to ask. What's with the hair?"

Louisa grabbed her pony tail with her free hand to examine it and rolled her eyes. "Pink wouldn't have been appropriate for court."

Beatrice gave her a look like she isn't quite sure what to make of the last comment.

"I'm kidding." laughed Louisa. "My granddaughter is studying to be a hairstylist. She needed a model for her finals and talked me into it."

"It looks lovely." Beatrice said as she tried not to laugh.

"It looks like hell. You can only imagine how overjoyed I was to learn that she used the wrong product and the purple is not washing out any time soon."

"Oh my. Did she at least pass?"

"You are able to see my hair???"

The two women laughed even louder.

"What you won't do for the happiness of your children." smiled Louisa through her tightly gritted teeth.

"We do what we can."

"I have to tell you Bea, this case is starting to become a real pain in my ass."

"Oh?"

"Yeah. Francis has all the documentation upstairs. But I think that we have logged a minimum of fifteen or sixteen phone calls from your step children. They are all asking a variation of the same questions, which all centers around the size and timing of their inheritance."

"I'm sorry about that Lou. I have told them not to bother you."

"I don't mind some of the calls. It's pretty standard in these situations. It is obvious that they are not sharing any information with one another."

"I can't say."

"The worst offender is the daughter. Is it LaRue? Why can't I get her name right?"

"LJ?"

"That's the one. Does she have a substance abuse issue?"

"Well, that's not…"

Before Beatrice could finish, Louisa jumped in. "Never mind. I really do not want to know. Who am I kidding? Of course I want to know. Does she?"

Before Beatrice can answer, Louisa jumped in again. "Of course she must. No one in their right mind would call as much as she does. She often slurs her speech when she calls. Talking so slow it's hard to make a word out. And then other times she speaks so rapidly, I must miss every other word."

"What does she say?" Beatrice asked earnestly.

"That's just it. I don't know. Sometimes, she talks about the love she had for her father. The love that she has for you...and all of her brothers and sisters...and her kids? At least I think she has kids."

"You don't' know the half of it!" Beatrice thought to herself.

"She will start to talk about how she needs to take care of them and then she feels like she is going to get screwed over. I try to get her to focus in on the process that we are following and then she is off on another tangent. She is very upset about being forced to sell the lake front property."

"Lou, it's not actually on a lake."

"I seem to remember you telling me that. Anyway, she keeps referring to it as the Magical Fairy Land. From the way she describes the place, and the specific details about the amount of money he spent developing the property, she gave me the impression that it's probably worth quite a substantial amount of money."

"Oh believe me...it isn't."

"Well, either way, once the calls stopped, I thought we were free and clear, That was until I received a letter this week from the law offices of Cynthia Tseng-Smythe."

Beatrice shot her a look of confusion and offered another cigarette which Louisa gladly accepted and lit. "Thank you. I graduated law school with Miss Cindy Tseng. Total pain in my ass, by the way...always trying to one up me and never successful pulling it off, I might add. She was like one of those annoying greenhead flies that come out and ruin your July beach day...just buzzing around trying to suck your blood. She does have the most beautiful complexion though….porcelain like skin…has a lazy eye. I never knew which one is looking at me. "

"What did the letter say?" asked Beatrice more concerned with this new complication.

"LJ hired her. Not happy with the impromptu yard sale and the tossing of personal belongings. Blah. Blah. Wants to put a halt to selling off any more assets and see if we can come to a mutual understanding before having to get a judge involved."

Beatrice let out a frustrating exhale of smoke. "What's that mean?"

"That's what we are going to talk about today."

Beatrice took another deep dive into her pocketbook and ultimately produced three packages of drug store photo prints. "Knew I would find them. I want you to see just what everyone is fighting over."

Louisa put down her briefcase, put on her half framed reading glasses that were in her jacket pocket and opened the first package of photos. She stared at each picture intently for a minute or so before moving on to the next and then the next. On a few pictures she squinted and shook her head in disbelief. Not saying a word. The only sound that she made was an occasional 'Tsk' or an exhale from her cigarette. Beatrice studied Lou's poker face hoping that it would give her some clue to what her lawyer was thinking. When she was finished looking at the last package of photographs, Lou took the last puff of her cigarette and dropped the remains on the sidewalk and stamped it out with her red high heeled shoe.

"This is the magical fairly land?"

"Mmmmhmmm."

"You've got to be fucking kidding me?" said Louisa trying desperately to keep her anger in check.

"I wish I were." apologized Beatrice. "The pictures don't paint the whole picture."

"Oh I don't know about that? It looked like he lived in a landfill."

"There was the smell."

Lou grunted disgustedly. "I am not sure I want to hear…this is totally unprofessional and none of my business, but I have to ask…"

"Why did I marry him?"

"Well, yeah."

"That's a great question, Lou. I wish that I had an easy answer…because I don't. Looking back at it now, I can tell you that I must have been crazy. I know that I wasn't in my right mind. I drank my way through most of that marriage. All the signs were there. I just chose not to look at them."

"What do you mean signs?"

"He had these incredible mood swings. If he were on a high, he was loud and gregarious, funny, entertaining and generous. Thoughtful. He would go out of his way to make sure that everyone was included. He'd plan these lavish feasts or daytrips. Foods and places that I have never heard of. And then, without any warning his mood would change. He would focus in on the minutest of details to prove someone wrong. He became short tempered, mean, violent. The highs were delightful. The lows were a nightmare. Almost always afterwards he would take to bed for a week at a time."

"Did he ever seek medical or psychiatric help?"

"There was a time we tried medication, but…he never acknowledged that there were any issues. When he snapped back, he swept the whole thing under the rug."

"Why did you put yourself through that?"

"I was barely thirty five when my happily ever after went to shit in a hand basket after seventeen years of marriage. I had four kids, no money, no marketable skills, no one to help watch my kiddos if I were able to find a job and a car with two bald tires and a rejection inspection on it."

"Didn't you have family that could help out?"

"Two brothers. Both were knee deep in their own issues. And my mother…well, let's save that when we have much more time on our hands."

"Didn't you have any friends that could help?"

"I'm sure if I asked. But I didn't want to. I had a lot of great friends. But they were all happily married and here I was something of a marriage failure. I was embarrassed and humiliated. I didn't want to retell my story over and over or hear any more details about their suspicions that they refused to share while I was married. I didn't want to be pitied and I didn't want to be a third wheel so I found myself making one excuse after another not to go out or meet for coffee."

"But him?"

"I know that it seems strange. It was strange to me as well. But truth be told, he made me laugh. He took me out. He showed me different things. It was an escape and that is what I needed more than anything else at that time. There were some great times and there were a lot of shitty times as well. I overlooked the shitty times, because with his mood swings, I knew that eventually a better time was right around the corner."

"Must have been a tough life."

"I'm not going to lie to you; it wasn't a walk in the park. With each low, I lost more and more of my self-esteem. Looking at me know, I bet you couldn't tell that I used to be fearless?"

"How so?"

"I wasn't afraid of anything. No risk was too big. When I was in junior high school I used the payphone outside of the principal's office to have me and my friends dismissed early so we could take the bus to the beach."

"No you didn't."

"Three calls. Three different voices. I sounded just like my friend Betty's mother, it was scary."

"You never got caught?"

"No. If I wanted something, I went after it...especially when it came to boys. I was a terrible flirt. Where I grew up, there was a lake. It was pretty big. About a mile and half long. It had a town beach on each end and a lot of the high school kids got summer jobs there as lifeguards. There was this one guy...Dickie Caldwell. He was a wide receiver on the football team and all the girls wanted him."

"Where you a cheerleader?"

"No. Captain of the Majorettes." Before Lou could finish her giggle, Beatrice jumped in. "Don't laugh, back in the day, it was a highly coveted position. I still have my baton."

"You are kidding me."

"No ma'am. Back in the day, I was it on a stick. And I set my eye on Dickie. His dad owned a small roofing company in town, so during the summer when he wasn't at practice, he would hump packages of shingles up and down the ladders for his dad and the rest of the crew. On the weekends, he worked on his tan as one of the lifeguards. By the beginning of August, he was one of those gods of summer you would read about in those romance novels. The other girls would sit around the base of his chair trying to make small talk as he kept an eye on the people in the water. We didn't have a lot of money growing up, so there was no way that my one piece hand me down bathing suit could compete with the bikinis the other girls were wearing."

"What did you do?"

"Thought outside of the box. Back in those days, people were not allowed to swim from one end of the lake to the other unless they were accompanied by a lifeguard."

"You didn't."

"Oh yes I did. Every Saturday for a month, I swam across the lake with Dickie rowing right alongside. Butterfly stroke, back stroke. You name it. I did it."

"You were shameless."

"Yes. But I was the one wearing his ring that season."

"What ever happened to him?"

"Last I heard, he and his boyfriend were giving airboat tours of the Everglades. Can I pick them or what?"

Both women laughed again uncontrollably and Beatrice took one last puff before she extinguished her cigarette.

"Lou, I want you to know, that they weren't all shitty times with Freddie. There were some good times and I did love him in my own way. What you need to understand is that my life with him was as messy as those pictures that I just showed you. When the shitty times significantly outweighed the bad times, I knew that I had to make a change. It wasn't easy. And looking back on it, I should have never put myself or my children in that situation. I was weak and felt like I was backed into a corner. I am truly ashamed. It took a toll on all of us, especially my daughter. I don't want you to think that I am greedy..."

"Bea, you don't have to explain..."

"Yes. Yes I do. I want you to know why I am pushing to get this resolved as quickly and as cheaply as possible. Towards the very end, we would fight. We would fight a lot. And more often than not, it would get very physical."

"Did he hit you?"

"Yeah. But usually only after I hit him or threw something at him. I'm not proud of it, but a lot of times, I would start it. I'd be filled with liquid courage...seems like the only time that I would stand up for myself was after a few beers. I'd get bitter; I'd get mean...and then watch out world."

"There is no excuse. Why are you excusing his behavior?"

"I'm not, really. I'm just owning up to my part in all of it. He would take off and stay with his parents. Sometimes it was overnight; sometimes it would be for a couple of weeks."

"When did he leave for good?"

"It was after....it was after...it was bad. You know what Lou? Let's save that story for another time, too."

"Ok Bea."

"Just know that when he finally left, he left me, he left us in worse condition than when he found us. Physically, financially, and emotionally. Each day that I stayed with him I lost bits and pieces of myself. My self-esteem, my fearlessness slowly eroded away. I felt embarrassed and ashamed and pathetic. A first class failure. I would rarely leave the house."

"What changed?"

"Grandbabies." said Beatrice smiling. "My daughter pushed me to get my first job in twenty five years. Talk about nerve shattering. It wasn't much. I cleaned bedpans, and washed dishes at a nursing home. But it got me out and off welfare. Now, I slice cheese at the deli counter of a very high end grocery store that no one can afford to shop at full time. I am barely making ends meet and if it weren't for Christopher I would have lost the house a long time ago. The other kids help out when they can, but they have families of their own. I want to make sure that I have social security so that my kids can worry about their own babies. I want to be able to go into a store and not have to choose between the electric bill and a birthday gift. I know that it might seem awful to some people, but I think for everything that he put me through, Freddie owes me. Do you know what I mean?"

"Absolutely." said Lou as she put her arm around Beatrice's shoulder and led her to her office. "Let's go talk about how I am going to mop the floor with lazy eye Cindy."

Both woman laughed as the door closed behind them.

An Epilogue Of Sorts

She was determined to make this a surprise party to remember. It's not often that your mother celebrates her eightieth birthday. And it certainly isn't often that Beatrice actually had the money to pay for it.

Louisa Nickels was true to her word. The money that Beatrice received from cleaning up Fred's estate put her just slightly north of the poverty line for the first time in decades. She was able to pay off a few bills, make a couple of overdue repairs to the house, and buy herself a new to her car that was only two years old. She even had enough left over money to start a very small nest egg in the bank in case of rainy days. Thanks to a three thousand dollar win on a scratch ticket, even after the state and local taxes were paid out, it was enough to throw the party for her mother. Beatrice felt like she was an heiress.

Beatrice was insistent on owning and planning every detail of Nana Flossie's surprise party. The lovely girl with the long dreadlocks, neck tattoos, and multiple piercings at the Paper Store named Janice, who insisted that she had no last name, just like Cher or Madonna helped her design the perfect invitation. Janice talked her into using thermography style printing which involved sprinkling resin on the invitation.

There were several additional and more complicated steps about how the ink and the resin bond together which Beatrice simply chose to tune out. She just cared that the invitations looked simple, elegant and that Flossie's name was written in her favorite shade of pink.

It wasn't difficult convincing Artie Papadopoulos to close his restaurant down on a Monday night, which was traditionally slow, in order to host the party for his favorite and most popular waitress. After all Flossie had worked for him for over thirty years. Although she cut her hours way back to just two lunch shifts a week. The true negotiations came into play when Beatrice had to convince Mrs. Papadopoulos to let Cooper back into the restaurant. It took some creative haggling which involved a dozen roses, a heartfelt apology from Cooper and a promise that he would not have a drop of liquor to drink before or during the celebration. To make sure that he kept his word, Mrs. Papadopoulos would be Cooper's date for the evening.

The reason that Beatrice didn't want a formal sit down dinner for the occasion had nothing to do with the cost but more to do with making sure that Nana Flossie had a chance to mingle with every one of her guests. A cocktail party would allow her that flexibility. Artie promised to put out a few scattered high top tables around the room and if guests wanted they could certainly take advantage of the curved double button tufted high back booths in oxblood leather that outlined each of the walls of the restaurant. Artie felt that he was giving his patrons the feeling that they were a private table in some posh Las Vegas night club. Each of the tables would be covered in crisp white linens and pink vases filled with daisies and baby's breath, Flossie's favorites. Together Beatrice and Artie worked out a menu that consisted of hors d'oeuvres and other finger foods, which would allow guests to graze throughout the event as they felt the need. They agreed to a couple of stations that were strategically placed throughout the room to maximize flow and the rest of the food would be passed by the staff who volunteered to work the party for no money. Artie convinced Beatrice that they should only serve a limited menu of wine and beer and he offered to front the costs of a pink champagne fountain, because he knew that Flossie would love it.

The guest list consisted of a few of Flossie's closest friends, a couple of her favorite customers, and the rest was filled out with relatives; aunts, uncles, and lots and lots of cousins, many of whom Beatrice hadn't spoken too in a very long time. She lost touch with some over the years just because that's how life works sometimes. Others stopped talking to her. While some of the details were a bit hazy, Beatrice was pretty sure it involved a couple of intense conversations after she had six or seven beers. Either way she knew that this party would involve eating some crow. She was naturally a little anxious, but she was prepared to do so in order to make sure that Flossie had a great time.

She was happy that her older brother Joe had flown in from Florida with his new wife and that his children and grand children would be coming as well. It had been years since Beatrice, Joe and Cooper had been in the same room. For the weeks leading up to the party, she warned both of her brothers to play nice and be civil to one another. Beatrice reminded each of them that this party was not going to be a platform to rehash any of their unresolved issues and believe me, there were many! They needed to be the perfect hosts and give their guests the appearance and the impression that they were all one big happy family.

She was most happy that Kevin, his wife, Allison and the boys made it back from Japan for the party and even more excited that they were all staying with her, although she had forgotten what it was like to have three very rambunctious rough housing children living in her little house by the golden pond. She had also forgotten what it was like to have so many people living under one roof and having to share the one and only bathroom! She missed the utter pandemonium of it all and she missed the noise...some of the time. Thankfully, Christopher kept the medicine cabinet stocked with extra strength ibuprofen.

The morning of the soiree, Beatrice decided to forgo her usual spot on her perch and opted to take her coffee and cigarette on the back deck which overlooked the golden pond. She was feeling a little nostalgic when she saw her grandsons hop into the boat and row off in search of bull frogs and water moccasins just like Kevin used to at that age.

"Do not take that boat out of this cove!" she shouted knowing full well that they were going to ignore her.

"Promise Nana!" the three boys shouted back in unison as they rowed away.

She laughed to herself as she watched the boys struggle to direct the boat in pursuit of the water snake which swam quickly away from them. Once the boat disappeared from her view, Beatrice yelled into the house.

"Kevin. They have escaped again!"

Kevin came bolting out of the living room door and on to the back deck as he pulled a blue tee shirt over his head. "Goddammit! Boys you best be getting your asses back here pronto!" he screamed as he ran down the stairs towards the golden pond.

Beatrice let loose with a big belly laugh at the sight of Kevin chasing after his boys.

"How many times have I had to do that?" she thought to herself.

She was proud that her middle son, whom she never thought would live to see the age of eighteen mainly due to the fact that she came close to strangling him with her bare hands on more than one occasion had turned into such a great husband and father. She almost felt sorry for Kevin because it was just a matter of time before he would no longer be a step ahead of his boys. Karmically speaking, it was a phone call that she could not wait to receive.

"This is not a negotiation!" Beatrice heard Kevin scream. "Did I give you the impression that you three had a choice in this matter?!! If you know what is good for you, you will get that boat back here right now!"

Beatrice sat there finishing off her coffee and smoking her cigarette just enjoying the rest of the morning's entertainment.

The guests were to arrive at the restaurant by five thirty, each prepared with a story, a memory, and their favorite photograph of Flossie to share. Beatrice insisted that we all be there before then in order to help set up and handle any last minute details that may pop up.

"You look handsome, Michael."

"Thanks, Mom." I replied as I kissed her cheek. "Look at you! Hubba Hubba."

"I know. Can you believe it?" Beatrice smiled as she twirled around, her eggplant colored silk dress rose slightly above her knees. "I look good, don't I?" she said as she dramatically placed her hand on her heart.

"That's Mom's subtle way of asking you to comment on her nails." Christopher said sneaking up behind me and handing me a beer.

"Hmm?" not sure of what I was looking at.

"I had them done you idiot!" Beatrice gushed as she showed off her new French manicure. "Allison took me this afternoon. My whole life, my mother made fun of the dirt underneath my nails. Well not tonight!" she laughed.

"Are you wearing heels?" I asked. "You seem taller."

"Yes. And, yes they are killing my feet. She better appreciate everything that's all I can say."

"I am sure that she will, Mom." added Kevin, who was wearing his dress uniform.

"Thanks honey." Beatrice said as she kissed Kevin. "You look so handsome in your uniform. Right out of a movie. Where are the boys?"

"It's an enclosed room. How much trouble could they possibly get into?"

"Kevin, would it have stopped you?" I teased.

"Fuck." Kevin grabbed and downed my entire beer. He handed me the empty bottle before darting off looking for his sons in the hopes of preventing an inevitable disaster.

"You're welcome." I said sarcastically, just as an irritated Carrie joined us with her equally angry eldest child tagging right behind.

"You look beautiful Mom." Carrie said as she kissed Beatrice. "I apologize now. This one is in a mood."

"Hey squirt, you clean up nicely." Christopher teased his niece hoping to solicit a reaction and got none.

"Ooooo, it's chilly all of a sudden." I added.

"What do you say to your Uncle?" Carrie asked her daughter who just stood there with a snarl on her face and her arms crossed resting on her chest.

Beatrice put her arm around her oldest grandchild and hugged her tight. "What's the matter, baby? What did your mean old mommy do now? You look very pretty by the way."

"Oh. Miss thing is pissed because she's grounded. Gimme a swig of that." Carrie said as she grabbed Christopher's beer.

"What did you do now, kiddo?" Christopher asked.

The teenager's only response was the 'if looks could kill death stare' that she clearly inherited from Carrie.

"I caught her in a lie."

"No!" Christopher and I dramatically responded simultaneously.

"Knock it off you two. I don't care if it's a party, I can still kick your asses!"

"What did you do, honey?" Beatrice asked soothingly.

"Nothing." Her granddaughter answered sweetly.

"Oh, look she speaks!" snapped Carrie.

"Carrie..." Beatrice said in a familiar tone that clearly meant for Carrie to take it down a level or two.

"No. This one hasn't said a word to us since we grounded her Friday night. Instead she has chosen to follow me around where ever I go and pout."

"Classic Carrie move." I said.

"We are going to have to take points off for lack of originality, kiddo." Christopher chided.

"Why did you get grounded baby?" Beatrice asked.

"Because my *mother* likes to treat me like a baby and has to control every aspect of my life!"

"Why don't you tell your grandmother the whole story?? You see, the school pep rally is coming up this Friday. So over the weekend a bunch of the kids on her team were going over to this girl's house...some girl who I never met...I think her name is Stacie, Macie, or Tracie...something like that. The girls were going to make posters and supposedly work on some skit for the seniors. I talked to the girl's parents...or so I thought...and they were going to be home... bunch of kids working on a project...didn't think anything of it. Until I got a call from the police department asking me to come to the house and pick her up. Turns out that it was a huge party."

"No!" Christopher and I dramatically responded simultaneously.

"So help me God, I will kill you both!"

"That doesn't sound like you Paige honey. What were you thinking?" Beatrice asked sincerely.

"I was thinking that I just wanted a little fun. I am tired of living under a microscope. *She* needs to know everything that I am doing. What do I have for homework? What are my teacher's names? Who my friends are! What they like! What do their parents do for work! I feel like I am living with the director of the FBI!"

"Honey, it's just because your mother loves you."

"No! It's because she has nothing better to do than ruin my life! She is the worst mother in the world! And I hate her!"

Beatrice lightly slapped her granddaughter across the face.

"I will not allow you to talk that way about your mother." Beatrice said with a very calm voice. "You haven't a clue about all that she has been through and what she has done for you and your family!"

As her granddaughter started to cry, Beatrice put her arms around her and gave her a tight hug. "No tears, baby. You have nothing to cry about."

"She makes me so mad."

"S'ok. I make her so mad sometimes too."

"You do?"

"Darling, let me let you in on a little secret…mothers and daughters have been fighting with each other since the beginning of time. And before you say it, you will be doing the same to your daughter one day. I promise. But you need to do me a favor and lay off your mom a little…because from my perspective, in the last four generations of women in this family, she is the only one that got the mother thing right."

"That's not true."

"Oh, it is. You see my grandmother was so worried about making her husbands happy, she didn't see or maybe she just over looked all the problems with my father. Who knows? If she paid a little bit more attention, I might have had a different life."

"What about Nana Flossie?"

"Oh, she was the bravest. She loved me and my brothers so much, she would rather have us living with other relatives than be in a potentially dangerous situation. And I was so determined to have this idyllic home life that I was completely blind to what was actually happening until it was almost too late." Beatrice took her granddaughter's face into her hands so that she could look directly into her eyes. "Your mom spends all of her time making sure that you feel safe and that you are having a happy childhood...something that I am ashamed to admit that I could never do. She has created some great memories for you and your sister and brother. Sure she may get it wrong from time to time...it's not like you came with a manual when she took you home from the hospital. But she is doing her best. And I promise you, it's better than I did. So look around. You are surrounded by love and by a lot of relatives...some we love...some we love a little less. But in the grand scheme of things, that's all that really matters. So this is what you are going to do." Beatrice wiped the tears from her granddaughter's eyes. "I want you to go over there and apologize to your mother and stand next to her. Nana Flossie will be coming through that kitchen door any minute now. She thinks that she is here to help out for a special party, so she will be dressed in her uniform. After everyone yells surprise, she is going to be happy and then she is going to be very angry because she isn't dressed. That's when you and your mother will take her into the ladies room, where there is a pink Chanel suit that she had always wanted to own. I want you and your mother to help Nana Flossie get ready for her second entrance."

"But you should be the..."

"No honey. Your mother will need you to help her. So do me a favor. You make sure that my mother looks pretty."

"I love you Nana Bea."

"I love you more."

The End

Made in the USA
Columbia, SC
13 May 2018